HOTEL BERINGIA

HOTEL BERINGIA

A NOVEL

MIX HART

TIDEWATER
PRESS

Published by Tidewater Press
New Westminster, BC, Canada
tidewaterpress.ca

978-1-990160-38-7 (paperback)
978-1-990160-39-4 (e-book)

LIBRARY AND ARCHIVES CANADA CATALOGUING IN PUBLICATION
Title: Hotel Beringia : a novel / Mix Hart.
Names: Hart, Mix, 1966- author.
Identifiers: Canadiana (print) 20240383079 | Canadiana (ebook) 20240383443 | ISBN 9781990160387 (softcover) | ISBN 9781990160394 (EPUB)
Subjects: LCGFT: Novels.
Classification: LCC PS8615.A7547 H68 2024 | DDC C813/.6—dc23

DISCLAIMER

This is a work of fiction. Names, characters, businesses, institutions, organizations, places, and events other than those clearly in the public domain, with the exception of some well-known historical events, are either the product of the author's imagination or are used fictitiously. Where real-life historical events appear, all incidents, dialogue, and characters, are products of the author's imagination and are not to be construed as real representations of the event, or to change the entirely fictional nature of the work. All opinions expressed in the work belong exclusively to fictional characters. Any resemblance to persons living or dead is entirely coincidental

Canadä

Tidewater Press gratefully acknowledges the support of the Government of Canada.

For the Arctic wolves and bears

I

Charlotte's black bob hangs straight and dreary like the Vancouver rain; her pale face looks like death in contrast. She plugs herself into the earphones and closes her eyes. She's either hungover or premenstrual—either way, her mood is silent in its fury. It was her idea that we apply for the waitressing jobs together—an "Arctic adventure." A chance to be the sisters we once were—fearless and sometimes maybe even dangerous. I'm not fearless anymore, though Charlotte is probably more dangerous than she's ever been.

The hotel recruiter was keen to hire us as a sister-unit, to take the edge off the isolation. The irony is the isolation worries me less than my companion does. I assume Charlotte's heading to the Yukon for the same reason I am—to escape. Only she and I know that she won't be returning to university in the fall. She failed too many courses and UBC officially banned her for a year. The fact that my parents don't know she flunked out is suspect; her silence could mean she is building toward a histrionic extravaganza, to be revealed at a later date.

No one knows that I'm seriously considering not returning to Ottawa to finish my journalism degree. I'm in career limbo—indecision is viewed as a weakness by my parents—and I don't want them to use it against me. Until I figure out what my next life move is, I am a writer. Dr. Gallant's words are imprinted on my brain: "One is not a writer unless one is writing. It is a present state of being." I open a leather-bound journal, a rare gift to myself, and write, *Arctic Summer 1988,* on the inside cover and then turn to the first page. The pristine page looks too hopeful. I hate to mark it with my ramblings. I close the book.

"What happened to Dad?"

"What?" Charlotte pulls out one earphone and furrows her brow, warning me that whatever I've got to say better be worth interrupting the Air Canada playlist.

"Dad never made it to the airport."

"Probably didn't want to cut short his morning run." Charlotte pops her earphone back in.

I didn't want to come home this summer, but I had nowhere else to go. While I was in Ottawa, our family unravelled. Mom got the house and Dad moved into a high-end suite. We, the daughters, were inconsequential, as we are over the age of eighteen.

Despite being two years apart in age, Charlotte and I were often confused for twins. Mainly because our parents refused to let us cut our long, blond hair. People would marvel at the similarities between us until we hit puberty. Puberty changed everything—pubes and periods were the least of it. Suddenly, our bodies were public domain and a form of entertainment: who's blonder, prettier, thinner, taller, had longer legs, a straighter nose, smaller nose, bigger bum, larger breasts. The constant critique of our physical appearance damned the sisterhood into a slow, excruciating death. Charlotte has progressively become less sister–friend and more competitive foe. She cut and dyed her hair two days ago, as though trying to distance herself from me before we even touch down in the Arctic.

The plane glides low over a huge indigo lake, a monstrous eyeball watching those that dare enter the sacred north. The water is surrounded by coniferous-treed bluffs, too small to be considered mountains but too high to be called hills. The plane shakes and jerks through atmospheric potholes.

We disembark on the runway. I descend the narrow stairs in a pleated miniskirt and strappy sandals, as a Hollywood star from another era might, I imagine, when arriving at an isolated movie location. The sky is different—softer—and the clouds too high above the earth, as though we've arrived on a neighbouring planet, farther from the sun. The wind is peppered with icy rain that whips my hair against my sunglasses and lifts my skirt. I stride toward the tiny airport, trying to absorb all the Arctic possible from the tarmac.

The Whitehorse airport is a single room. It would be impossible to miss meeting up with someone, so impossible that one would have to actively avoid making eye contact with everyone in the room. The balding, beer-bellied man holding the cardboard "Hotel Beringia" sign is probably waiting for us. Charlotte slowly clomps her hunched-back self toward him, and my heavy backpack and I drag along behind her.

"You the waitresses from Vancouver?"

Up close, he has stained teeth and a floppy mouth, the type of mouth I avoid for fear the breath is toxic.

"Yes, Rumer Rantanen . . . my sister, Charlotte." I don't extend my hand.

"Larry, manager, Hotel Beringia," he says with the same degree of ardour that we demonstrated when we hauled ourselves toward him. He nods once, turns, and then walks as quickly as a man with a massive belly can toward the airport exit.

"I guess we're supposed to follow," Charlotte says.

We squeeze our backpacks in the rear of a long white van, behind boxes of groceries and flats of soda cans, and then settle ourselves into the first row of van seats. Larry wedges his belly behind the wheel. He jerks his head toward the woman sitting beside him. "Louise—hotel cook." Louise half turns her head and nods.

"Hi," Charlotte and I say in unison.

Louise has the mother of all cowlicks on the rear crown of her head, accentuated by a third of an inch of white roots rebelling against the black dye job—an unnatural shade, blacker than black, oddly comparable to Charlotte's.

The back of Larry's head seems benevolent enough: shiny, bald on top with a dingy base of limp, taupe-coloured hair. I imagined him a lot more elegant. The hotel recruiter called him Laurence. The name Laurence conjures up visions of *Laurence of Arabia* and the icy blue eyes of Peter O'Toole. A guy named Larry wouldn't even pass as an extra on the film. What kind of man would choose to call himself Larry over Laurence? I bet Larry is well aware that he's a disappointment, but he's likely been a disappointment to so many, for so long, that he could give a toss.

Louise turns to face us. She's as weathered as Larry. Her face is lined with worry, booze, and too many cigarettes, or maybe all three. She pulls a pained smile. Her lips part slightly, unable to fully cover protruding front teeth. The teeth don't detract from her overall attractiveness. They make her face more interesting, like Queen frontman Freddie Mercury. "I hope you two brought something to wear other than miniskirts. Sometimes we get snow in May."

I do a quick mental inventory of my packed wardrobe: one pair of jeans, two pairs of shorts, four mini-dresses, and the skirt I'm wearing.

Whitehorse disappears from view. Aspen bluffs line the highway with an occasional conifer. Small inky lakes, with splotches of tropical turquoise, appear intermittently among the trees. "How far to the hotel?" I shout into the front seat.

"Roughly twelve hours. Six to Dawson City and then six more up to Beringia," Larry shouts back.

The van is the only vehicle on the narrow Klondike highway. We gain altitude, gradually climbing toward the faraway sun. We're on the top of the world, driving on land higher than the highest mountains. The sky is an impossibly saturated deep ocean blue. It's as if I'm seeing the colour of blue for the first time—everything before was an imposter.

Louise's shaky hand lights a cigarette. The speed with which Larry follows suit is an indication that he's been in nicotine withdrawal for the past few hours. We drive by a sign that says "Montague Roadhouse, 10KM." A pothole in our lane jerks the van over the faded centre line and jars my bladder.

"Could we stop at the roadhouse?" I shout up front.

"What for?" Larry asks.

"I'd like to use a bathroom," I say.

After several long minutes during which I contemplate the contrasting pleasures of an urgent hot pee and a cool iced tea sliding down my parched throat, Larry pulls the van onto a dirt road, beside a derelict log building.

"Is this the roadhouse?"

"Make it quick," Larry says.

Louise unrolls her window, takes out a cigarette and lights it. I step from the van into a cloud of Louise's exhaled smoke. "Toilet's in back."

The roadhouse is gutted and roofless. Its old walls are tightly fitted logs. They remind me of the interlocking toy set that Charlotte and I used to play with when we were little. I climb through an empty window and into what must have been the entrance hall. Shreds of wallpaper hang in torn patches from the wood. A rusted wood-burning stove lies belly-up in deep grass.

"Outhouse is *behind* the roadhouse," Louise shouts.

"What bloody century have I landed in," I mumble as I step over dismembered stovepipes and then crawl through a window at the back of the roadhouse.

Leaves rustle from behind the outhouse—not the whisper of

trembling aspens in the wind, but forceful thrashing, bushes parted with weight. "Charlotte?" I hover above the toilet seat and read the message scrawled in charcoal on the inside of the privy door: *No time to explain—pull up your pants—leave immediately.* The sound stops for a moment and then a branch snaps. I pull up my underpants, wait for silence, and then sprint to the road.

The three of them are standing in a row, outside the van, hunched over like high school students smoking at recess on a chilly day. Somehow, in my five-minute absence, Charlotte has assimilated into the odd couple's road-hard culture. With their skinny legs and matching hair colour, she could almost pass for Louise's angsty teen daughter.

"Since when did you take up smoking?"

Charlotte shrugs and takes another drag. I channel my annoyance with my sister to take on Larry. "Why would they call this place a roadhouse? It's misleading."

"Did a little exploring, did ya?" Larry smirks. Louise laughs.

"I heard something behind the outhouse."

Charlotte glances up at me and then at Larry.

"There's nothing out here but bears." Larry drops his cigarette and extinguishes it in the dirt. "Montague's the only roadhouse left on The Overland route. In winter, only way from Whitehorse to Dawson was by sleigh. Skinners drove horses twenty-mile days. So there'd be a roadhouse every twenty miles. Highway changed all that," Larry says.

"When did they build the highway?"

"Montague was in operation forty years ago."

"Forty?" I don't hide my incredulousness.

"Montague Roadhouse ain't so different from Hotel Beringia. Montague died when the gold was gone. Beringia's turn'll come, once the black gold's gone."

Larry pulls the van onto the highway. He looks into the rear-view mirror, shifting his gaze from Charlotte to me. "Roadhouse would'a turned you girls away. They didn't allow single women." Then he glances at Louise. "*You* would've had to marry me— what do you think about that, Lou?"

Louise stares out the front window. If she responds to him, I don't hear it.

The back of Larry's neck turns dark pink.

I lean toward Charlotte. "Was that a proposal?"

"What?" Charlotte says, seemingly oblivious to the drama unfolding in the front seat.

"You'd still be cleaning toilets in Dawson if it weren't for me," Larry says.

"The kitchen's short-staffed. You can't afford to lose me," Louise says.

Larry expels a rattled cough. The van zigzags across the centre line. He coughs again, a reiterative, shallow hack. His head bobs dangerously close to the steering wheel, then he suddenly thrusts it back and gasps as his head hits the headrest. After what feels like an eternity on the highway to hell, with Larry in the throes of death at the wheel, Louise hands him a flask. He takes a swig, and another, and then hands the flask back to Louise. His glassy eyes catch my stricken gaze in the rear-view mirror. He mutters something and his purple neck returns to a slug-grey shade.

The van suddenly swerves into the oncoming lane. Larry's looking at me in the rear-view mirror. "Prospectors travelled by sleigh on The Overland trail in winter, but come spring, they braved the Yukon River," he shouts and then turns his head to look out his side window. "Shot through them Five Finger Rapids in handmade boats." The van swerves back into our lane.

I peek at the turbulent river below. Turquoise water rushes toward a serrated rock island in its centre. The water swirls and crashes in voluminous waves and frothy spit onto the soaring stone blades. I'm instantly transported from the smelly van interior into the thrilling icy currents. I unzip my carry-on pack, pull out the journal and scribble with a trembling hand: *Yukon River, Five Finger Rapids—I am drawn closer and closer to the omphalos of the action, the collision of rock and river—a fervour that is consuming and violent.*

We leave the Klondike Highway and turn north onto the Dempster. "We're not going to stop in Dawson City?" I say.

"Not this time. It will add eighty K to the trip. We still have nearly five hundred K ahead of us," Larry says.

I want to wake Charlotte for this momentous occasion, but I'm afraid to chance her mood. The infamous Dempster was the one thing that interested Dad when he found out we got the job. He said it's practically a rite of passage to say you survived driving it . . . the only Canadian highway to cross the Arctic Circle. He didn't mention that the Dempster is a dirt road.

"We're the first settlement north of Dawson City. Hotel is at sixty-five degrees, just this side of the Arctic Circle. Hotel sits on a rare slice of bedrock—only bedrock for miles. Hotel's good but the Dempster's another story— they shovel shale on it all summer long to keep it afloat," Larry says.

"Is the highway gravel all the way to the Arctic Circle?"

"Local shale. Two metres thick. Ice underneath," Larry says.

The van stinks of cigarettes and salt and vinegar chips. No one's had chips. Everyone is asleep except me. Larry's head is upright but whether he's conscious is debatable. We snake through a valley surrounded by tree-covered mountains with towering rock precipices on one side of the road, and smooth, tundra mountains on the other. The van loses speed as we climb the precarious Dempster, leaving the valley below. The light is otherworldly and the view epic in scale: acres upon acres of unremitting mountains in every direction, each with a personalized weather system of either cloud, rain, mist, sleet, or sunshine, simultaneously hovering over every range for eternity. It's as though we are on a planet much bigger than Earth. I am humbled into insignificance. The van is a noisy, dusty flea on the back of planetary splendour.

Dark clouds suddenly overtake the van, and we're pelted with rain and sloppy snow. The moisture instantly turns the highway into muddy slush and deep puddles. The van slides dangerously close to the Dempster's sharp edge. "Highest point of the Dempster . . . continental divide. All rivers north end at the Beaufort Sea, all rivers south dump into the Pacific," Larry shouts as we slip and slide. Below, the river valley is shrouded in misty sunlight with double rainbow arches straddling the mountain ranges. I open my journal and scratch: *The rainbow is my talisman. I will survive this journey.*

The van slows as we crawl past a herd of white sheep with curved horns that trot along the ditch. "Dall sheep—unique to the Arctic," Larry says.

"What's unique about them?" Charlotte says, in a voice with the varying pitch of someone not yet fully awake.

"Not many of them left—come down to drink at Engineer Creek. They get calcium from the water."

"Are they a protected species?" I ask.

"Nothing's protected if you have money," Louise says.

"We get a lot of big game hunters at Hotel Beringia—hunting's part of Yukon life," Larry says, staring into the mirror, as though daring me to object.

"The hotel's not a hunting lodge, is it? We were told it caters to the bus tour and cruise ship crowds."

"I don't see any sea around here, do you?" Larry laughs.

"We have had a steady increase in bus tours the past few years. Odd one's been an extended shore excursion," Louise says.

"What ports do the ships dock at?"

"They bus them from Skagway to Dawson. A night at Gerties and then up to Beringia for a night. They fly 'em home from Whitehorse."

"What do they come to see at Beringia?" I ask.

"They bus 'em up to say they've stood at the Arctic Circle. Give 'em some kind of Arctic explorer certificate to take home and frame like a bunch of kindergarteners."

"Larry!" Louise snaps. "It's not just the Arctic Circle. They come to see the tundra, the wildlife."

"We cater to the ancient sea tourists—hotel sits on top of a three-hundred-million-year-old sea. You girls see those mountains on the right? Those mountaintops were once islands in the sea. The dinosaurs in that sea turned into oil and gas, and oil men need a place to stay."

"The hotel houses oil workers?" There's a hint of anticipation in Charlotte's voice. She's probably picturing a buffed-torso rig worker.

"Not anymore. They gave up. Too hard to get the oil and gas out. But she'll be filled again soon, once they find a way—George, he's our oil man." Larry laughs and coughs.

"Poor old George," Louise says.

"What's the story on George?" Charlotte asks.

"He was on a new Eagle Plains rig. Wasn't on the job a month, they told him to climb up and take down a raven's nest. The crew forgot he was up there . . . fell twenty-five metres. Learned to walk again but his short-term memory's shot," Larry says.

"He remembers some things, especially things from before the accident," Louise says.

"Can't remember a damn thing from one minute to the next."

"What does he do at the hotel?" I ask.

"Not a damn thing."

"That's not true. George works front desk and night watchman."

"Night watchman. Ha! That's a good one."

The wet snow stops abruptly, as though we cross an invisible weather line, and the Dempster is dry and dusty again. Louise's head nods in and out of sleep. I wobble my head in time with hers. Charlotte's repressed laughter escapes in a snort.

"Your résumé said that one of you has first aid training," Larry says to the rear-view mirror.

Charlotte and I exchange glances.

"Yes—I do," I say, cautiously. I don't tell him that my first aid is two years old, and I took CPR in high school.

"If somebody gets hurt anywhere north of Tombstone, to the Territory border, we're the ambulance. We need someone to help with the patient until they're helicoptered out. Would you be interested?"

"Maybe. I mean, sure—in an emergency. I'm curious, what kinds of emergencies are common up here?"

"Grizzly took a guy off his bike last August. He was trailing behind his group. Found his wheels on the side of the Dempster but no guy. His remains were found a quarter mile from the highway."

"Where did that happen? Near here?"

"About thirty K south of the hotel."

"That is horrific. Did you see the body? I mean, was it your ambulance that picked him up?"

Larry studies me in the rear-view for a moment before getting irritable. "Yeah, it was us. You'll be notified if and when we need you."

Charlotte leans over the seat, toward me. "Doesn't sound like much of an emergency. The guy was already dead."

"I don't think I could handle the dead," I say.

"I don't know, the dead would be less work."

The van slows and then turns into a large parking lot. We drive past a corrugated-steel garage with two gas pumps and stop in front of a two-storey, Klondike-style clapboard building—the kind with a false façade that makes the building appear taller than it is. It is lake-blue with white trim and looks out of place on the tundra, like a corked bottle washed up on a desert island beach and you hope to God there's something decent inside.

Larry opens the mud-caked rear door of the van and drops our backpacks on the gravel.

"Your living quarters are in there," Louise says, pointing to an orange construction trailer beside the hotel. "Door's open. Pick a room. Toilets and showers are down the hall, on the left. Come to the restaurant in the morning, sometime between ten and eleven. Susan will show you the ropes."

Larry jumps back into the driver's seat and speeds toward the garage in a cloud of shale dust. Charlotte and I stand alone in the empty parking lot. Charlotte runs her hands through her short bob and pulls out fingers draped in hair. "Where did Louise go?" she says as she releases the hair into the wind.

"Inside the hotel, I think."

Charlotte clomps toward the trailer, bent over under the weight of her backpack.

The screen door swings wide open with the wind. I race up the few stairs to catch it before it slams shut. The place has an abandoned vibe to it. The air is cool and dusty. Sunlight streams through a window at the opposite end of the trailer's long hall. I drop my packs and scan the doors for a washroom symbol. I push open a door with no knob and fumble to find a light switch inside the windowless room. Fluorescent lights buzz and then illuminate a row of toilet stalls. I lock the door out of habit and sit on the frigid seat.

I wash my hands for a long while. The hot water is ecstasy. My hair looks like fried angel's hair pasta and my eyes are bloodshot. The crop of duress pimples on my forehead rivals Charlotte's stress-shed. I exhale fog onto the mirror until it covers my face.

Charlotte sits on a narrow bed next to piles of neatly folded sheets and blankets. Across from her is a bunk bed made of four-by-fours. She holds up a quarter. "We'll flip for the single bed—I call heads." She rises momentarily from her claimed territory to look at the quarter on the linoleum floor. "Heads."

I slouch on the bottom bunk's bare foam mattress. "I can't sleep here. I can't even sit up without hitting my head."

"Sleep on the top bunk."

I stand to examine the top bunk. "It's less than two feet from the ceiling." I walk to the window and turn the electric heater to the highest setting. "What time is it?"

"Two-thirty—a.m."

"Weird. The sky's as bright as if it were two p.m. in Vancouver."

"Where's the bathroom?" Charlotte asks.

"Down the hall, door with no knob. Can you look for an electric heater and turn it on? It's freezing in there."

The trailer vibrates like a kazoo played by the wind. The window has no curtain. The night sun illuminates my bunk. I turn my face toward the wall. Prickly pillow feathers press into my cheek. Charlotte hasn't returned from the bathroom. When stressed, Charlotte gets constipated. I read that people have died on the toilet from constipation. If that's how she goes, so be it. I'm too tired to check on her. "Look after your sister," Mom said to me at the airport. Dad a no-show. He would have said the same. Both probably relieved to be free of the responsibility that is Charlotte for the summer.

Charlotte's voice startles me awake. "Why don't we get to live in the hotel? They said we would at the interview." She is lying on top of her bedding, combat boots pointed toward the ceiling.

"They said a lot at the interview. I highly doubt all the YTG are seniors who eat nothing but dessert." I kick the plywood above me. "I'm sleeping in a shoebox."

"Shut the lid."

II

I wake up shivering in the XXXL men's undershirt I wear for pajamas. Somehow my pillow and wool blanket ended up on the floor. I crack my forehead on the upper bunk as I step onto the cold linoleum. "Fuck!" I say in a delayed whisper. Charlotte's quiet snores don't skip a beat. Yesterday's cigarette probably irritated her respiratory tract. I wrap myself in the wool blanket, creep across the hall, and peek inside a doorless room—an attempt at a lounge. The vending machine is empty and there's nothing on the TV except grey crackling fuzz. I pull four tacks from a bulletin board on the wall and head back to our room.

I unroll the collage–poster that I made from magazine photographs that inspire me: models in billowy evening gowns flitting through historical European cityscapes, Hemingway's Key West studio, a Frida Kahlo painting. I use the end of my deodorant stick to hammer the tacks into the wall. Charlotte raises her head and opens her squinty eyes. "What the hell. What are you doing?"

"It's eight. I thought it would be okay—I'm the one who should be tired. Your bed creaks every time you move."

"Well, you snore like a goddamned chainsaw. I had to turn off the heater. The air's so fucking dry in here."

There is something about being accused of snoring—a humiliation that cuts deep. I unearth my beach towel, take my toiletry bag and head for the shower.

Charlotte's thick hair shoots out from her head like rough lines of charcoal on a sketch pad. She pulls her straightening iron over the charcoal wisps and then unplugs it. Her hair sits on her head like a voluminous sooty mushroom, but I say nothing. She lines up her hairspray, deodorant, and perfume on the floor in front of the mirror. I leave quickly before her aerosols take the room. The wind slams the trailer door shut behind me.

A huge dog bounds toward me. I slow my steps to a shale-shuffle and watch, through wind-blown hair, as a guy in the parking lot lights a cigarette instantly, as though the wind doesn't exist. He's attractive in a shaggy-haired, surfer-boy way. The attractiveness could be accidental and due to total neglect. The sandy highlights in his hair could be grease and his tan dirt. I freeze as the dog sniffs my crotch forcefully then turns its gaze across the highway at a small herd moving on the tundra. The hotel's front doors open. "Ireland, come here!" a deep male voice booms from the direction of the entrance. The dog trembles, not wanting to take its focus from the animals, and then trots reluctantly toward a lanky, black-haired man in a red plaid flannel shirt. He's older, striking, with short, dark hair, a finely chiselled face, and crinkly dark eyes. The man watches the moving beasts, holding onto the dog's collar to keep it from the herd. "Migration began a few weeks ago. These are the stragglers." His voice is low, smooth, and melodic like a public radio host.

"Caribou?"

"Yeah. Porcupine herd. Heading to the calving grounds, Beaufort Sea. Longest land migration on earth. Cows have gone ahead. These are bulls and yearlings."

I wrap my arms tightly over my chest. "How long will it take them?"

"They average about twenty K a day."

The breeze smells of hair spray and perfume. Charlotte's managed to put on full makeup in record time. "Is that a wolf?"

He takes in Charlotte with a subtle grin. "Half wolf, half Irish wolfhound."

"Looks like a wolf. I'm surprised the caribou don't stampede," she says.

"It's the two-legged predators they're watching out for. Dempster makes them easy targets. Anyone can shoot from the highway. Harder to track a Caribou on the tundra."

"I can't believe how close they are to the hotel," she says.

"Caribou been migrating a long time before the Dempster and the hotel existed."

A small crowd of guests or tourists has gathered in front of the hotel entrance with their cameras. I leave Charlotte to flirt with the man and his dog and weave my way through the tourists toward the hotel. The surfer dude has disappeared. A little boy in bare feet and baseball-themed pajamas stands alone at the edge of the parking lot. I pull open the front door and gasp as I am greeted by a disembodied caribou. The head is a predictable shock, as if I've entered a theme park haunted house, and a fake corpse suddenly appeared. An older man, with thick black eyebrows and freshly trimmed, silver-black hair, glances up from the polished wood front desk. "Welcome," he says. He is a smiling sun with round cheeks, and I have to smile back. A golden eagle's outstretched wings take up the entire wall above his happy face.-

I wander past a bookcase, the public washrooms, a shiny staircase, and down a hall to the Lost Patrol Saloon. I step inside; the doors swing shut behind me. The room has a heavy, lingering scent of yeasty beer, whisky, and tobacco. More disembodied heads line the saloon walls. I recognize the round-horned sheep's head as an endangered Dall. The floor-to-ceiling wall of windows at the rear of the saloon is the only space free of the dead.

The bar doors swing open. "Jesus, it's a morgue in here," Charlotte says.

"Why would anyone want a dead creature on their wall when they can see the living version in their front yard?"

"Like Tom said, a lazy ass who shoots from their truck."

"Tom—the old dude with the wolf-dog?"

"He's not that old." Charlotte presses her face to the wall, reading the inscription below a black and white photograph before moving on to the next.

I join her at the wall and then follow her around the saloon, studying the old photographs and reading the story about a Yukon outlaw called the Mad Trapper. I pause at the picture of a corpse, the Mad Trapper's face frozen in a self-satisfied half smile. "He's the creepiest thing in this room."

"The Mounties got their man."

"I guess we can be thankful that they didn't stuff him and put his head on the saloon wall."

"I have a feeling that they would if they could. I can picture it over the bar."

"They shot him at Eagle River, just north of the hotel. We should check it out."

"Yeah. On our day off."

I walk toward the wall of windows. There are no manmade structures, no major landmarks, only distant, undulating mountains dotted with miniature spruce trees. "This view is pure wild! Those must be the Ogilvie Mountains. Larry said the Ogilvies are behind the hotel and Richardsons are in front."

Charlotte sits in the leather club chair. I fall into the chair across from her. After twelve hours in the van and another six on a foam mattress, the soft leather feels luxurious. "Do you think that smiling man at the front desk is George, the one with brain damage?"

"Probably. Who else would be that happy about working here?"

"You know, despite the dead, it's kind of relaxing in here, like a library."

"Instead of books, there's booze."

"Don't get any ideas. You're barely legal."

Charlotte rolls her eyes and gets up from the chair.

I drag myself from the comforts of the chair to sort through an assortment of snack-sized chip bags in a basket on the end of the bar as Charlotte pounds out an aggressive rendition of "Chopsticks" on the player piano—despite holding a Grade Eight from the Royal Conservatory. "Do you think the chips are free for staff?" I shout above the noise.

The saloon doors swing open and a large, middle-aged woman in distressed jeans marches her voluptuous bottom behind the bar. She wears the extra weight like armour. It's a take-me-as-I-am-because-I-could-give-a-fuck statement before she bodychecks you out of her way. A single white lock hangs rebelliously at the front of her short, dark hair. She looks startled to find us in the empty bar. She reaches beneath the counter with muscular arms and heaves a plastic tray of washed glasses onto the top. Her billowy sleeves sway as she wipes the tall beer glasses with a dish towel.

"You look like your sister," the woman says in the silence after the stupefying piano solo. I detect a faint French-Canadian accent.

"Really? You can tell we're sisters?"

She nods. "Same face, different hair. That and there's . . ." She squints her eyes, as though trying to find the right word, and then butts her fist together. "How do you say, *discorde*?

"Discord. It's the same in English."

"There is *discorde* in your energy," she adds.

"I'm Charlie." Charlotte reaches her hand across the bar. In my entire life, I have never heard Charlotte introduce herself as Charlie, to anyone.

"Rumi," I say to mock Charlotte. "Rumer, actually."

The woman looks unamused. "Odette. I prefer Ode." Her fragrance is noticeable but subtle, a scent that could go either way, a

European men's cologne, or a citrus women's. Charlotte disappears through the saloon doors.

"Your sister is in a hurry. Better catch her." It's not a suggestion.

Charlotte stands at the dining room entrance. The white-on-white dining room walls and wainscotting are a stark contrast to the crypt-like saloon. "Looks like they spent the wad decorating the bar."

"I suppose we should be thankful they ran out of money."

"Yeah. Dead heads watching everyone eat would kill the appetite."

"It would make you wonder what's in the burgers. Impressive rendition of 'Chopsticks,' by the way."

"Get a load of Yukon Cornelius."

I shift my focus to the two men seated in the middle of the dining room. They are beards, penetrating eyes, and abnormally large hands that dwarf the mugs they grasp. "Who?"

"Yukon Cornelius. He looks like the lumberjack in that retro, stop-motion Christmas special. The one with the gay elf."

"You're right. He has the same hair. All he needs is the toque."

"There's something sexy about a man in plaid."

"If you're into Paul Bunyan."

Yukon Cornelius lets forth a bellow of a laugh. He glances up, meets my gaze, and pauses with curiosity. If I look away now it will be too obvious. The blood leaves my head like a retreating ocean wave, warning the beach that the next wave will be monumental. The blood rolls in like a tsunami. My flooded face burns red hot. I turn and causally walk to the lobby to escape the awkwardness. The smiling man is gone. The lobby's deserted except for dead beasts. I creep back down the hall and survey the dining room.

Charlotte's talking to a woman in a dowdy red skirt and apron. The woman looks animated and pleased to be in conversation with Charlotte—who's probably introduced herself as Charlie. The mountain men are getting up from their table. The prospect of small talk with Yukon Cornelius aborts my plan to join the waitressing conversation. I hurry through the front doors and then break into a run for the orange trailer.

Charlotte flops on her bed. "Susan thought it was weird that you just took off."

I know she's referring to the woman she was talking to in the restaurant. The name-drop is to inform me that she's already ahead of me in the hotel's social hierarchy. "When do we start?"

"Today at two."

"How long are the shifts?"

"They're seven hours—there's only two a day. Seven to two and two to nine. We're on again tomorrow morning."

"We haven't even been here twelve hours!"

"They're short-staffed."

"How many waitresses are there, besides us?"

"There was supposed to be someone on our flight up here, but she bailed at the last minute. Two more were supposed to already be here, but their flight got cancelled because of wind or something."

"We're it?"

"There's Susan—I heard she's involved with some hottie up here named Rob, the hotel mechanic."

"That dumpy woman in the red skirt?"

"She's better looking up close," Charlotte says, her words quietly trailing to a nearly inaudible range. Now I know it can't be true; Charlotte doesn't even believe it.

"Who told you that he's hot?"

"Louise mentioned he looks a little like John Kennedy Junior."

"I'll believe it when I see it. Where does Susan stay? Are we the only suckers in the trailer?"

"There's another trailer, bigger, on the other side of the hotel. They live in there."

The screen door creeks open and slowly shuts; soft footsteps in the hall and then three knocks on our door. I open the bedroom door as the screen door squeals shut. I step over the smoothly folded plastic garbage bag at my feet and look out the window at a boy on a bicycle, peddling like a mini tornado through the parking lot. It looks like the kid I saw this morning, in his pajamas, watching the caribou. I pick up the bag and pull out two long, red skirts and two long-sleeved, white sweaters. “How lovely. We’ve received a bag of polyester from a kid on a bike.”

The loose sweater hangs awkwardly and a thick elastic on the skirt bunches all the fabric at the waist. I hoist the red polyester skirt a few inches above my knees and roll the waist, hiding it underneath the waistband of the acrylic V-necked sweater. A golden eagle, the Hotel Beringia’s emblem, spreads its embroidered wings across my right boob.

“You look lumpy,” Charlotte says.

I unfold the skirt and let it drop to its intended mid-calf length.

Susan’s smile fades as we approach. She looks me up and down. “The dining room is usually quiet once breakfast is finished. Lunches are hit-and-miss—depending on highway traffic. It picks up again by late afternoon.” The English accent works in her favour—she’s an Arctic exotic. She speaks quickly, with a cheery yet cold smile, directing her explanations toward Charlotte, as though I’m invisible. Her brown hair is an undetermined style of floppy curls that she must have spent hours perfecting. The result is so dull I can’t even call it ugly. She shoos a giant fly from her unremarkable face as she natters on to Charlotte, pointing at various locations in the dining room, oblivious that the fly is poised to enter the tunnel-like curl atop her head. I want it to crawl inside. I float in and out of focus until she says, “We pool our tips and split them with the cook.”

I laugh aloud, an unconscious reaction.

Susan turns to acknowledge my existence for the first time. "You find that amusing?"

"No. Quite the opposite, actually."

"Do you have waitressing experience?"

I've never waitressed a day in my life.

"Yes," Charlotte says. It's a stretch. She worked at a Dairy Queen drive-in for a total of two weeks. They fired her because she refused to abide by the serving sizes. Her sundaes were like Gaudi sculptures and her blizzards like cement—all topping and very little ice cream. Susan tosses her manicotti curls abruptly, possibly sensing Godzilla the fly has set up shop in one of them.

"When do you expect the other waitresses?" I say.

"They're coming from Old Crow, a fly-in-only community. Who knows when they'll get out." She looks directly at Charlotte. "Come, I'll introduce you to Eugenie, kitchen manager—she's from Old Crow too, actually."

A short, plump woman, with a black ponytail slipping from a white hairnet, stands with her back toward us, rolling dough on the kitchen counter. "I found the sisters," Susan says.

Eugenie turns, holding a large wooden rolling pin in her hand. Her features are smooth, rounded, and her skin the colour of tea. "My new servers! And not a moment too soon. You two are the talk of the hotel."

"I hope that's a good thing," I say.

"We don't often have two pretty sisters from the city waitressing up here." I detect an accent in her voice. Her inflection is like a low, calm stream. Eugenie sweeps her finger up and down. "I see Sebastian's delivery service was on time."

"Your uniforms," Susan says, monotone.

"The little boy, that was Sebastian?"

"Yes, my son. They might not be the latest fashion, but they will save your own clothes from getting ruined. I see you're on breakfast shift tomorrow. We usually have only one waitress on early shift, but you two are new. We'll see how it goes. I'd get an early night if I were you. You won't have much time between shifts. Use it wisely. Don't let YTG convince you otherwise."

"YTG?"

"Over half a dozen single men with nothing to do on a weeknight," Eugenie adds.

"Don't frighten them, Eugenie. Yukon Territory Government—highway workers. Don't worry, you'll have the pleasure of serving them every morning," Susan says. I can't tell if she's being sarcastic. "If you think the YTG are wankers now, you should see them on a Friday, or better still, in the winter." She unties her waitressing apron and throws it into an open bin. "I'm off, then."

"And here she is—your cook tonight," Eugenie says. Louise walks into the kitchen through a delivery door that opens to the outside. Her hair is freshly dyed, a more natural dark shade, the colour of coffee beans. She's wearing a white chef's jacket and fitted black jeans that accentuate her wide-spaced thin legs.

Charlotte rearranges the ketchup bottle and the salt and pepper shakers on each table. It's a fake make-work project if I've ever seen one.

"One of you might want to get in here and finish up the dishes before things get busy," Louise says.

I turn around to see where her voice is coming from. She's standing at the order window looking bored. Two giant men walk into the dining room. It's Yukon Cornelius from this morning. I take a plastic-covered menu from a stack beside the till and open it in front of Charlotte. "It looks like pretty basic greasy diner fare. Though, I admit, today's dinner special is starting to smell good. Lasagna."

"Go." Charlotte nods her head toward the table where the mountain men have seated themselves.

"You go. You're the one with experience. I'll wait for the tour bus and the hordes of seniors that should be storming the place any minute."

"Get out there."

"But it's Yukon Cornelius."

"An inexperienced waitress can get away with anything. No one expects much. All you have to do is smile." Charlotte pushes open the kitchen door. It swings shut behind her. She's not coming out.

I approach the men's table and then place a menu in front of each of them. I smile just enough to confuse everyone—the waitress with the Mona Lisa smile. "Can I get you something to drink?" I force myself to glimpse at their faces. Yukon Cornelius seems pleased with my question. He has the most startling pale turquoise eyes. My face instantly warms.

"We'll have a couple of pints," his swarthy companion says. His thick, wavy black hair is cut in a long, trendy man-bob. Up close, his dark beard is more *Miami Vice* shadow than mountain man. "And two burgers." He hands me back the menu without looking at me.

Charlotte has reappeared at the till to needlessly restack the menus.

"They want pints." I glance at their table. "What do I put in the pint?"

"They want draft. You get it from the bar."

I put their order in, then push open the saloon door, relieved to find Ode sitting behind the counter, working on what looks like accounting. George, the smiling front-desk man, sits across the bar counter from her, holding an empty glass.

"I need two pints, please—drafts."

Without looking up, Ode says, "We open at four. Before that, you pull your own pints."

It's past four, but I pull the lever like I've seen people do on TV. It flows like root beer. I block Ode's view of the pints as I slosh them back and forth between the glasses to get rid of some of the foam. I take the pints toward the dining room.

"Stop! Bring those back here," Ode says. She dumps my pints and pours two fresh ones. I'm not sure whether to be insulted or to thank her.

There are two new tables: eight middle-aged people in spandex and a single woman in a booth by the window. "What's with all the spandex?"

"Cycling tour."

"You take that guy." Charlotte nods toward a middle-aged man, with a substantial moustache, in tight Wrangler jeans who's moving with an elegant swagger that can only be described as a sashay toward the small table near the till.

I place a menu in front of Mr. Moustache.

"It's nice to see a friendly new face in here," he says.

"The staff aren't usually friendly?"

"Winter's hard on the crew up here. It's always a pleasure to meet the new summer staff."

"Coffee?"

He nods. "What brings you to Beringia?"

"I don't know—I mean, aside from the oblivious: needing money for school in the fall. I guess it's an adventure, somewhere new. A hotel on the Arctic Circle seems sort of exotic."

"I like your spirit—keep walking toward wild." He smiles so broadly that his moustache is pulled straight across his face.

"Wild?"

"Given the choice between known and unknown paths, choose the unknown. It will scare the bejesus out of you, but it will be your greatest teacher." *Bejesus.* I never hear that word anymore. My dad used to say it when we were little. "You know what? I'd like a pint as well as the coffee. And I'll take the special."

"Sure."

The mountain men haven't touched their platters. Miami Vice motions me over with his hand. He lifts his bun to reveal a blackened patty that was once a frozen puck. Yukon Cornelius lifts his bun to reveal a lump of coal.

"What the bejesus! Is that what I served you?"

Miami Vice sits back in his seat, "Who else?"

Yukon Cornelius raises his thick eyebrows, as though apologizing for his mate's tone. His eyes are smiling, maybe amused by my retro language. I can't blame him, I almost laughed out loud when Mr. Moustache said it.

"I can't believe she sent these out, sorry," I say as I collect their plates.

Charlotte sidles up to me on my way to the kitchen with the burnt burgers. "What's with the mountain men?"

"I'm handling it."

In the hot, greasy recesses of the kitchen, Louise throws two new frozen patties on the grill. She smacks the burgers with the steel spatula as though she's beating them and calls them "motherfuckers."

The middle-aged woman by the window doesn't even have a menu yet. Damn Charlotte, I thought she could handle one more on top of the cyclists. I rush to the table and place a menu in front of her, prepared to be told off for the tardy service.

She smiles as I place the menu on the table. "Thank you." It's a genuinely kind smile, the rare variety usually found only on kindergarten teachers.

"I'm sorry it took so long to bring you the menu. It's our first day."

"Not to worry. You're doing fine. The restaurant is busy tonight." She has an unusual accent that sounds like a mixture of Eastern European and French. She tucks one side of her chin-length, toffee-coloured hair behind her ear. "Do you know what? I have already decided on the special. May I order it now?"

"Of course."

"I would also like an iced tea—no sugar."

"One lasagna special and an iced tea—no sugar. Ah, sorry, we don't have iced tea."

"A tall glass, full to the rim with ice, and a cup of hot black tea is all I need."

"I can do that. Are you on vacation?"

"Work trip."

"Where is home?"

"Vancouver is where I currently reside—Montreal is home." It fits. Even makeup-free, dressed in cargo pants and lace-up leather boots, she embodies culture.

"What sort of work brings you up here?"

"I'm an archeologist with Simon Fraser University. Excavating northwest of here.

First trip up this year. Unsure what shape the site will be in."

"That's so cool. What type of things are you looking for?"

She leans toward me, as though she's sharing a secret. "Very old things." She winks.

I laugh. "What sort of old things?"

"Bones. Boring old bones."

"I doubt that they're boring."

She laughs. "You are right. They are not boring at all."

"How far is your site from here?"

"Not far the way the crow flies. Inaccessible by land—a helicopter will take us in the morning, if the wind cooperates."

"I'll be back with your order as quick as I can—sorry, again, about taking so long."

She nods and lowers her eyelids in understanding. "You are doing your best." She leans out of the booth and points behind me at the pitchers of ice water beside the stacks of glasses on the buffet counter. "I'm just going to help myself to a glass of water, if that's okay."

“I can bring you one.”

“I got it. You go ahead and place my order. Do what you need to do.”

“Of course, sorry.”

The saloon doors are hooked wide open for business. The quiet library-bar has vanished, and the Wild West has come to life in the Arctic. I count only two women in the place and Ode is one of them. The rest of the tables are filled with all sorts of men. A cowboy sits on a bar stool strumming his guitar, belting out an acoustic rendition of “Pretty Woman.” Under the wide-brim hat, straight black hair hangs down one side of his forehead. It’s Tom, the dog’s dad—the cowboy can sing.

The only other woman in the saloon is elegant, yet decidedly masculine, with straight, shoulder-length, light brown hair and narrow eyes—Clint Eastwood with ovaries. Happy George, sits on the bar stool next to her.

“I’ll have another Coke when you’ve got the time,” he says to Ode.

“Sorry, George, you’re cut off. Two colas a day is the limit. You’ve got to watch the sugar. We don’t want your wife marching in here. How about ice water?”

George turns to Clint. “Good to meet you. What brings you to the Yukon?”

“I work for highways, George,” she says in an accent that sounds Australian.

“Could I have a pint for Mr. Moustache?” I ask Ode.

“Ha!” Ode laughs. “Is Frank in there?”

“Handlebar moustache and Wrangler jeans?”

“That’s him.”

“I remember you. I can’t recall your name,” George says to me.

“Good on you, George—you always remember the pretty ones.” Ode winks at me.

"I'm one of the new waitresses, Rumer," I say to George and then turn to Ode. "Could I also get a stein of ice—full to the top?"

Ode places an ice-filled glass on my tray and nods toward the saloon doors. "You better get that out."

I carry the tray through the bar, trying not to spill it in front of the watering hole of hungry eyes that follow me. Charlotte stands at the saloon entrance. "What are you doing?" I say as I pass by with the tray. She doesn't answer. She's transfixed by the singing cowboy.

"Here you are, Frank," I say, putting the stein down without spilling a drop.

He smiles and then nods. "Thank you very much."

Two burger platters sit on the narrow order window counter. The new patties are as scorched as the first set, but I'm not brave enough to ask her to redo them again. I take a steak knife and quickly scrape some of the black off, then drop the burgers in front of the mountain men. Then I rush behind the buffet counter, pour hot water into a small teapot, throw in a tea bag for the old-bone scientist, and leave it to steep. I peek at the mountain men's table. They seem to be having a serious discussion. *Please let it not be about the burgers.* Let them be ravishingly hungry gluttons that eat the burgers in giant bites without opening the buns.

"I can't believe it's already nine. The first shift flew by," I say as Charlotte sorts through the tip jar.

"Not fast enough for me. Those rich European cyclists? They left me nothing! Zero tip. Assholes."

"Cheapskates. Mischa, that archeologist, gave me a five-dollar tip—over fifty percent of her bill."

"How do you remember her name?"

"It was on her credit card: Dr. Mischa Lempicka. I like how it sounds. How much American did we get in total? Their dollar is worth more than ours right now."

"Forty-eight."

"Nice."

Charlotte whispers, "I divided the American between us. Left Louise the Canadian."

"Fair. She's the reason the mountain men left me nothing. She burnt their burgers twice."

Louise leans against the stove, smoking a cigarette, slouched forward and done-for. She needn't take it so hard. I think the shift was pretty much a success: the mountain men ate the entire second go of the hamburger platters without sending them back, and in the interest of health and safety, they probably should have.

There's no way we're getting out of here before midnight. I've never in my life seen so many grimy dishes. I take a bite of an oatmeal chocolate chip cookie.

"Is that your dinner?" Louise asks.

"Yup."

She shakes her head disapprovingly.

"When is the dishwasher supposed to arrive?"

"Huh?" Louise's tired face morphs into a scowl.

"I mean dishwasher person, not machine."

"Don't hold your breath." She glances at the clock above the freezer. "You get time and a half after ten," she says and then steps toward the outside door exit. She turns before opening it and says, "Goodnight," like a defeated sigh of camaraderie, as though saying, "Welcome to Hotel Beringia."

III

Men with scratchy faces begin to file unenthusiastically into the dining room. I scan the surly, silent crowd. Judging by the facial expressions, they are an assortment of escaped criminals, highway workers, northern truckers, and possibly, the odd tourist—trying to sober up from last night's bender.

"The Dempster seems to be pulling in an awful lot of sorry-looking creatures today."

Eugenie laughs. "Be nice. They're YTG. The hotel is home." She opens the oven and takes out an extra-large pan of delicious-smelling buns.

"Cinnamon buns?"

"Sticky buns—where's Charlotte?"

"On her way." Eugenie hasn't noticed my updated uniform, or if she has, she's refrained from commenting on it. I used my travel scissors to hack off the bottom of the skirt and hand-stitched a new hem that falls between mini-skirt and knee-length.

"Don't look so worried. YTG serve themselves breakfast and take a bag lunch to go. Your job is to make sure the breakfast buffet is topped up, the coffee pot's full, and clear away their dishes. Best get to it." She nods her head, two quick nudges, toward the kitchen door.

I pull out the used coffee filters and throw them in the garbage while taking furtive glances at the YTG tables. They're a quiet crew. I read their silence as sadness, as though there is no hope that the day ahead will provide any moments of joy. The surfer dude could be a rough-looking sixteen or a skinny thirty-year-old. Aside from him, the only other semi-attractive highway guy is Tom, the singing cowboy. I count the assorted faces: seven men and the woman from the bar last night: Clint Eastwood with ovaries. I peek my head in the kitchen door.

"Who is the YTG woman?" I ask Eugenie.

"Caroline. She's the boss, highway forewoman."

Charlotte arrives fourteen minutes late, mushroom helmet seared into submission and her eyes freshly lined in coal black. Her skirt is shorter than mine. She hacked hers off too, though hasn't bothered to hem it. Tom watches her with his crinkly, cowboy eyes. He has to be close to our dad's age. Charlotte turns twenty in September but looks younger. Maybe he's a pedophile and freakishly into her new macabre image.

A bald head, attached to a thick neck and tattooed arms, thumps his coffee cup on the table and then holds it up as Charlotte passes. She ignores him. I ignore the cup-thumper too. Eugenie said the highway workers serve themselves the buffet breakfast and I am not going to break protocol for someone so rude. I head to the kitchen to see if there are more sticky buns to bring out. The cup thumping continues behind me and then a deep, angry voice shouts, "Hey!"

I turn to glance at his table. Charlotte strides past the cup-thumper like he's not even there. She walks past me, into the kitchen. Witnessing rude waitress behaviour somehow feels worse than actually being a rude waitress. I take the coffee pot to his table and force a tenuous smile. His hazel eyes flutter on the edge of cruel as I lift the pot tentatively. He slams his coffee mug onto the table-top, pushes his chair back, spits out, "Bitch!" and then stomps his heavy work boots out of the restaurant.

I remain frozen, coffee pot in hand. Charlotte darts from the kitchen, eager to feed on what's left of the drama.

"I don't get it. I ignored Cup-Thumper once. You ignored him at least twice. I'm the one who finally came to refill his mug."

"He gets that I don't give a shit. He thinks you might."

"I do give a shit. I ignored him on principle—Eugenie said the YTG's serve themselves and I'm not going to baby every lazy ass who throws a tantrum."

Tom has been watching the drama with a slight smirk on his face. He pushes back his chair slowly, stands, stretches his arms wide, and then takes a convoluted path out of the dining room, slinking behind us. "Looks like the Barbie dolls have attitude." The words roll off his smooth tongue. It takes tremendous self-control not to flip him the finger.

The restaurant is empty except for handlebar-moustached Frank. I cleared away his plate and cutlery ages ago. He shows no signs of paying the bill that I placed on his table. His jean-on-jean wardrobe and seventies 'stache are over a decade out of fashion and yet, somehow, he pulls off the look without seeming pathetic. I wipe down his table while he sits, nursing his coffee like a dying man. He glances up at me. His wide smile is genuine, innocent of my critical thoughts—suddenly, I regret wiping the table.

There's a woman behind the front desk. The name tag says SERAPHINA.

"There was an older gentleman working here yesterday," I say.

She looks up from the desk. "George. What do you want with my dad?"

"Nothing, really . . . what's with the saloon's name—The Lost Patrol—Is there some sort of Yukon history there?"

"White history." She breathes in loudly and sighs as though she's been asked the question too many times. "Four Mounties thought they could travel from McPherson to Dawson without a guide." She looks bored.

"It seems like it would be hard to get lost around here. There are virtually no trees, lots of mountain ranges to follow—you can see for miles from any high point."

"That's what the dead Mounties thought. Too arrogant to hire our people as guides."

"I was thinking of doing a little hiking around here on my day off."

"Don't step on the tundra. It takes a hundred years to regrow," she says.

"I'll stick to the Dempster," I say, worried that she thinks I'm some clueless city girl and worried that she might be right. "I'm Rumer, one of the new waitresses, by the way."

"I know who you are."

"I just finished my first early shift. We're crazy short-staffed until the Old Crow waitresses arrive. If they arrive."

"You're talking about my sisters."

"Oh, do you know when they're arriving?"

"My sister moved to Whitehorse with her band."

"Is there another sister coming then?"

Seraphina seems unusually fixated on the washroom doors. I glance behind me to see what it is she finds so distracting. A toilet flushes. A guy in a mechanic's steel-blue jumpsuit emerges from the men's toilets. He's in his early thirties, athletic build, short, thick, dark brown hair, parted on the side. He strides through the lobby like he's some kind of wonderful, side glances at the front desk and then looks me up and down. He runs his hands through his hair before pushing open the front door. The front doors close but whiff of gasoline remains.

"I'm guessing that was Rob."

Seraphina shudders as though wanting to shake off Rob's strut. "Yeah," she says, sounding tired.

I spot Eugenie's kid outside in the parking lot with the dog,

Ireland. I push open the doors and then stand on the edge of the front step.

"Sebastian, isn't it?"

He nods. "People call me Seb." He picks up a substantial piece of wood and throws it out of the parking lot. Ireland bounds into a ditch of purple fireweed to find it.

"Ireland's lucky to have a friend like you."

"He's my dog."

"I thought he was Tom's."

"Tom adopted him from *me*. He was mine first. Tom calls him Ireland, but his name is Shorty Bear—Bear for short. My mom says he's too big for our place now. He lives with Tom—temporarily."

"Does that confuse him, having two names?"

"No. Bear is smart. He knows four languages: Gwich'in, English, wolf, and dog."

"That is impressive."

"He's half wolf."

"How'd that happen? Where'd you find him?"

"My uncle. He's a trapper in Old Crow. He has Annie, Bear's mom."

"Annie's a wolf?"

"No, she's Irish wolfhound. She keeps the wolves away from my uncle's lines—my uncle says that wolf-dogs have the brains of a wolf and the courage of a dog."

"How old are you, big boy?" I say after Bear drops the stick at my feet.

"He's two."

"Whose yellow camper is that?" I say, pointing to an older, faded motorhome parked at the end of the lot.

"Tom's. Bear sleeps in there sometimes."

"It's the same yellow-gold colour as the Barbie camper I got from

Santa when I was a kid. Well, I got the tent trailer and convertible; Charlotte got the camper."

"You believe in Santa?"

The kid looks to be around eleven, too old to believe in Santa, but I can't risk it. "A little?"

Sebastian retrieves the stick from my feet. He throws the stick farther than I ever could. Bear disappears into the short trees on the opposite side of the highway.

"Are you homeschooled?"

"Pretty much—what are you going to do now, on your break?" he says.

"How do you know it's my break?"

"My mom told me."

"I'm guessing you know all the comings and goings at the hotel."

"Pretty much—my mom's the hotel chef."

I smile. He makes it sound so much classier than the greasy spoon I just stepped out of. "Hotel chef? Lucky. I bet she cooks all sorts of delicious treats for you."

"Sometimes—she's usually too busy." We glance across the highway in unison, checking to see what's keeping Bear "I got a new bike."

"Nice. I wish I had one."

"You don't have a bike?"

"I do, back at home in Vancouver, but I didn't bring it with me."

"You could borrow a hotel bike." Sebastian looks directly at me. "My mom does—all the time." He nods quickly for emphasis.

"Maybe I will." Judging by Eugenie's plumpness, I have doubts about the "all the time."

He turns his gaze to the ground and pushes shale around with the toe of his worn cowboy boot. He looks up and slaps his thigh several times. "Come on, Bear." Bear bounds from the ditch. Sebastian takes off running. Bear gallops past the lanky boy. I watch them until they round the corner at the far end of the hotel and disappear from view.

Charlotte stomps out the front door.

"You forgot to take off your apron."

She looks down. "Shit."

"I feel bad. I think Eugenie's son wanted to ask me to go on a bike ride with him, but I brushed him off."

"Keep him away from me. I didn't come up here to babysit—Susan predicts they'll be busy tonight. She said you could work a double shift if you want."

"She wants me?"

"She asked me, but I said no."

I glance and the trailer and then back at the hotel. "I guess I'll do it."

I flop onto my bed and roll toward the wall, away from the light streaming through the edge of the sheet-curtain that I tacked over the window. Burnt burgers, scalding soapy water, banging pots, shouting European accents, and disembodied heads jostle for footing in my mind. I shut my eyes. The images remain.

"Pull the sheet over the edge of the window."

"You," Charlotte says, lying in her bed that's right next to the window.

"You're right there."

Charlotte makes a fumbling attempt to close the sheet without bothering to look to see what her hand is doing. "How late do you think the saloon stays open?"

"Probably until they all pass out."

"Is last call in the Yukon the same as in BC?"

"No clue."

"What time is it now?"

"Almost eleven."

My eyes refuse to stay closed. They keep sliding open just enough for the thin crack of light to irritate my fried mind. I take off my nightgown and pull on a blue T-shirt that I tie-dyed myself and jeans.

"Where are you going?"

"I don't know. I can't sleep when it's so light out. I'm going to take a walk and clear my head. Want to come?"

"No."

The parking lot is the fullest I've seen it, probably because it's a Friday night. I pass the surfer dude. I smile in greeting. "Watch for the grizzly," he says. His Eastern European accent is a shock. I expected him to sound southern Californian.

"You saw one? Where?"

"Behind the hotel."

"When?"

"It was there in the morning."

"Okay. I'll keep a lookout for it, thanks. Was it big?"

"Big enough."

I wait until he's inside the hotel and then trot to the far side of to check out the staff apartments. It looks like an extended-length, doublewide trailer. At least they've tried to match the aluminum to the vibrant blue wood siding that's on the hotel's fake front.

"Can I help you with something?" I recognize Larry's irritable voice coming from behind me.

"Just out for a walk. I wanted to see where the staff apartments were for myself."

"Snoopin'," he says gruffly, a cigarette hanging from the corner of his mouth.

I step to the side, giving him leeway as he shuffles past. I sprint around the corner to the parking lot, safely out of his jaundiced view. The deserted highway continues indefinitely in two directions. We drove the southern route to get here. The north is unknown.

Walk toward wild.

I step north. The Dempster feels like a typical gravel road beneath my feet, yet knowing there's ice under the shale makes each step slightly more exciting.

The wind is like a spiritual vacuum; it sucks my mind clean. I no longer hear the abrasive echo of the banging pots and pans and sizzling of hot grease. The tundra is tempting; I long to experience the sensation of bare skin on vines, over ice. Seraphina seemed to think it was more than a bad idea. Not only will I destroy the delicate moss and lichen, but I might also drift aimlessly, overconfident in my ability to traverse the Arctic.

I slip off my runners and step from the shale. My feet sink onto a damp, living carpet—a tangle of roots, moss, tiny leaves, and needles. There are so many spaces, textures, layers, in each luxurious step. I try to step lightly, like a caribou, yet I feel like a terrorist, annihilating a miniature world with each step. I slip silently across the spongy carpet until my feet connect once again with the sharp and dusty rocks of the Dempster. This carpet is not designed for human feet. Apes aren't meant for tundra.

I continue north, alert for grizzlies. The Richardson Mountains are illuminated in the distant sun's rays. I imagine the mountains as they once were, three hundred million years ago—islands in a vast sea. The warm sun, blue sky, and empty tundra convince my mind that I'm walking through a comfortable dream, but the truth is that it's around midnight and I am a lone human in the middle of nowhere, miles from the hotel. I turn to look behind me. In the distance, on the crest of a hill, it looks like there's a large animal on the road. It's coming toward me fairly quickly on four long legs. If it's a grizzly, it's young and starving. As it gets closer, the colour turns to grey. The wolf shows no signs of stopping. I wave my arms over my head and shout, as though it's a stray dog. "Off!" I bellow in an unnaturally deep voice.

The animal looks familiar. "You! I thought you were a wolf! Bear's the name, isn't it?" I pat his long, wiry back. "You have no idea how ironic your genetics are, do you?" It feels as though I have been exploring for only minutes, but my watch says it's almost one a.m.

Bear and I walk back to the hotel together. He holds his head high, pausing periodically when he picks up a new scent, to gaze across the tundra. He gets how spectacular it is.

I creep into the trailer. The room smells of Charlotte's heavy floral perfume and fresh nail polish, but she's gone. I check out the bathroom. "Charlotte?" What if she went out looking for me but turned the wrong way, like the Lost Patrol? I sprint back to our room. Her combat boots are stashed under the bed next to her only pair of runners. There's no way she went further than the hotel without decent walking shoes. I collapse into my bunk and wriggle out of my jeans. I flip open my journal.

1:15 a.m., Saturday, May 28, Dempster Highway: I walk, immersed in an ethereal world of never-ending light and air infused with the scents of whatever minute, fragrant plants cling to the permafrost—breathing it in feels like a tall, cool drink of primeval oxygen.

I awake intermittently, the room smelling of stale macaroni and cheese. In my sleepy thoughts, I decide that there must be a garbage truck parked outside the trailer.

The late morning sun paints a stripe of light across Charlotte's face. Black lipstick is smeared on the pillow next to her head. She's asleep in my black knit mini-dress, and my strappy high-heeled sandals are lying on the floor beside her bed. It's not mac and cheese that I've been smelling. Charlotte vomited on the floor and on my shoes.

"What the hell? I've been smelling your puke all night!"

Charlotte rolls over. "Shhh."

"My shoes! Get up and wash them—now! The leather is probably ruined. Get up!"

She acts dead. I grab my toilet bag and towel. "You better have this cleaned up by the time I get back."

I pop into the quiet saloon before afternoon shift starts and pour myself a half club soda, half Coke on ice, and sit at the bar. Caroline sits further down bar, perhaps keeping Ode company while she restocks the place. I fantasize I'm at European pub, chatting with a few locals before starting the hard slog as an underappreciated waitress.

"My first Monday, but up here, it feels like any another day," I say.

"Not for Caroline. First Monday off in a long while, isn't that right?" Ode says.

Caroline half smiles and nods once.

Ode cuts open a large cardboard box with a utility knife. She straightens to standing and pauses to catch her breath. "I'm going to start doing that for George."

"What?"

"Watering down his cola," She taps the side of her nose and then squats beneath the counter and then lifts a box of pub snacks onto the bar.

"Are Rob, the mechanic, and Susan a couple?" I ask.

"They're not married. But yeah, they've already moved themselves into a staff apartment for couples." Ode air quotes the word "couples" and then adds, "Only reason he shacked up with her if you ask me. Singles don't get to live in the staff apartments."

"Where do single staff live?"

Carolina and Ode exchange a look. "In the hotel," Ode says.

"Where?"

"Down at the end of the hall, past the guest rooms on the first floor."

"Why are Charlotte and I the only staff in the trailer?"

"Isn't there a chambermaid out there?"

"Someone leaves an old cookie tin full of makeup on the bathroom counter, but I've never actually seen her in there."

"You're seasonal. Trailer would be too cold to heat in the winter." Caroline says.

"So, if we stay the winter, we get to move into the hotel?" Caroline is staring into her mug, so I look at Ode.

"Most likely. You planning on staying?" Ode says.

"No. Are the couples apartments that much nicer than the hotel rooms?"

"Bigger and there's a living area, separate bedroom, and you have your own kitchen. I suspect Susan makes Rob home-cooked meals. Waits on him hand and foot."

"Did they know each before Hotel Beringia?" I ask.

"Doubt it. Susan came over here as a nanny from England," Ode says.

"What's she doing way up here? There are no kids up here."

"Why so curious? If you have any ideas about romancing Rob, don't."

I laugh at the word "romancing" and then say, "God no."

Ode throws a tea towel across her forearm and walks toward me, sizing up my energy, no doubt. She leans over the counter and whispers, "A little bird told me that she was sleeping with the children's father. The mother found out and threw the nanny to the curb." She straightens up and wipes down the counter. "I'd have done more than throw her to the curb. I'd have thrown the old prick out with the British trash while I was at it." She whips the tea towel against the counter to stress her point.

"You don't know the facts," Caroline says.

"I think I do." Ode holds her chin high.

Charlotte walks into the saloon, in uniform with full makeup on.

She fills a pint with Coke and then takes a seat in one of a coveted club chairs by the back window. I take my soda and collapse into the leather chair opposite Charlotte.

"Cheers." I hold up my pint.

"I'm sick of all the whining. I've worked with men all my life," Caroline says loudly.

"We should shut up and take whatever scraps the oppressor throws our way, eh?" Ode shouts.

"I manage."

"You manage? Just getting by in a man's world is enough for you? Yeah, well, you've embraced your masculine side. What about the rest? The feminine side better not rear its head—you know I'm right. The feminine is only allowed when the patriarchy wants to fuck it."

"Shhh, keep your voice down," Caroline scolds.

"They're women. They can handle the truth. Women's role in the Arctic was to serve food and sex to gold-mining desperados. Nothing's changed," Ode says to Caroline, and then shouts to us, "Klondike geishas—that's what they hired you two for. Don't put up with it!"

Charlotte leans across the table. "Is she drunk? The bar's not even open yet."

"She seems sober. Do you think she's right? Is that why they hired us?"

Charlotte takes a sip of her cola, ignoring the question.

"Why didn't I see it? Dessert waitress, tour buses, living in the hotel, it was all a cover. They hired us as eye candy for the highway workers."

"It was a sales pitch. No one *wants* to work here. Ode's just jealous. She wants a piece of you," Charlotte says.

"Shut up."

"It's a valid assessment. You know she's having a fling with Caroline?"

"Who said that?"

"Louise. I overheard her call them dykes."

"She said that—to their faces?"

"No. She was bitching to herself as she cooked."

"I wouldn't take that as the gospel. According to Louise, we're all motherfuckers."

"Apparently, Caroline is from a wealthy Australian family—I can sort of see what Ode sees in her but what does she see in Ode?"

"How'd Caroline end up here?"

"Running from her past—she left a couple of kids and an ex in Australia."

"You've talked to Caroline?"

"No, Tom told me."

"Tom? You talked to the old guy?"

"He's not old."

"Too old for you. I would not trust that guy."

"You don't even know him."

"What if Ode's right—about the sexism?"

"You're a YTG geisha," Charlotte says.

"Never! Crap, it's work time—go check if anyone's in there."

"Okay, but you'll have to take my glass to your lover, Ode," Charlotte slides her empty glass across the table.

"I'd take her over Tom. Seriously."

I take our steins to the counter as Charlotte disappears through the saloon's swinging doors and then reappears in less than a minute. "Hey, Rumer, the mountain men are back and they're asking for you."

My stomach instantaneously knots. "Truth?"

"Yes and no. They're back, but they're not asking for you."

I follow Charlotte into the kitchen, pretending not to notice the two tall mountain men seated in a window booth.

I watch them from the safety of the order window. "Yukon Cornelius has bare feet."

Charlotte joins me at the window. "He's kind of hot."

"Should we say something to him?"

"Like what?"

"Something like, 'no shirt, no shoes, no service.'"

"Go for it."

His turquoise eyes follow me as I bring menus to their table. "Excuse me, but the health authority is very strict about its rules on footwear. Sorry, you'll have to put on some shoes."

"But the sign at the entrance said to remove muddy footwear." His face transitions from startled to pissed-off.

Who put up that fucking sign, and how did I miss it? "Yes, well, sorry, but you'll have to put the muddy shoes back on." I hurry to the safety of the kitchen and then spy on him through the order window. He pulls his long, awkward legs out from under the table, slowly stands, and walks out of the dining room. I glance at Miami Vice. He doesn't look too worried. He adjusts his chair and stretches out his long legs beside the table, like he's getting comfortable for an extended wait.

Yukon Cornelius appears at the dining room entrance wearing big, mud-caked, leather sandals. He lopes to his seat like a giant boy after being scolded by his teacher, mud flying in every direction.

"Nice one," Charlotte says from the order window.

I swallow my meanness; it slides into my stomach like a heavy ball of mud.

I take the mountain men's order, too distracted by maintaining my warrior façade to pay close attention. I've written down that Yukon Cornelius ordered a peanut butter and jam sandwich on wholewheat. What grown man orders that? I don't have the courage to go back and ask if it's right. I dash to the saloon to pull them pints, which manifest as my best pints to date: a perfect ratio of liquid to foam.

The mountain men's order waits at the window: a Reuben sandwich, two daily soup specials, and a PB and J sandwich on wholewheat.

The men eat quietly, without incident, and then take off without leaving a tip. Again.

"What all did you say to Yukon Cornelius? He looked gutted and left a shitload of mud balls all over the carpet."

"I said too much." I walk out of the restaurant before realizing I'm still on duty. I spot the mountain men in the lobby, standing across from the front desk. Hopefully, they're not complaining about me, and if they are, I hope it's George that they're talking to. I make a hairpin turn, sprint toward the saloon, and push open the doors. Caroline and Ode have disappeared—the room is empty. "Fuck off," I say to the Mad Trapper, as though he is responsible for turning all who gaze upon his dead face momentarily insane.

The mountain men are long gone. Seraphina's behind the front desk and talking with a middle-aged, attractive, Indigenous woman. "What can we do for you?" the woman asks.

"Mom, she's the waitress," Seraphina says.

"Oh." The woman sizes me up with a critical expression.

"Rumer." I extend my hand across the desk.

"I'm Doris. Rumer—what kind of a name is Rumer?"

"I don't know. Mine?"

"Never heard it before," Doris says abruptly.

"Who were those tall guys?"

"Who?"

"The tall men who just passed through the lobby."

"She's talking about Leo and Malik," Seraphina says.

"Scientists."

"Why are they at the hotel?"

"They live here off and on in the summer," she says.

"Do they work near here?"

"I don't know."

"Where are they from?"

"Whitehorse. Why do you ask so many questions?" Doris asks.

"No reason, only curious."

"I think Malik's from Vancouver, Mom."

"Rumour has it, the new waitress has a thing for Leo's feet," Doris says and then laughs. It sounds like a cackle. Seraphina tries to maintain her straight, stone-cold face but turns away, shaking with laughter.

I stare at them deadpan and then turn to walk back to the restaurant.

"Hang on. Leo left this with George the other night. Said it was for the new blond waitress," Seraphina says, then unsuccessfully stifles a laugh, and hands me an envelope.

I open it behind the buffet counter . . . a ten-dollar bill. Last week's tip. He was generous despite the double burnt burgers, and I was such a bitch today. I stuff the bill into my bra. No one is the wiser.

Charlotte stands on one leg scratching with her other foot like an itchy flamingo while taking the orders from a family with three super-tall teenagers. My guess is they're Dutch. Charlotte stops writing and smacks her arm wildly, at a mosquito I presume. After killing the thing, she resumes taking their order. She switches legs and continues her bird-scratching with a foul expression on her face.

At nine-thirty, I clear away a table of trophy hunters' blood-streaked plates and don't ask if they want to refill their beer pitchers. It doesn't seem to inspire them to leave. They push their chairs away from the table and sit, in matching camouflage pants, with outstretched legs, as though they own the place.

The kitchen reeks of burnt meat and animal fat. Dirty dishes everywhere. Louise sits quietly on a chair, next to the refrigerator, smoking. Charlotte stands on the opposite side of the galley kitchen, holding a burning cigarette between her fingers. I avert my eyes, not giving her the satisfaction of my disapproval.

"They ate in slow motion, gnawing on rare steaks and bragging about killing grizzlies and now they won't leave. I turned off all the lights, but you can't tell. It's still daylight in there."

Eugenie shuffles into the kitchen, wearing beaded moccasins. "Why's everyone in a huddle back here?"

"We're trying to encourage the trophy hunters to move into the saloon." I say and then mumble, "I hate trophy hunters."

"I'd keep that to yourself. They're part of the reason you and I have jobs," Eugenie says.

"It's tragic irony. They come to our country to slaughter the animals that they've wiped out in their own countries. They won't be satisfied until every creature, other than themselves, is dead."

Eugenie takes in what I've said with a contemplative expression. "You could say the same thing about colonialism."

"True, I guess." I am taken aback by Eugenie's conviction.

"We're completely out of milk. Louise, you told Susan to put in an emergency milk order?" Eugenie says, instantly back in no-nonsense, kitchen manager mode.

Louise nods. "I did."

Eugenie pins next week's schedule to the board.

Charlotte rushes to the board as Eugenie leaves. "A new name—Maxine—on a shift with you next week," she says pointing at me.

"Must be one of the waitresses from Old Crow. I was beginning to think they made her up."

Tom's voice booms from the saloon, singing "It's Hard to be Humble." I plug in the vacuum, drowning him out, as I follow Leo's trail of chunky, dried mud from the pile under his table, through the dining room, and into the hall. I stop once I reach the lobby entrance. Leo's pale eyes and hurt, childlike expression, flash in my mind. My face burns with the memory.

Charlotte has hardly made a dent in the pots and pans. I struggle to shove the vacuum back into the supply cupboard. "It's ten-thirty. So much for seven-hour shifts."

"Come here." Charlotte opens the door of the dish sanitizer. It's stacked full of dirty dishes.

"Why'd you shove them all in there? They're filthy."

"They said we'd have a dishwasher. We don't."

"It's a dish sanitizer, not a dishwasher. The dishes need to be clean before they go in there."

"It's their own fault. Hand me the bottle of dish soap."

"Are you serious? What if we break it?"

"I'm not unloading it. If you want to put everything back in the sink and hand wash it all, you're on your own." She holds a gloved hand, palm up, like a surgeon waiting for a scalpel. "Soap."

I place the bottle of soap in her palm, a silent agreement that we're doing this, aware that no good will come of it. "This reminds me of the time we faked my death. Remember? I lay at the bottom of the basement stairs, sprawled out with my eyes closed. You shouted for Dad to come quick, that I'd fallen down the stairs and died."

"Oh God, I remember now . . . holy shit, did you get in trouble!"

"According to Dad, me, pretending to be dead was a more heinous crime than you, reporting my death."

Charlotte squeezes the industrial-strength liquid dish soap inside the sanitizer, shuts the sanitizer door and turns it on.

The night never comes, yet the morning comes too soon.

YTG are lined up like irritable cattle, waiting for their first drink of the day. The joke is on them. I am no Klondike geisha and I pity the YTG worker who raises his mug today. I don't even try to force a robotic smile. They don't tip and no one looks beyond the rim of their coffee mug except Tom and his pervy eyes that follow Charlotte's every move. I ignore him, and him and him—make that the entire table except for the surfer dude. I heard Tom call him Ilya. My eyes take a rest on Ilya's face, and the morning feels a little more tolerable.

Eugenie's pissed-off voice radiates from the kitchen. "Rumer, get in here now!"

I assume Louise has fucked up the food delivery and there is no milk. I open the kitchen door, then slip and fall into an ocean of frothy, white bubbles. Eugenie points to the open dish sanitizer, where more bubbles are still falling to the floor. "Get this cleaned up now!" she shrieks. Bubbles are everywhere. Like little balls, they roll into every corner of the kitchen. I right myself and find a mop in the supply cupboard. Cold, soapy water dribbles down my legs as I mop.

The kitchen door suddenly swings open. "What needs to go out?" Charlotte asks, so innocently, with her wide Charlie smile, that even I question whose idea the dish sanitizer was.

"Someone put dish soap in dish sanitizer last night," Eugenie says.

I don't so much as glance in Charlotte's direction.

Eugenie looks directly at me. I meet her gaze and then she turns toward Charlotte. "The sanitizer does not use soap. It sanitizes the dishes with steam. You do nothing but line up the already clean, washed dishes, facing the back and then turn it on—any questions?"

Charlotte shakes her head slowly. She looks bored. I'd be pissed if I were Eugenie.

"No questions. Got it. Sorry about that. We thought it needed soap to sterilize them," I say.

"No! Never put soap in the sanitizer. I'll let it go this time, you're new," she says in a forgiving tone that I imagine she uses on Sebastian, and then she adds, "If the dish sanitizer breaks, it will mean more hours in the kitchen for you two."

I get ready for morning shift while Charlotte sleeps— before her aerosol assault gasses me out. I grab my journal to jot down something before I forget. *Wednesday, June 1: The French have a word for beautifully ugly: jolie-laide. Ilya is jolie-laide.*

Charlotte raises her grumpy head off her pillow and squints in my direction. "What time is it?"

I glance at my watch. "Crap. It's six-fifty-five."

"Seriously? Fuck! Why didn't you wake me up?" she says as she tosses off her blankets.

"Sorry. I got distracted writing." I stuff my journal under my pillow and bolt from the trailer.

The kitchen is unusually quiet. "Morning," I say. Eugenie ignores my greeting and then turns around and points to the kitchen bulletin board. I turn to look at it, confused. There's a hand-written note pinned to it.

Charlotte enters the kitchen and abruptly stops, sensing the awkward vibe. She turns to exit, as though her entrance was a mistake.

"Charlotte, you stay," Eugenie says. She wipes her doughy hands on her apron and walks to the board. She stands behind me and reads the note aloud: "I have never encountered such poor service in my life. If the waitress would have cracked a smile, hell might have frozen over."

I laugh. "Sorry," I quickly add.

"The note continues in the same vein," Eugenie says.

The note has got to be about Charlotte. She is the shittiest waitress I've ever seen. She scowls at all customers except Tom. I, at least, pull out a fake smile for the tourists. Charlotte smirks at me. She thinks the note is about me. I walk to the bulletin board. "Scratchy, heavy-handed printing . . . definitely male. Probably some lonely, bitter dude."

"The fact remains that the customer was dissatisfied, very dissatisfied. What can we do to make sure this doesn't happen again?" Eugenie says calmly. She's too nice. She deserves a better waitress than Charlotte. She might even deserve a better waitress than me.

"Maybe his shoes were muddy," Charlotte says.

I flash her my middle finger.

"That note has YTG all over it," I say, once Eugenie's inside the walk-in refrigerator looking for the milk that I pray Louise told Susan to order—any more disappointments this morning and Eugenie might change her mind about going easy on us.

"I bet the bald guy wrote it," Charlotte says.

"Cup-Thumper? Maybe. Though, it could have been one of the Europeans who witnessed your mosquito-slapping fest the other night."

Charlotte sidles up to me as I change a coffee filter. "She's rearranged the schedule."

"Who?"

"Who do you think? We don't work together again for a while."

"Was it the bubbles?"

Charlotte shrugs. "Maybe she wants to separate us to figure out which one of us inspired the poison-pen letter."

I pick up a bottle of hot pepper sauce and pretend to pour some over the giant bowl of fruit salad on the YTG breakfast buffet.

"Do it," Charlotte says.

I unscrew the lid and sprinkle a few drops on the fresh, cut-up fruit and then stir the salad with a large serving spoon.

"More," Charlotte whispers. She snatches the hot sauce and shakes it liberally all over the fruit bowl. I give it a quick stir.

The YTG make their way down the buffet line. Tom smiles at me as he fills his bowl, as though we might be friends. I smile back . . . yes, let him think that we are.

Ilya doesn't take any fruit salad and neither does Caroline—thank God. She's bright. If she tastes it, she'll know what we've done.

"Do you think we overdid it?" I whisper.

"Nah, most of them smoke. Their mouths will burn but they won't know why."

Charlotte takes a full coffee pot to Tom. He's asking her something about the coffee. She looks inside the coffee pot, swirls it around and then laughs. She smiles her wide-toothed, Charlie grin—maybe his Barbie comment was not far off. He hasn't touched his fruit salad. *Eat, you fool, eat.*

"What was Tom saying to you that was so funny?' I ask as Charlotte places the coffee pot back on its burner.

"He wondered if we brought the coffee with us because it tastes better since we arrived."

"God, that's so lame."

"He was trying to be nice."

I glance at the YTG tables. Tom is eating the fruit salad.

"Rumer, YTG sandwiches are ready," Eugenie calls from the kitchen window.

I sort the sandwiches into the brown paper bags already half-filled with an apple, two cookies, and a juice box. Today's sandwiches look good: turkey and lettuce, or ham and cheese, on Eugenie's homemade bread. I wonder if YTG know how lucky they are that Louise doesn't make their lunches.

"Make sure you put the lunch bags with two sandwiches on the red tray," Eugenie says. "Got it," I say, pretty sure I accidentally put the single sandwiches on the red tray last time.

"The boys that do the hard physical labour get upset if they mistakenly grab a single sandwich."

It's weird to hear her refer to the YTG as "boys." A few of them are older than she is.

I deliver the bag lunches to the buffet. Ilya takes a double sandwich bag and then glances my way and nods his respect. I smile as though I packed his lunch myself. Tom grabs a single. I turn my back toward him and fumble with the condiments. "Thanks for breakfast. I like things spicy," he says to the back of my neck as he walks past.

IV

Maxine arrives eight minutes late for her first shift. She's a skinnier version of Seraphina, with the same thick, straight, hair. She's wearing tight jeans and a fitted, red, spaghetti-strap T-shirt. She is beautiful, but to be fair, it's not until you put a woman in a mid-calf-length, red polyester skirt and a baggy, white acrylic sweater that you know how attractive she truly is.

"You've waitressed before, right?"

Maxine shrugs.

"Okay, the menus are stacked here. But don't take them out to the YTG workers unless they request them. We encourage them to eat the breakfast buffet. Though some of them are arrogant and insist on ordering from the menu regardless—and we pool all the tips and split them evenly at the end of the shift."

"Yeah?" she says, not even remotely interested.

"Was Eugenie able to find you a uniform?"

"Yeah. I got one."

"Why aren't you wearing it?"

"It's ugly." She walks to the buffet counter and grabs the coffee pot. Maxine smiles as she pours coffee for every one of the sorry-faced YTG workers and each one rustles up some sort of smile for her. Maybe northern life has changed me—I'm already hard with brittle edges. The thrill of being second-to-top waitress, after Susan, wasn't that great anyway. I only owned it out of default; anyone could beat out Charlotte and her penchant for wild mosquito-scratching fits.

Frank sashays into the restaurant. I leave the YTG with their preferred waitress and make a beeline to his table and arrive a moment before he does. "Hello, Frank."

He pulls out his chair. "Good morning." He takes his seat as I wait, poised beside the table. "How goes the battle?"

"The battle is going, Frank. What brings you back to Beringia?"

"Work. I drive a truck. Everything that's in the kitchen refrigerator, that's me."

"Cool, literally." I smile and nod until it starts to look obvious that I'm stalling. "I need to ask you a small favour. There's a free breakfast in it for you."

Frank makes a circling gesture with his hand, encouraging me to reveal the favour.

"Someone left a horrible note, a disgruntled customer, saying how terrible the waitresses are up here. Is there any way that you would write a counter-note, saying how wonderful the Hotel Beringia waitresses are and leave it with the front desk? It would really help out our morale."

"Sure. Get me a pen and paper, I'll do it now."

I am delightfully surprised by his eagerness to be a part of my plan and I rush to the front desk for stationery. George and Doris are together behind the desk. George smiles. "Hello, dear, how may we help you?"

"Could I borrow a pen and a piece of hotel stationery?"

Doris' nostrils flare open as she stares blankly through me. Suddenly, she raises her arm and hits George on his shoulder. He closes his eyes and shrinks away. "For heaven's sake George! You've been in the cashews again."

"I have not!"

"Don't you lie to me. I can smell it. The entire hotel can smell it!" She addresses me. "You smell that?"

A noxious, sulphuric scent suddenly hits me. "I smell *something*."

Doris holds up a nearly empty package of salted cashews. "How many of these have you had?" Doris asks George, then turns around and yells into the store, "Sera, hide the cashews again. Your father found them!"

"Not the time and place, Mother!" Seraphina says from inside the store.

Doris turns her attention back to me. "Sorry about that. George can't have cashews. If he finds them, we all pay dearly for his mistake."

"Just a pen and paper."

Doris slaps a pen and piece of paper on the desk. "There you go. Get out of here while you still can."

I place the pen and sheet of paper in front of Frank. "Okay, Frank, on the house, anything you want this morning."

"How far did you have to go to find a pen? You sound like you just ran a marathon."

"Not that far. It's a long story. What can I treat you to this morning?"

"This calls for a real breakfast. Hand me a menu, would you?" I wait beside him while he studies it. "Kodiak Breakfast, please."

"Omelet, bacon, sausages, hash browns, two pancakes with whipped cream and seasonal berries. Are you sure you can handle all that?"

"And a coffee, please and thank you."

Louise stands in front of the stove, holding a porcelain coffee mug between shaky hands. "The Kodiak? Who needs all that artery-clogging shit at this hour?"

"Well, technically, it is breakfast food. It's on the breakfast menu." She has no idea I'm offering it to Frank for free.

"We have no berries. Call Eugenie and tell her we need fresh seasonal berries—do it now or Frank's getting squat on his pancakes."

I use the phone on the kitchen wall.

"On it," Eugenie says and then abruptly hangs up.

Frank picks up the pen and stares at the headed stationery. I take the coffee pot to his table. The paper is blank. Sebastian suddenly appears out of nowhere, runs at top speed and jump-stops in front of me. "Delivery," he says loudly and then hands me a bag of frozen berries. The innocence of Sebastian's enthusiastic delivery contrasts with the morose adultness of Hotel Beringia.

"So much for Sebastian's discreet delivery service," I say as I hand Louise the bag of golden-hued berries.

"Kids . . . I tell ya," Louise says. Her smile is one of genuine affection, and for the first time, I see a softer, gentler version of Louise—the Louise she might have been before life became hard. I don't want to become hard like the calloused bodies who've drifted north to hide inside the hotel walls

Eugenie walks into the dining room in her moccasins at the end of the shift. Her usual shuffle has been replaced with peppy little steps. "You've met Maxine?"

"I have. So great to finally have her here."

Eugenie smiles as though she personally wrapped Maxine in pretty paper and delivered her to the dining room. She walks her unusually chipper self into the kitchen without even a side glance at Maxine's casual attire.

I hear Eugenie and Louise discussing something in the kitchen. Eugenie sounds optimistic. I saunter behind the buffet to listen at the order window and watch Maxine sort through the tip jar.

"There's always two sides to a story." Eugenie's tone is outright jolly.

"Every cloud has a silver lining." Louise sounds as though she's channelling Eeyore from *Winnie the Pooh*.

I reluctantly leave Maxine with the jar of cash and dart around the restaurant, gathering together enough dirty dishes to fill a tray to take into the kitchen.

Frank has done me proud. His letter has replaced the shitty waitress complaint.

I am writing to say thank you to the friendly waitressing staff at Beringia. As a hotel regular, it is always a pleasure to sit down in the dining room, after a long day on the road, and be greeted by warm smiles and courteous service. Best service in the Yukon!

I read it and then nod. Eugenie's face is lit with genuine belief in the worth of her staff. I should feel guilty, but I don't. I guess because I believe in the letter too, even though I basically paid Frank to write it.

Maxine gives herself every single American bill. She doesn't even attempt to explain, just pockets them all, and I am too cowardly to challenge her.

The YTG don't seem as antagonistic today, all hunkered down awaiting the evening's supper special: spaghetti Bolognese. Maybe it's because Susan is the one serving them their tossed salads and soups. She natters on in her perky British. Tragically, some of them appear to be invested in her jolliness. They sip their soups, half smiling, absentminded and glassy-eyed, as though they're watching a dumb sitcom on TV. Though, a few of them look as though they wish she'd shut her beak. To me, most of them are scruffy faces with no names. I've resisted learning their names to remind them, and myself, that I am no Klondike geisha.

A portly, middle-aged man in a safari shirt beacons me over to his table by the window. He clears his throat. "Is there someone working here who can serve me?"

For no other reason than to prove the nasty Note-Writer of the North wrong, I approach his table with my Mona Lisa smile: I will take his crap and hand it back to him on a platter. "Thank you for your patience. I'll bring you a menu."

"Not necessary. I know what I want."

"What would you like?"

"I'll settle for the burger platter with bacon, no cheese, and a Guinness. Tell Louise not to burn it."

I pause, trying to remember if we have Guinness as I glance outside at Sebastian, tossing a baseball in the air and trying to hit it with a bat.

The Indiana Jones wannabe clears his throat loudly. "Today?"

I bring Fatty Jones a glass of lukewarm water, no ice, and then peek out the window to see if Sebastian is still out there. Sebastian's bat lies on the ground, but he has vanished along with the ball. "Someone needs to get out there and toss him a ball," I say, pretending that Fatty Jones doesn't exist.

"Are you going to jump on that order or what?"

I continue my outside gazing for a moment more and then take a detour to the kitchen. I run my hand along the window's ledge, scoop up a handful of dead flies, and then tuck them in my apron pocket.

Louise sits on a stool in front of the open rear loading door. Her hand trembles slightly between cigarette puffs.

"Who's the rude dude in the safari outfit?"

She looks at me with bloodshot eyes. "Spare tire and round glasses?" Her voice sounds raspy.

"Yeah, and a pathetic little ponytail."

She walks over to the window. "Ponytail's new. Tony, or should I say, Dr. Jones. He comes up every spring on his way to Old Crow." She places her burning cigarette in the ashtray beside the stove.

"Seriously, his name is Jones? What does he do at Old Crow?"

"Fuck all. Claims to be excavating for fossils. He calls himself an archeologist but he's just a prick."

"He is very rude. The hotel seems like a sort of northern base camp for scientists."

"Like Larry said, we got things in the ground that the whole world wants, and all the greedy balls in the world are on us." She laughs. "Meant to say eyeballs, but balls works too." She nods toward the order window. "That one has, or had, a court order against him to stay away from another scientist's site."

"Why? What did he do?"

"I don't know. You know, I always thought universities were for intelligent adults, something I should have aspired to . . ." She shakes her head. "The way academics carry on up here, the back-stabbing, sneaking around, seems more like junior high to me."

Louise unintentionally prepares the perfect burger for Fatty Jones: just blackened enough to hide crumbled fly parts, but not burnt enough to be sent back. I deliver the protein-plus burger platter with my trademark smile. I place the platter before him and say, "Or what."

The restaurant is empty. All the YTG have transitioned into the saloon. The music and loud voices trick me into thinking I need to get in there because I might miss out but the realist in me knows I'll end up having to deal with drunk YTG who think they might have a chance with me. Two big-hair guys walk into the dining room. They ooze urban sophistication: brightly coloured leather jackets, cigarette-legged jeans, and leather boots. I take two menus and head to their table.

Susan slides in front of me so suddenly that I step on the heel of one of her nurse-style Oxfords and get a full whiff of her stale hair and the spray she uses to keep the sausage curls intact. She places a menu in front of each of them. Her movements seem slow and exaggerated. I want to snatch the menus from her white hands and slap them on the table. Their English is rough. I can't place their accents, but from what I can make out, they drove up from California.

Across the room, some dipshit in a ball cap takes a table. He holds up a coffee mug and glances my way, smiling. *It's near closing, buddy, as if I'm happy to see you.* I take a menu and a pot of coffee to his table. "Coffee at this hour?"

"I've got to stay awake. I want to be in Whitehorse by morning."

"You're going to drive all night?"

"I'll pull over if I need a break."

Susan's high-pitched giggle reverberates through the room. I glance at the mystery hotties' table.

"Why don't you take a picture? After that, you can wipe up the coffee."

In my distracted stare, I missed his mug. "Oops, sorry." I pull a wad of napkins from the dispenser to absorb the mess.

Susan is on the hotties like a determined horsefly. I can't think of a reasonable excuse to sidle up to their table. As annoying as Susan's British charm is, she's coming off as sincere. An unexpected drop of lonely hits the bottom of my stomach, and then another, until a puddle forms. I want her to talk to me in the way she talks to the mystery guys. I want a chatty, British friend.

I leave Susan with the hotties and head for the kitchen. It's Friday night, and for better or for worse, I am getting out of here by nine. Fat sizzles and spits as Louise lowers a basket of fries into the frier. She watches it as though hypnotized as it calms into a bubbling mantra. I pull on a new pair of yellow rubber gloves.

Charlotte lines her eyes in charcoal. She's let her hair dry in its natural curls—blond roots anchor the loose black springs to her head. "A couple of mystery hotties came into the restaurant. Hardly speak a word of English, but so hip. Could be Italian, Brazilian . . . All I know is they're something southern and sexy. They rode up from California. The motorcycles parked outside the hotel entrance look expensive under all the mud."

"I know. Susan already told me."

"When?"

"I ran into her in the lobby, like ten minutes ago. She invited me to girls' night at her place."

"Girl's night?"

"Starts with appetizers and then we'll probably hit the saloon."

"I just got off shift with her. She never said anything about it to me."

"You don't even like Susan." She pulls on her combat boots.

"I would if I could."

"No wonder you don't have any friends."

"Like you do?"

Charlotte stomps from the room, leaving the bedroom door wide open.

"Close the fucking door!" The porch door bangs shut.

My throat tightens. It hurts to swallow. I reach for my journal. *Friday, June 10: Charlotte is back to her old tricks. We are high-school twins once again and Hotel Beringia has room for only one of us.*

Tom's acoustic cover of "Always on My Mind" hits me like a combat boot to the stomach. It can't be a coincidence that he's singing one of Charlotte's favourite songs. George smiles like the sun as I pass.

"Welcome." His genuine humbleness feels tragic tonight.

"Thank you, George."

I want to be stepping into a club anywhere else tonight. The saloon is fuller than it's ever been. The acoustic guitar and the scent of polished wood and beer are instantly intoxicating. I head straight to the bar to order a drink before I recognize everyone and decide to abort the night. I turn to scan the room. Too late, the window of wonder has closed. Nearly every face is one I know. Tom looks shrunken, like a child strumming a too-big guitar. Louise smokes while Larry drifts in and out of consciousness, a sleepy smile on his face. A group of international bear hunters, about to terrorize the Yukon, have pushed two tables together—their legs hang wide and sprawled, their laughter harsh and amplified. Rob sits alone at a table, smirking like a lounge lizard. A cluster of YTG sit at a table together. They seem awake, a few of them are even smiling. *Ugh.* Fatty Jones sits on his pompous ass at the far end of the bar, next to a stuffed wolverine.

The disappointment of the night must register on my face. Ode walks to the end of the bar to address me before all the others. I watch the long chain earrings sway from her many ear piercings. "What can I get you?" she asks, with that odd combination of aloofness and intimacy that bartenders seem to excel at. "Your usual? Half-soda, half-Coke?"

Even though I know she's doing her job, I can't help but feel, for the first time in a long while, that I might have a friend. "A glass of red wine—Bordeaux. Put it on my tab. Thanks." Ode holds up a bottle of red blends. As she pours my glass, her bracelet's charms threaten to drown themselves in the wine.

"Larry looks like he's passed out," I say.

Ode shrugs. "He's been with the hotel since it opened. Never left the north." She leans over the bar and says into my ear. "Grandson of a Klondike prostitute. His grandfather made a fortune on the gold rush. Built hotels and brothels in Dawson. Sold everything before it went bust. Left his favourite lady of the night knocked up. Took the fortune back to San Francisco and built a hotel empire in California and New York. By blood, Larry's rightful heir to a fortune."

I nod, considering whether to trust Ode's Klondike lore.

I take the wine glass over and sit at the empty table next to YTG—across from Ilya. Ilya's fingers play with an American dollar bill. In my opinion, he's the most attractive man up here. Maybe I'm the only one who thinks so. I take a sip of wine. Ilya leans forward and hands me a small object, a ring. On close inspection, it's made from the dollar bill he was playing with; he's woven it into a perfect band. I place my wine glass on the table and slip the ring on my finger. I take another sip of the bitter wine. My nose starts to drip from the sulphates or whatever it is in crap wine.

The mystery hotties have arrived, their voluminous hair visible as they move through the crowd. I strain, without making it obvious by standing, to see if they've found seats. Susan's girls' night groupies pile through the door: Charlotte, Susan, Eugenie, and Crystal, one of the chambermaids. I feel slightly vindicated by the small number of groupies, and how brief the girls' night get-together at Susan's turned out to be. Her appetizers must have sucked—all those wee little spotted dicks and blood puddings gone to waste.

Crystal joins the hotties at the pool table. She bends forward over the table to take her shot. One of the hotties pokes her in the bum with the end of his cue. His friend thinks it's funny. If I were her, I'd thrash his flat ass with the pool cue. If he does it again, I'll do it myself.

Tom introduces his next song, an Everly Brother's cover: "Claudette." He has Charlotte's full attention. I get the appeal—a ruggedly handsome singing cowboy—but he's in his late forties and his black hair is probably a dye job. Ilya's fixated on the saloon entrance. His eyes are alert and glisten with excitement, the first glimpse of emotion I've seen from him. Seraphina stands just inside the entrance, scanning the room. She doesn't seem bothered by being excluded from Susan's exclusive club and she sways slowly along with Tom's song. Her thick, long hair moves with her. Ilya cannot take his eyes off of her. Rob is watching her too. His smirk is gone, though the intense stare is equally creepy. I take a sip of wine. It sounds as though Tom sings "Charlotte," not "Claudette" each time he repeats the chorus. He is definitely singing, "Pretty little thing, *Charlotte.*" I nearly spit the bitter mouthful onto the floor.

I make my way toward the bar. And place my half-finished wine glass on the counter.

Ode attempts to refill my glass. I put my hand over it. "No—thanks. I think I'm done."

"You're not missing anything."

"What do you mean?"

She throws my wine in the sink. "Susan's party of four. You're well out of it. Party's already over."

Ode is right. Eugenie sits at the "girls' night" table alone. Her expression is one of uncomfortable boredom, a silent scream that says she'd rather be home in her moccasins watching TV. Charlotte is at the far end of the bar, nearest the pool table. Tom stands next to her. He lights a cigarette and passes it to her. She takes a long drag, then takes a drink from whatever's in the glass in front of her.

ACDC's "Highway to Hell" suddenly blasts into the saloon. I glance toward the jukebox to see who put it on. A tall silhouette standing near the entrance catches my attention. Yukon Cornelius, Leo, is back. My face burns instantly.

A hunter shouts, "That's a shitload!" as I slip past his table. He stumbles to his feet, knocking over a chair in front of me. His anger seems to deflate as he bends over and attempts to right the chair and then struggles to walk straight. I follow him out of the saloon. He leaves the stench of alcohol and BO lingering in his trail.

The lobby is quiet. George sits behind the desk. His head hangs forward. "Hello!" He manages a wide smile with his eyes closed. His eyes slowly open and he raises his eyebrows as though surprised to be alive. "How can I help you?"

"I'm good." The night's been a bust but I'm not ready to admit it. I take a seat on one of the loveseats. The fabric is new, but the frames are old and small, most likely built for skinny, gold-fevered bodies.

A toilet flush sounds from the open door of the men's public washroom. The drunk hunter wanders out. He didn't wash his hands. He staggers in my direction and stops in front of the loveseat opposite mine. He points his index finger at me, raises his thumb, like he's about to pretend shoot me, and then falls back onto the loveseat. It skids backward, scratching the wood floor, and creaks a few times before settling still. I wait for the loveseat to collapse under his stalky frame. His eyes close.

"Murderer," I say loudly, then wait in terror that he might be conscious enough to hear me. He answers with a long fart. "You're the shitload," I add.

He replies with a thundering snore and then snorts three times and falls silent.

"What was that?" George asks.

"Trust me, you don't want to know."

I walk out of the hotel, inhale the fresh Arctic air, and exhale a saloon's worth of second-hand smoke. The parking lot is full: all the YTG vehicles are back, two semis, a helicopter, and a lot of tourist vehicles. Out of curiosity, I decide to check out the row of big, orange, YTG vehicles. I hoist myself onto the step of the biggest truck to peer inside. The door is unlocked. A dog barks.

"You can get in if you want."

Sebastian's in his pajamas and his feet are bare.

I jump from the running board. "What are you doing up so late?"

"I wanted to see Bear."

"Does your mom know you're out here?"

He looks nervously at the hotel's front doors. "Probably not. You won't tell her, will you?"

"Probably not."

"You can get in the truck—I can take you for a drive if you want."

"You know how to drive this thing?"

He nods.

"For real?"

He nods. "Yeah, Rob lets me drive the YTG trucks sometimes—the ones that come into the garage for a repair."

"Where do you drive them? Around the parking lot?"

"Pretty much, and sometimes on the highway." Sebastian steps onto the running board and opens the driver-side door. "You coming?"

"No. We are not going for a drive."

"I can go and find the keys."

"No. Definitely not."

"We can sit in it. I can show you how stuff works."

"I don't think it's a good idea."

"Come on. I'll show you."

I glance toward the hotel. "You'll go right home after?"

He nods. "Okay."

Sebastian slides over to the passenger seat. I climb in behind him and close the door. I clutch the wheel, pretend to drive, and then pick up the CB and say in an American accent, "Got a Smokey on my tail."

"That's a ten-four, big buddy!" Sebastian says. Bear barks and then Sebastian ducks. Eugenie is leaving the hotel through the front doors. "I better go home." His voice has the appropriate amount of fear for a kid who snuck out of the house at midnight.

"Go—quick. She's not looking this way."

Sebastian bolts from the passenger door and slinks his way behind the parking lot of cars, Bear hot on his trail.

Leo stands on the hotel's front steps as though he's waiting for something or someone. He's on the move, striding across the parking lot toward the helicopter parked near the garage. I feel like a kid caught pretending to drive the family car. I scrunch down in the seat, praying he hasn't noticed my idiot head sitting aimlessly inside the parked YTG truck. I peek at the view in the side mirror. He's still rummaging around in the chopper. He steps out with a blue backpack in his hand. I lower my shoulder onto the truck seat and wait for him to pass.

Leo squints through the driver's side window. "Hello?"

"Yes?" I say, as though I'm still on waitressing duty.

"You okay?"

I sit up and roll down the window. "Yeah—I was . . ." I don't tell him I was pretending to be a truck driver with a little kid who was supposed to be at home asleep in his bed.

"You're new up here." He says it like a fact.

"I'm just up for the summer."

"You a student?"

"Yeah."

"UBC?"

"No, well, I was, but then I moved to Ottawa. Carleton." Damn, his eyes are intense. I put my hands on the wheel and focus on the parking lot in front. "You work up here?"

"In the summer. I'm based out of Whitehorse. Though, I've been living in Vancouver for the past couple of winters—working on a PhD."

"What kind of work do you do up here?" I avoid his turquoise eyes.

"Limnology—water science."

"The water around Beringia?"

"Some. I work all over the western Arctic."

I nod, oscillating between feeling protected and then trapped inside the truck cab.

"The Beaufort Sea?"

"No, freshwater sources—I'm interested in what's under and above the tundra."

"The permafrost?"

"Yeah, but indirectly, through stream flow. Permafrost influences stream flow. Tundra is like a roll of living insulation. It floats on top of a slab of solid ice and protects the earth's freshwater sources from big, dirty feet like mine."

Flames of shame scorch my cheeks. I ramble off a half-baked question before I'm able to calm myself down. "So how is the earth's water situation doing? I mean . . . is the tundra doing her job?"

He laughs. "Yeah, she's doing her job, but she can't work miracles. There's been a trend for the last twenty years. We've—UBC's—been up here since the seventies. The Arctic temperature is slowly and steadily rising."

"So, you're a PhD candidate at UBC?"

"Yeah."

"Cool. So, you're saying that the permafrost is melting?"

"More of it is becoming active. The layer that melts in the summer and freezes again in the winter is growing."

"That can't be good."

"As the permafrost melts, organic matter starts to decompose. There's some scary shit thawing."

"It doesn't sound good."

He shakes his head. "It's not."

"What kind of scary things?"

"Some of the organic matter in the ice is tens of thousands of years old. As they thaw, so do the diseases that killed them—there are a lot of implications. By the way, I'm Leo," he says, and leans in, closer to the open window. His breath smells of beer. He extends his hand through the open window. His blue cotton shirt sleeve is rolled up to expose a tanned forearm covered in blond hairs. Just the right amount—not too hairy but just hairy enough to cause my heart to suddenly speed up.

I shake his hand. "Rumer." It hurts to say it. My name links me to the waitress with the Mona Lisa smile. Her wrongdoings are now mine.

"Rumer. How do I know that name?"

"Rumer Godden, the writer—my mom grew up reading her work and became obsessed with the name."

He nods, as though thoughtfully considering my ramblings. "I'll see you around—Rumer." He turns and struts his big feet back to the hotel.

I wait until he's inside the hotel before I bolt from the truck. I crawl inside my shoebox and close the lid.

The low hum of a refrigerator truck vibrates my brain. I get up and peer out the window. "Franklin's Expedition" is scrawled in fancy black writing on the cab door of the eighteen-wheeler making the godawful hum. It has to be Frank's truck. He must fancy himself an Arctic explorer like the ill-fated Franklin Expedition. That was a hundred years ago; decade-late Frank shall henceforth be known as century-late Frank. Blast Frank. Why did he have to park right outside the trailer? I'm beginning to think the room at the front of the trailer may not have been the best choice after all.

Still no Charlotte. I should go and check to make sure she's still conscious somewhere, but I cannot risk running into turquoise-eyed Yukon Cornelius.

I awake to the rattling snores of someone who drank way too much last night but at least she held her liquor this time. My watch says it's 6:50 a.m. I get out of bed to look out the window. Frank and his Expedition are gone.

Charlotte sits up in bed. "Why didn't you wake me up?

"Didn't know you wanted me to."

Charlotte grabs her toiletry bag, her eyes at half-mast, and drags herself from the room.

I hear the trailer door squeak, soft footsteps, and then gentle knock sounds on the bedroom door. More knocking. "Who is it?"

"Me," Sebastian says. There's a long flat box under his arm.

"You're up crazy early for a guy who drives trucks after midnight,"

He laughs nervously. "Maybe. My Mom said that you're free this morning."

"She did?"

"Yeah."

"What do you have there?" I nod toward the box.

"Battleship—want to play?"

"It's a little early for Battleship, isn't it?"

"Not really. It's an easy game. All you do is sit down and relax and play."

"All right. One game. I'll just run inside and get a tea to go. You wait in the TV room across the hall—can I bring you anything to eat or drink?"

"No thanks."

The morning air is fresh yet tepid. My bare legs feel comfortable in cut-off jean shorts.

The lobby is disserted. A toilet flushes. Doris emerges from the men's toilets. She stops, plunger in gloved hand. "Off to work at this hour?"

"No. My day off. Going to grab a tea."

"Can you tell me, Rumer, were there trophy hunters in the restaurant last night?"

"I don't think so—they ordered from the saloon. They were in the saloon late. Why?"

"Trophy hunters have big shits. They eat shit, make shit. Every time it's the same. Toilet's backed up from here to eternity."

"You just killed my appetite—for life."

Charlotte walks through the front door, her hair a frizz-bomb and her expression foul. "Thanks a lot." She says it like a fuck-you. She storms through the lobby and into the restaurant. Her sweater is accidentally tucked into the back of her skirt.

She looks lumpy.

I sit cross-legged on the dusty sofa and watch as Sebastian opens the Battleship box.

"Do you sleep on the top or the bottom bunk?" he says.

"Bottom."

"I'd sleep on the top if I had a bunk bed."

"Yeah, that's what I thought too when I was your age."

"You had bunk beds when you were a kid?"

"We did. I slept on the bottom then too—I wanted the top, but Charlotte had a shit fit—sorry for the language—and my parents gave in to her."

"Charlie's lucky. My mom never gives in to me when I have a shit fit."

I laugh. "Me neither. But Charlotte used to have asthma—she outgrew it—she'd have an attack whenever she threw a tantrum. My parents would give her whatever she wanted just to calm her down."

"You could have the top bunk now."

"I could . . . It's not as great as it looks. I'd have to sleep with my head turned to the side."

"Why?"

"Because if I rolled onto the back of my head my nose would be flattened against the ceiling."

Sebastian chuckles to himself. "Don't worry, your nose isn't that big."

"*That* big?"

Sebastian clutches his stomach and laughs at his own wit. I fold my arms over my chest and try to look bored, but his laughter is contagious.

"I do impersonations too," he says.

"You do?"

"Want to see one?"

"Someone I'll know?"

"Yeah. You'll know him."

"Okay."

Seb pushes his wire glasses under his eyebrows and says in a theatrical, slow, idiotic voice. "Hello, my name is Larry. Larry? Hey, that's my name too!"

My cheeks ache from laughing. "Stop, Seb! You're killing me. Okay, let's sink some ships—A 8."

"Miss. E 6."

"Miss. B 5."

"Miss. B 8."

"Hit! Damn. J 9."

"Miss. C 8."

The screen door squeaks. Heavy footsteps enter the trailer. The footsteps stop and knocking sounds from across the hall.

"We're in here!" Sebastian calls.

Leo steps into the doorframe. His head is flush with the top of the frame. He looks as startled as I am. A clean, sandalwood soap smell follows him into the lounge.

"These are for you." He extends his arm toward me. He's holding a bouquet of wildflowers.

"You're not supposed to pick Yukon wildflowers," Seb says.

"I picked them from the ditch. I thought roadside was fair game."

"No. You can get a fine."

"They are beautiful, thank you." I turn toward Sebastian. "It does look as though he's picked every type of flower on the tundra. Should we let him off with a warning this time?" Seb shrugs. I turn to Leo. "We won't report you if you can tell me all their names."

"Deal. You recognize this one—fireweed. The purple, lupine. Pink, shooting stars. Fluff is Arctic cotton."

"That's a grass, not a flower," Seb says.

"I would have gathered more but it's still early in the season," Leo says.

"How do you know so much about Yukon wildflowers?"

"When you spend so much time out there, you pick it up."

"I know them all," Seb says.

"I don't doubt that—Seb and I are sinking ships."

"It's your turn," Seb says.

"I'll go put these in water first. Be right back."

There's nothing to put them in but an empty glass. I take the flowers to the bathroom, fill the glass, and gently place the bouquet in the makeshift vase. I take it to my room and put the arrangement on the milk crate that I use as a bedside table.

Seb sits rigidly in the middle of the sofa with his arms folded tightly across his chest. Leo stands just inside the lounge door, against the wall, like a guest whose presence is unwelcome and thus has not been invited to sit.

The trailer door opens. Eugenie calls, "Sebastian?"

"He's in here," I say.

Eugenie hurries to the lounge and peers inside. "There you are," she says, out of breath and obviously relieved. "Where have you been? You were supposed to come to the restaurant for pancakes."

"I'm sorry, Eugenie. He's been with me."

"Oh, well, that's okay then—Leo? Is that you?"

"It is. Hi."

Eugenie seems a little bewildered. She shakes her head and opens her eyes wider, as though to clear the confusion and then looks at Sebastian. "I bet you're hungry."

"A little."

"Come on then." Eugenie beckons to him with an outstretched arm.

I turn to Leo and whisper, "I thought she knew where he was."

We wait in silence until the screen door settles shut. "Actually, I came to see if you'd like to ride with us, to check out some caves."

"When are you going?"

"Right away—about twenty minutes."

"How are you getting there?"

"There's only one way. We'll land the chopper near the caves and hike to them."

"The helicopter? I've never been in a helicopter."

"Is that a yes?"

"A maybe. What caves?"

"Ancient caves. Wear shoes that you can hike in. And don't worry, I've got Deet." He attempts some sort of awkward upper-body dance move and then abruptly freezes, waiting for my answer.

I glance down at my bare feet. "Okay, the Deet sealed it."

V

"You sit up front with Malik. It's your first ride. The view's best up there."

I put on the earphones.

We lift and fly above the highway. I spot Sebastian below, pedalling furiously on his

bike, following the chopper, and Bear running behind. I watch them until the chopper gains altitude and takes a wide turn to the left.

"Caves are not far, about an hour flying time," Leo says.

I give him a thumbs up.

We fly over the Eagle River. From the air it resembles a drizzle of hot cocoa flowing over green felt. We leave the familiar Beringian valley, soaring over smooth sandstone mountains, velvet tundra, and then alongside taller mountains with jagged limestone ridges that burst from their apexes like spikes along a giant dinosaur's back.

"Caribou," Malik says. He's positively civilized in his Ralph Lauren polo shirt. He even smells urban, like expensive men's cologne. Malik looks too suave to be hanging out with the likes of Leo in his Ron Jon Surf Shop T-shirt and blond beard. If I didn't already know that Leo smells of sandalwood, I would peg him as weedy.

"On that snow patch," Leo says.

Malik turns the chopper toward the mountain. Directly below us are three caribou standing in the only patch of snow left on the hillside.

"In summer, they stay close to snow. The cool air keeps flies off. Not as much spring snow up here as there used to be," Leo says.

We hover over vast vibrant green forests that never end—wilderness in inordinate abundance. There is no sign of human life for as far as my eyes see. We take a wide turn over the ocean of green spruce trees, toward a rocky protrusion on a mountain top. The dark shadows slashed between the rock meridian could be caves. Malik cuts in tightly toward the mountain and then gradually drops the chopper onto a small, cleared section on the hillside. Two goat-like trails lead from the helicopter landing site—one heads straight up the mountain and the other down, into the river valley.

I pull on my daypack. "How high up are we?"

"About a hundred and fifty metres."

The mountains compete with the sky in their ceaseless magnificence. "This is what Earth is supposed to look like. Humans have been here a relatively short time—what have we done?"

"It's called progress," Malik says, all teeth and mirrored sunglasses.

"I call it tragedy."

Leo pulls on a backpack and leads us up the narrow trail in beat-up hiking boots. I follow behind Malik and his expensive-looking hikers.

Leo waits in front of a shallow cave. "What river is that down there?" I ask.

"Porcupine," Malik says.

"It's the Bluefish, a tributary of the Porcupine," Leo says.

"What caves are these?"

"Bluefish," Leo says.

"Like the river."

The caves are obviously an archeological site. There is little room to walk with all the roped-off areas and shallow excavation pits on the narrow ledge.

"Why are we here? Is this a work trip?"

"More of a cave-of-interest," Leo says.

"What does that mean?"

"The caves are off limits unless you have a permit. This is one of the only places in the Canadian Arctic that we don't have permission to land."

"Why? Are they protected?"

"They're in the excavation process."

"What exactly are they looking for?"

"Bones, tools—ancient things of interest. They're among the oldest, human-inhabited caves in North America. If we don't touch anything or walk inside the ropes, we're cool," Leo says.

"So, whose site is this? The archeologist, Jones?'

Leo stops, turns slowly. "You know Fat Fuck Tony?"

"Not really. I had the displeasure of making his acquaintance in the hotel restaurant."

Leo's face relaxes. "I'm sure you put Tony in his rightful place."

I grimace, remembering the dead flies.

"I knew it," Leo says.

"Careful, the Fat Fuck is married to your queen," Malik says.

"Who, may I ask, is your queen?"

"Ana Basoalto—and she is a queen," Malik says, rolling the L with his tongue. I glance at Leo for clarification.

"My PhD supervisor," Leo says.

"Let's go," Malik says, as though he is Leo's boss. Malik wears a headlamp, and glasses that magnify not just his eyes, but his authority. I thought Malik was just the pilot, Leo's Arctic chauffeur, but there is obviously more to their relationship than helicopter rides.

"Don't worry. We're good. Won't be here long." Leo says. His hand touches my shoulder reassuringly. His touch lingers as I watch him pull on a headlamp and pull a large, professional camera from his pack.

"I'll be here."

I sit on the alpine slope and study the layers sliced open by science: soil in graduating shades, sprinkled with rock and on close examination, bone. A long, curved bone protrudes from the soil. It could be a giant tooth or claw, perhaps from a short-faced bear or big cat. I'm sure the archeologists would have removed it by now if it was a significant find but still, it takes discipline not to touch it.

"We're heading to the next cave," Leo says. It's not an invitation.

"I was thinking of hiking down to the river—did you bring anything to drink in that? I forgot to bring water." I eye Leo's pack on the ground.

"There's a thermos of water and a few snacks. Here, take it—help yourself. Stay alert—there are big carnivores out here. The only humans they encounter are hunters and trappers."

"Noted. I'll stick to the goat trail—that way you'll at least find my body."

Once they've rounded the corner into the next cave, I check out the pack: a warm bottle of Coke, a banged-up Thermos full of cold water, and a bag of four bruised apples. I stuff the Thermos lengthwise through my hoodie pouch and vow to take a sip only if I am near death by dehydration.

I pick up a spruce branch lying by the trailside and use it as a walking stick to keep my running shoes from sliding on loose rocks. The trees are thinner and much taller than the tiny trees near the hotel, but sparse. It shouldn't be too difficult to spot an animal. I hear nothing but the breeze and then a buzzing sound: a horsefly has found me. I pick up my pace, slipping, sliding, jarring my knees and hips, yet successfully prevent myself from falling.

Relief flows through me as the sound of fast-moving water increases in volume and I reach the rocky riverbank. I glance up at the caves. It is hard to believe I've climbed so far down in what feels like a short time. I walk along the silt bank until I reach a narrow gravel beach. I slide my feet from my runners, pull off my socks and then wade into a shallow pool at the river's edge. My feet ache instantly. The water is thick with spring debris. I creep over sharp rocks toward the only boulder on the bank and haul my butt onto its flat top. I look up at the rocky caves, from where it probably tumbled to its current resting place, as my numb feet thaw on the sun-drenched stone.

The moving water silences all other wilderness sounds. I replace relief with vigilance; the brown river is no less wild and unknown than the path I took to get here. I doubt Leo could hear me if I screamed. I turn in a full circle, looking for carnivore's eyes sizing me up as prey. Oddly, it's a sabre-toothed cat's eyes that I imagine watching me, despite knowing the big cats have long been extinct. I unscrew the Thermos lid—water looks clean. I take a sip and then another, wanting to believe that the water is fresh, the bottle sanitized, and that no one has taken a drink out of it yet except me.

I pull my journal from my pack. *Saturday, June 11, Bluefish Caves: The Bluefish River glistens like spider's silk in the valley below. The alpine air is heavy with scent, yet intangibly immaculate: infusions of sweet blossoms, spicy conifers, and lightly smoked wood, in an ocean of oxygen.*

Something bites my bottom. I slide over, prepared to hit whatever it is with the Thermos. A crack along the top of the rock pinched my butt cheek. I follow the fissure with my finger, over the top and down the front of the rock. The crevice continues to narrow until it becomes submerged in the river. Something is stuck in its cleavage. A smooth, oblong stone, or maybe a bone. My fingers are too short to reach it. I jump to the bank and search for a skinny stick to poke into the fissure.

The stick dislodges a nest of small twigs, pebbles, and mud from inside the crack, into the river's stream. I push the stick deeper, edging the narrow stone upwards. Once the tip is out, I pull on it with my fingers until it's released into my clutch. The narrow object is about six inches long and the colour of a walnut shell. It has a knob-like head with faint lines etched into it that resemble two tiny round eyes, a protruding nose, and a horizontal line for a mouth. It's like a little modern sculpture. God knows how long it's been stuck in the boulder crack and how it got there. I stuff it inside my hoodie's pouch and slip on my socks and shoes. From my riverbank perspective, there is no sign of the mountain men above.

Once I reach the helicopter, I take out the sculpture and hold it in my sweaty palm while I scan the trail above for life. I should be able to spot Malik in his polarized sunglasses—little spotlights on the mountain. I don't really know either of the mountain men. They could be midnight-sun tomb raiders, masquerading as scientists. The breeze turns into a wind. Leo makes his way down the trail. He looks grave.

"What's wrong?"

"The wind's come up. We should get going. Have you seen the Thermos? I thought I put it in the backpack, but I can't find it."

"Shoot! I must have left it down at the river. Sorry. There should still be a Coke in there."

"Malik finished it off." He throws the backpack onto the ground, then changes his mind, unzips it, pulls out a camera bag, and then gently takes the camera from his neck.

"Do you want me to hike down and look for the Thermos?"

"Forget it."

"Where's Malik?"

"He's coming."

"Did you find what you were looking for?"

"Not really, no," He steps toward me. I hold the unusual stone behind my back, and then stiffen, afraid he knows that I've found something of interest or worse, he's going to attempt some sort of affection. "What's wrong?" His breath is dry and foul.

"Nothing—I can tell you're dehydrated."

"Yeah?" He steps back. "How?" He is already irritated by my imagined answer.

I don't let him down. "Your breath."

"Ouch." He turns away from me and picks up the backpack.

We fly back the same route we came. Malik is less animated, more antisocial than on the ride up. Leo is quiet in the back. I probably hurt his feelings about his breath. It is something I'd say to my sister—it slipped out so naturally—and I can't think of any reasonable way to come back from the insult. If I lie and say that his breath isn't that bad, he won't believe me. If I bring up the subject again, it will be like rubbing salt in the wound.

The figure lies inside my hoodie front pouch. I slip my hand inside to stroke its smooth, oblong form. The scientists are focused on the caves. No one is focused on the river. If it came from somewhere else, and washed downstream when the river was deeper, it could possibly have been stuck in the rock for years—thousands of years. If I hadn't walked down the mountain, and waded in the river, the sculpture would never have been found.

I pull my small backpack from under my bed and lift a heavy sock from the bottom of the pack, then jump onto Charlotte's bed and sit cross-legged. The oval sculpture slips from the sock and onto my lap. The two lines on its sides look like arms, the W etched on the front resembles breasts, and there's a V carved into its crotch area. On the back side, a line separates two bountiful butt cheeks. I slip it back into its sock and take out my journal. *June 11, Bluefish River: The Bluefish goddess might hold spiritual significance. Maybe I shouldn't have liberated her from the crack in the boulder. Maybe she was never meant to be found.*

VI

Heavy panting from behind, sounds closer and closer. "No, Ireland! Go home! *Go home*!" Charlotte shouts. He refuses to listen.

"Stay, Shorty Bear, stay," I say. He sits on the highway and whines. The wind is strong enough to keep the mosquitos at bay but gentle enough that it doesn't blow our bikes into the ditch. We ride north. The highway's lined with lilac and fuchsia fireweed—the colour dependent on whether the flowers are in full sunlight. Charlotte pedals in slow motion. I'm surprised her bike's upright at that speed. I stop and wait for her to catch up.

She pulls up beside me and tucks her hands into her armpits. "I'm sweating . . . in the Arctic. How is that possible?"

"There's a hole directly above us. The ozone is thinnest around the Arctic Circle this summer."

"How do you know that?"

"It's been in the news. One of the scientists and I were talking about it. The tall guy with the beard."

"The guy you made put on his shoes? Yukon Cornelius?"

"Yeah. He's actually a limnologist."

"Whatever that is—I thought you hated them."

"You say I hate everyone. Maybe it's you who hates everyone."

Charlotte jumps back on the bike and pedals hard, leaving me in shale dust. I almost confessed the helicopter ride to her. It would be a mistake to mention it. She won't care about the ride or the river. It will be my time with Leo and Malik that will obsess her. If she thinks Leo's remotely interested in me, she'll instantly be interested in him. She'd be in heaven having the jealous old cowboy fight for her. I do not wish that drama on myself, however much I might delight in the few moments of panic that her startled eyes and Charlie smile would reveal when she discovers that she's not the epicentre of my life. Though my so-called independent life may have already ended before it began. The only thing Leo said to me after I thanked him for the trip was, "No worries," as though I'd invited myself.

Trees shrink and the old-growth forest of knee-high trees scatter, metres apart, as we edge closer to the Arctic Circle. I stop at the Eagle River bridge to peel off my T-shirt.

"You look like you're topless. Your bra's the same pink as your skin," Charlotte says.

"I'm not worried. Not one vehicle has passed us the entire trip."

"It's see-through."

"The hotel laundry soap is industrial-strength. It eats anything delicate."

Charlotte pulls up her sleeveless tank top and knots it above her waist. "How much farther to the Arctic Circle?"

"I don't know. Ten K?"

We turn off the Dempster and ride down a winding river road lined with poplar and spruce trees and into the Eagle River valley. We park our bikes on the narrow, rocky riverbank, next to the wide, frothing river.

I open my pack on sit on the wool blanket from my bed. "The river reminds me of hot chocolate—now I'm thirsty. Can you pass me a water?"

Charlotte opens the backpack lying beside her bike. "I forgot the water bottles."

"How could you?"

"I took them out to rearrange things. I guess I forgot to put them back in." She rummages in her backpack and takes out two cans of beer. "Catch."

"You remembered to bring beer but forgot water?"

"That's right."

"Is it any good?"

"Tom likes it—it's from Juneau." She takes out two mini bags of potato chips and tosses them onto the blanket. A large creature gallops down the river road toward us. My mind registers grizzly, and I jump to my feet. Bear darts past us and into the river. He splashes around playfully, takes a drink, and then bounds from the water and onto the bank, where he shakes the water from his wiry coat.

"Get it the fuck away from me, dog!" Charlotte yells.

"Does Tom know you don't like his dog?"

"Why would I care if he does?"

"I thought you fancied Tom."

"Fancied? What are you, ninety?"

"If I was, I'd be ripe to date him. How old is he—sixty?"

After a long pause, she says, "He's forty-eight."

"Wow, two years older than Mom."

"Face it, no man is good enough for you."

"Bring me a lion-hearted king who possesses both humour and humility." I quote a line from my journal, describing my perfect mate.

Charlotte scoffs. "Good luck with that."

"Look for gold teeth."

"Why?"

"Albert—the Mad Trapper. This is where they shot him. He was running when they killed him. They found a bunch of gold teeth in his pocket. He probably stumbled all over the place and a few could have fallen out."

"I don't get it. Why'd he shoot all the Mounties? No one really had anything on the guy. Just some hunters saying he was stealing from their traps."

"I guess that's the point. He wasn't called 'Mad' for nothing." I pull off my runners and socks. The rocks are large enough to step on with bare feet and minimal pain. I wade into the river. My legs ache instantly from the frigid water. "It gets deep fast." I gasp for breath between the words.

Charlotte slips off her runners, wades into the river, and lunges toward me, pushing my back. "Get in there and find us some gold teeth."

I stumble into the water. "Mary, Mother of God!"

Charlotte darts out of the frigid water as quickly as she entered. "Sorry," she says with a smile. "I didn't think it would be that cold."

"Yeah, right." I am too frozen to retaliate with anything more than a handful of river water tossed in her general direction. I take off my cut-offs and lie them on the warm riverbank rocks that glitter like gold in the sun. I hand Charlotte two small golden stones, the size and shape of flattened golf balls. "Here's your gold."

"Do you think they're really gold?"

"There's no way they'd still be here if they were." I open a bag of chips.

I take my T-shirt from my pack, roll it into a pillow, and then lie back on the blanket. The afternoon sun feels close, like a heat lamp directly above me. I sit up, crack open a can of beer, take a sip, and then lie down and roll onto my stomach to let the sun warm my back. The river rapids are like a punk lullaby. The beer bubbles up from my belly. "Excuse me," I say with my eyes closed.

Charlotte lies back beside me. "Have you talked to anyone back home?" I ask.

"No. Why would I?" she says.

"You have a point."

"Do you think Mom will sell the house?"

I open my eyes. "I didn't even consider that option. Crap. She better not. Where will you live?"

Charlotte sits up.

I push myself into a sitting position. "Don't worry. You could always bunk in with Dad."

"Yeah, right." Charlotte shifts, turning her back toward me.

"She won't sell."

"You don't know that." She crosses her arms tightly over her chest.

"Who would buy the place with all your goth rock posters plastered everywhere?"

Charlotte uncrosses her arms and turns to face the river. "I miss those . . ." I detect a slight smile. "Or all your shirtless Rex Smith posters," she adds.

"Hey! That was one poster, and it was up for about a year when I was twelve."

"It was up for more than a year and you were sixteen."

I bury my face in my hands and shake my head, smiling. "Don't remind me!"

"Remember his hair? He had this flowing Miss Piggy hairdo," Charlotte says and then pats the air with her hands, miming the voluminous hairdo.

I get giddy. "In my defence, he had an amazing six pack."

Charlotte's nearly at the top of the river road when I realize I can't find my shirt. "Charlotte!" I shout. She stops her bike and turns around. "Do you have my T-shirt with you?"

"I don't know," she shouts.

"Look!"

I watch her remove her backpack and unzip the top. "It's in here!"

Once I reach the highway, I pedal fiercely, spitting dust, trying to catch her. "Charlotte! Wait up! I need my shirt!" She ignores my shouts. Bear runs next to my bike, loudly barking every time

I shout "Charlotte!" I hear a loud motor from a massive vehicle behind me. I glance back quickly. It's a giant bus. Heat waves stream from it as it gains on me. I shake my hair to cover my face and then peek through the strands. A male tour guide stands at the front of the bus. The bus feels a mile long as it passes. Faces are pressed to the windows. If only I wasn't wearing the sheer, flesh-coloured bra. I wait until I no longer breathe shale dust and then hop off the bike and squat among the fireweed to catch my breath. Bloody Charlotte. She better not be in the trailer when I get back. That bitch better hide.

At six they arrive, not a tidal wave, more like a trickle of grey and blue heads. The elders want beer, wine, and decaf, tout de suite! "You have beautiful hair," an old man in a butter-yellow polo shirt says. I touch my hair just to make sure it's still pulled up in a tight, high ponytail.

"Thank you." His lingering smile makes me think that he's a delusional pervert who believes I was braless on the bike.

Charlotte's no longer in the dining room. I hide behind the buffet counter, watching the line of passengers fill their plates with a variety of cold salads that look suspiciously tasty. The fried chicken smells unbelievably good. I pray it's not pink inside for their sake. A busload of seniors with diarrhea on the Dempster would not be good.

I slip into the kitchen to see if Louise knows where Charlotte is, without making it obvious that she's currently missing. "Just you back here?"

"Who were you expecting?" Louise says, deadpan.

"No one."

"Where's your sister?"

"In the bathroom."

I sprint to the saloon to see if she's hiding in there.

Charlotte's standing at the bar talking to Tom. "What the hell, Charlotte! You've been in here all this time? You've been missing for half an hour. It's our first bloody tour bus and you take off."

"It's only been twenty minutes."

"Are you kidding me?"

"Relax, Rumer. Come, sit," Tom says with a slow smile and glassy eyes, as he pats the bar stool next to him.

"No, thank you—come on, Charlotte. The seniors need you in there."

"Sit your tight ass down, seriously." Tom attempts to pull out the bar stool next to him.

"Leave it, Tom. I'll be back," Charlotte says.

The screen door of the trailer bangs shut and awakens me from a light sleep. It's almost two a.m. Charlotte's bed is empty. She was vacuuming the dining room when I finished loading the dish sanitizer. I sit up in bed to listen. The trailer is quiet, no footsteps, no wind, no Charlotte. I need to pee. I open the bedroom door slowly and peek my head into the hall. The trailer door is shut tight; it must have been a dream. The hall smells faintly of gasoline. Frank better not have parked the Expedition outside. If that big-moustached idiot gasses me to death in my sleep, I'll awake from the dead and kill him.

I pee in the dark, leaving the stall door slightly ajar. It is the only darkness to be found at Hotel Beringia and there is peace in the blackness. The bathroom door opens. I stop peeing, mid-stream. "Charlotte?" She could be fumbling around in drunken confusion. "Maxine?" The door swings shut. Whoever opened it has left or is inside the bathroom with me. A drop of water falls from a leaking facet into the porcelain sink. I stand slowly, pee dripping down my legs, and then sprint for the door. Midnight sun fills the hall. The screen door bangs shut. I walk cautiously down the hall and stop in front of Maxine's room. I knock softly on the door. I knock louder. "Maxine?" She's not in there. I creep to my room and turn the knob slowly. No Charlotte. I take the blanket off the window to let in the sun. No semis in the lot tonight. I lock the bedroom door and then sit on my bed. I slip my head inside the giant undershirt. The warmth of my breath and smell of my own sweat are comforting.

The trailer trembles in the morning wind. Charlotte's bed is still empty. I grab my toiletry bag and head down the hall. I put my hand through the bathroom door and turn on the lights before I enter. The room looks as it always has, the bathroom counters clear, showers empty, and the curtains pulled open. I kick open each stall and then flush the toilet from last night's disrupted pee.

The sound of squealing breaks shakes the trailer. I rush to the end of the hall and open the trailer door as the squeal ends with a loud sigh. The refrigerator vibration shakes my eardrums. The wind snatches the doors and flings them fully open. Frank and his big 'stache jump from the driver's seat onto the shale. Charlotte stomps by his truck. The wind blows her hair from her cranky face, as she fights her way toward the trailer. I step aside as Charlotte climbs the stairs, and then follow her into our room.

"Where did you sleep last night?"

"Why?" she says, instantly defensive.

"Did you come into the trailer early in the morning, around two?"

"No."

"You didn't come in, even once, for a second, to use the bathroom or sit in the lounge?"

"Why?"

"I think someone was in here in the night. They opened the bathroom door while I was on the toilet and then they left. I think maybe they were hiding in the lounge."

"Okay, don't have a coronary. I came in to pick up something."

"You could have said something. I thought some pervert was in here."

"You weren't in the room." Charlotte squats, pulls out her toiletry bag from under her bed, and rifles through it. She selects a sandwich bag with a handful of small, white chalky pills inside and then stuffs it into her jean jacket pocket.

"What is that?"

"What?"

"The pills in your pocket."

"Fuck off, Nancy Drew."

"Are they Tom's?"

A sneaky smile spreads across her face as she stands. The smile fades into aloof superiority. "Tom called it. You are a tight ass."

"So where did you sleep last night?"

"At Tom's—not that it's any of your business."

"You slept in his camper with Shorty Bear?" I say to antagonize her.

"In the hotel." She says slowly, trying to incite envy.

"You bunked in with Tom and Cup-Thumper?"

"Wouldn't you like to know. Tom has his own room, pervert."

"Were you with him—Tom—all night?"

"We were together—all night long—satisfied?"

"Hardly."

I flop onto my bed and then gently kick the plywood above. I'm so bored, I'd settle for Sebastian showing up with a board game. I slide out my journal from under my bed, flip it open. A pen rolls from its pages and onto the bed. *Saturday, June 18: It has been a week since Leo loped his long legs into the restaurant . . . I can't believe I'm counting the days since I last saw Yukon-Fucking-Cornelius.*

The blue ball under Charlotte's bed looks like my tie-dyed T-shirt. I stretch my arm to retrieve it. It smells of her perfume and cigarette smoke. I scribble: *Loneliness floods in, and all it took was for Charlotte to become obsessed with an old cowboy.*

Muffled female voices and laughter sound from inside the trailer. I recognize one of the voices as Maxine's and the other as Seraphina's. It seems the sisters are throwing themselves a little party for two. I stand in front of the narrow mirror and imagine myself through the Stanley sisters' critical eyes: skin too pale to be considered beautiful, nose too European. The freckles on my nose and cheeks probably work against me. Nice eyes though, the colour of the Yukon summer sky after midnight, I like to think.

The lonely part of me wants to call home. I jump from the trailer steps and crunch across the parking lot, aware that I will probably regret it.

"It's nine here . . . that makes it eight in Vancouver?" I ask George.

"That's right. Vancouver is an hour behind." His hand reaches into a bag of something on his desk and he puts whatever's in it into his mouth and starts crunching.

"What are you snacking on?"

He holds up a bag of cashews.

I smile, nod, and then dial my mom's phone number and plop in the appropriate number of coins for a five-minute phone call. "Hi, Mom. You sound out of breath."

"It's your father. He's left me to cut the grass. It's nearly half an acre."

"Why can't he come over and do it?"

"Your father's too busy. Couldn't *possibly* get to it until next week."

"Just leave it then, Mom. No one will care."

"I can't leave it. It's starting to seed, and I leave tomorrow for the island."

"Holiday?"

"That would be nice. No, I'm hosting the writer's retreat."

"Oh, yeah, it's that time of year again."

"How are you? Why are you calling?"

"I'm okay. Can't a daughter call her mom?"

"Did something happen to Charlotte?"

"Why would you say that?"

"I don't usually hear from you unless it's bad news."

"That's not true."

Silence. "What I mean is, you don't usually call home unless you're in some sort of crisis."

Silence. "If you're referring to April, when Charlotte showed up in Ottawa to crash at my dorm during finals—"

"I wasn't. That had nothing to do with me anyway. You know Charlotte stole that money from your father."

"You and Dad were all keen for me to keep her, show her the capital."

"Why are you bringing this up? That was between you and your sister."

"It should have had nothing to do with me. I was in the middle of writing final exams."

Silence.

"My roommate was pissed that there were three of us in the room. I couldn't afford to feed her. You and Dad should have forced her to go home."

"You know she's never listened to me. And that is not the story we got."

I want to hang up but curiosity and rising rage glue me to the receiver. "What are you talking about?"

"Charlotte said you wouldn't let her stay with you. You threw her out onto the street. How do you think your father and I felt hearing that?"

"Charlotte was lying to you! You know I would never kick her to the street."

"You are the older sister, Rumer." Before I can come up with a reply, she adds, "You let us down."

"If you actually believe that I would kick Charlotte to the street, I have *nothing* to say to you."

"I don't think it's fair of you to dredge this up—after everything I've been going through with your father."

"She never even had to pay Dad back," I say.

Silence. "How is Charlotte?"

Silence.

"I don't have time for this. I have to cut the grass." Click.

I hang up the receiver and stand in shock for a moment as the phone drops my unused coins into the slot.

The saloon is quiet for a Saturday night. There's only one table with two guests. Louise sits at the bar holding a glass of translucent liquid that I doubt is water. "Rumer!" she shouts with drunk enthusiasm. Ilya takes a seat at a table near the back window. I sit next to Louise. A cigarette burns in the ashtray on the counter in front of her, its elaborately long tube of ash still attached. "I told Doris not to let Seraphina do any lifting in the shop. It will all be too much for her soon. Pregnancy will tire a girl out." Louise's left eyelid droops, covering the top half of her eye as she speaks.

"Seraphina's pregnant?" I say.

"Can't you tell?"

"No. She dresses in loose clothes—who's the father?"

"No idea."

"She hasn't said?"

"She said it's no one's business," Ode says.

"Good for her. I guess she's right about that," I say.

"Well, it is *someone's* business. Takes two to make a baby," Louise says, raising her cook-from-hell hackles.

"I don't know—if he'd make a crappy father, she wouldn't want him anywhere near her baby." I glance up at Ode to see if she agrees.

"A father has the right to know!" Louise shouts. She stands up and attempts to push in her bar stool with her vodka-soaked limbs, but it appears to be cemented to the floor.

"No worries, Louise. I'll get it. You have yourself a good night," Ode says.

"I . . . will . . . do that," Louise says and walks slowly from the saloon.

Ode picks up Louise's ashtray. She seems to be as impressed with its long ash tube as I am. She gently lifts the cigarette, holding it momentarily in the air. The tube stays erect for a fleeting moment and then collapses.

"Could I have a vodka cooler, please—lime."

Ode grinds the remaining cigarette into the orange glass ashtray. Ilya puts a loonie in the jukebox. "Abracadabra" by the Steve Miller Band begins to play. "I wonder about that one," Ode nods toward the club chair Ilya's seated in.

"Ilya? Why?"

"He's a little odd. Would you agree?"

I laugh. "Yeah, but you just described everyone up here—present company excluded, of course."

"He's Russian," she whispers.

"Yeah, so?"

"KGB."

"Ilya? I doubt that. He looks too young to be a spy."

"Maybe, but I heard they can rebuild your face, make you look ten years younger."

"Interesting theory."

"They say there are a lot of secrets hidden in Beringia. Under the ice, over the ice, either way, the truth doesn't come cheap up here. That's why I mind my own damn business."

I nod, unsure whether delusion is the prerequisite or post-requisite to surviving a winter at the hotel.

"What's the story on Charlie and Tom?"

I'd laugh at the irony of the question, but Charlotte is my Achilles heel, and the mention of her name immediately snaps me into protective mother-hen mode. "What do you mean?"

"He's bad news."

"How?"

"He has a history with the bottle and harder stuff too. Does your sister know that he's married with four kids back home in BC?"

I don't know whether to thank her for the tip or to stand up for Charlotte and defend her choices. "Yeah, well, Charlotte never listens to me. Though, I'm a not fan of his myself."

"I've noticed."

I almost choke on my cooler, surprised that my feelings toward anyone up here are observable. "I'm not her mother," I snap. After I say it, I realize how ironic the statement is. I've done nothing but mother her. Maybe because we're no longer capable of being sister-friends, it's the only other role left for us, aside from Cain and Abel.

"It might be good to remind yourself of that on occasion," Ode says and then opens the till and pulls out the tray of bills to count.

The vodka hits my brain, but I'm sober enough to know that continuing down sisterhood lane, in an alcohol-induced state, is dangerous. "So, Seraphina's pregnant?" I say to distract Ode with her weak spot for hotel gossip.

"She surprised us all."

"Do you know who the father is?"

"No—she tells no one. But my hunch is it was one of the truckers stranded up at Tuktoyaktuk with her."

"Abracadabra" ends, and Ilya walks out the saloon door. The door swings a few times, adding a touch of drama to his exit.

"There's a road to Tuktoyaktuk?"

"An ice road in winter. A truck fell through the ice and then a blizzard hit. A fleet of trucks were stranded up there for a few days."

"Why was she up there?"

"She caught a ride with one of the truckers. She said she went to visit a friend of hers who was working in Tuktoyaktuk. Though why she decided to go up in December, no one knows and she's not telling."

"Do you know when Seraphina's due?"

"Let me think, if the baby was conceived in Tuktoyaktuk, she'd be about six months. The baby could come sometime early September."

"Which trucker did she catch a ride with?"

"I think it was Frank."

I lean across the bar and whisper, even though we are alone in the saloon, "Do you think Frank could be the father?"

"Frank?" Ode practically shouts, and then lowers her voice, "Frank's a poof."

The cooler's too strong and probably full of preservatives—every muscle in my body suddenly aches. I leave the nearly finished bottle on the counter and say goodnight to Ode.

George sits behind the desk. His head bobs in and out of light sleep. I spot Ilya down the hall. He walks to the end where the staff rooms are located, and I hear the echo of soft rapping. The door opens and Ilya steps inside; it appears Ilya's found himself a lover, even if for only one night.

"Goddamn Russian," George mumbles. His eyes are half closed so I can't be sure if he's sleep-talking.

June 18: Ode's advice makes me realize how invisible I've felt in my own life. This is supposed to be our Arctic adventure, yet Charlotte's ongoing teenage rebellion has descended upon me like summer stock theatre with Hotel Beringia the playhouse. Charlotte's the lead—bad-girl ingénue—and I've accepted a shitty supporting role.

The loud chopping sound of helicopter blades pulsates inside my skull like a morning alarm. I bolt to the trailer door to see what looks like the water scientists' helicopter rise and then shrink to a small dot. They must have landed late in the night. Disappointment hits more slowly than anticipation. I carry the heavy ball in my gut back to bed with me.

I wake to a halo of brown sausage curls dangling above me. "Where's your sister?" Susan says accusingly, as though I have her hidden under the blankets on my bed.

"I don't know. Why?" I pretend to be awake and with it. "What time is it?"

"Seven-forty. She hasn't shown up for her shift. We need you."

"What day is it?"

"It's Monday."

"Charlotte will show up any minute. Can't you handle it?"

"I'm not on this morning. Eugenie called me in to deal with a kitchen emergency because Charlotte never showed. I can't stay. Get dressed—tell your sister she can do a double shift tomorrow when you see her." She marches out of the room in her nurse shoes.

"Ask Maxine!" I yell. The screen door bangs shut. Bloody Charlotte. I put on mascara, brush my hair into a ponytail, and pick my uniform from the floor. The sweater's pits are starting to stink. This will definitely be its last shift. The loose sweater hangs shapelessly from my boobs to my waist. I look lumpy.

Maxine is on the dining room floor. I don't get the big emergency. It doesn't look any busier than usual.

"Rumer, you're needed in the kitchen," Eugenie calls from the order window.

She never calls me into the kitchen unless it's bad news. If Charlotte has anything to do with it, the blame will drift to me.

Eugenie points to the long line of brown bag YTG lunches on the counter. "She left them on the counter all night. All night!"

"Who left them?"

"Louise made egg salad and chicken salad sandwiches last night and then left them on the counter—all night!"

"That's not good."

"We can't serve them—they're not safe to eat," she says between heavy breaths. I've never seen Eugenie upset. She's always the calm in all kitchen storms. She slaps mayo onto store-bought bread slices, then plops on a couple of slices of unidentified lunch meat and tops it with a slice of processed cheese.

"Do you need help?"

"Yes, I need help! Go through the lunches, take the sandwiches, and throw them out—all of them." Eugenie jerks her hands forcefully and then places her hand on her hips. She looks at me with wide, steady eyes that simultaneously plead for help and scream that she is one sandwich away from losing it.

Maxine walks into the kitchen. "YTG are wondering when their lunches will be ready."

"Soon," I say, placing the first of Eugenie's freshly made sandwiches into a brown lunch

bag.

"What was wrong with these?" Maxine says, pointing to the garbage bin overflowing with last night's sandwiches.

"They're spoiled. Louise forgot to put them in the fridge overnight."

"Shit—I sold one of those sandwiches. He came in early and took it to go."

"Shit is right. Let's just hope he doesn't die."

I'm pretty sure the large pan of uncut squares on the counter is for the YTG lunches. Eugenie's so frazzled, I'm almost afraid to bring them up. I gesture to the pan, "Do these need to go in the fridge?"

Eugenie's eyes bulge and then her face falls. "I nearly forgot. They're for today's lunches." She snatches a knife from the rack.

"I'll cut them, and you wrap them—thank you, Rumer. It's been a morning."

"My pleasure, peanut butter marshmallow squares are my favourite."

The breakfast crowd dwindles to a few tables, nursing coffees. I retreat to the tables by the rear window to wipe tables, refill condiment bottles, and gaze at the mountains. Charlotte walks into the restaurant with Tom. She's in uniform. Tom takes a seat at the empty YTG table. Charlotte makes her way to the back windows.

"You are relieved of your duties." Her eyes are glass balls in charcoal-lined sockets. Looks like she's sampled some of Tom's "hard stuff" for breakfast.

"Nice try. I'm finishing the shift. I wasn't hauled out of bed for nothing."

"It's my shift. You can go."

"I don't think so. Super that you showed up, though. Better late than never," I say in a fake English accent. "Why's he here?" I nod in the direction of Tom. "Shouldn't he be at work?"

"He's on holiday, starting today."

"Doesn't he have kids to visit?"

"Do you know how long it takes to drive to Prince George? He'd get there and have to turn around and come back."

"You don't have to make excuses for his shit parenting."

"Why is it any of your business what Tom does on his time off?"

"It isn't. Shouldn't be yours either."

"Go. You should leave."

"The restaurant is empty. We don't need you. Talk to Eugenie—she might want you to work the supper shift."

Charlie turns to walk toward the kitchen but changes her mind and comes back to my table. "I thought you might want to know—I heard Eugenie and Susan talking." She pauses. "Forget it," she adds but makes no move to leave.

"Don't keep me in suspense. What did they say?"

She stares through me, as though contemplating whether to go ahead with her next move to oust me from the shift. "Susan said that you aren't pulling your weight and if they weren't short-staffed, they'd have to let you go."

"Why would she say that? I work my ass off."

"That's all I know," Charlie says and then leaves. She likes to bully more than she likes to work. If the conversation between Susan and Eugenie ever happened, they probably said it about Charlotte. There's no rational way she'd come out ahead of me in a rate-the-waitress poll. Though there's not a lot of rational at Hotel Beringia.

Tom turns his head from side to side, suddenly aware Charlotte has left. "Where is that pretty little bubblehead?" he says loudly.

"I don't know, but my sister left the building." I quietly add, "Asshole."

I slip into a booth. There's a nice crop of dead flies to harvest along the windowsill.

"You know, you could give your sister a break." Tom is standing directly behind me.

"I thought you left."

"Sorry to disappoint." He steps to the end of the bench, trapping me in the booth.

"A break? What does that mean?"

"Cut her some slack."

"I don't know what you're talking about, but *you* should mind your own business."

"Your sister is my business."

My chest burns from a sudden jolt of adrenalin. I contemplate crawling under the table to escape him. "Whatever you say, old man. And by the way, she has a name: it's Charlotte."

As soon as my shift finishes, I take the shower that I missed out on due to the morning sandwich crisis. I take my time in the warm stream to consider my entertainment options, then shut off the water before coming up with anything. I walk to my room, barefoot and wrapped in a towel. Jovial voices sound from behind Maxine's door. Their laughter intensifies my loneliness—she gets along so well with her sister and parents. My bedroom door is ajar. I know I shut it when I went to take a shower. I push it open cautiously. Charlotte is lying on her bed in a T-shirt, cut-offs, and combat boots.

"Sounds like someone's having a good time," she says.

"Why are you in here?"

"I knew you'd be like this."

"Like what?"

"Hot, cold. No one knows where they stand with you."

I scoff. "Let me guess, you want to fuck around with Tom again tomorrow and want me to take your shift?"

Charlotte sits up. "No wonder Leo's terrified of you."

"Like you know anything about Leo—did you say something to him, about me?"

"Nothing, really—I only told him that you are not really into mountain men with beards."

"Why would that ever come up between you two? You don't even know him. He hasn't even been up here in ages."

A smug smile spreads across her face. "He's been up here—he asked me what your problem was." She gets up from her bed and steps toward the open door, turns, and then adds, "Why you're such a cold bitch."

I follow her into the hall, wanting to yell something but nothing comes to mind except "fuck off" and that seems pathetic.

Maxine's door opens and she steps into the hall, "Oh, it's you two—you two are always complaining," she says and then steps back into her room. The door closes and the laughter continues.

The porch door bangs shut. "Good riddance!" I shout. I step inside my room and slam the door shut. If Charlotte said something to Leo about me, I will die. If Leo said anything to her about me, I will die.

I take the bike that I've claimed as mine. Somehow, I've avoided even Shorty Bear. I don't call him for fear I'll alert his dreadful foster father. Escape isn't easy on a sunny night in a forest of hobbit trees. I turn south. The Dempster unravels beneath me like a carpet. I pedal fast, pushing through the night. Fireweed lines the highway, dotted with bunches of yarrow. As I ride, the flowers morph into fuchsia ribbon and white lace. I keep the speed high to maintain the illusion until I am too winded; as I slow, the colours settle into flowers again. The forest grows thicker and the trees taller. The universe is warming to my escape plan. I lift my feet from the pedals and glide into the deep green valley. My cotton dress billows open like a windsock—clothing is optional on the Dempster after midnight. "Marco—Polo!" I shout to alert all wild ears of my presence—a phrase spontaneously retrieved from in the recesses of my brain, from when I used to play the game with Charlotte in our backyard pool. I stop in a refreshing pocket of cool, moist, spring-bud-scented air. Grass sways, leaves quiver, things alive and dead fall or jump from branches. A creek crackles in its frigidity—so many small happenings that are undetectable unless it is past midnight, and one is alone on the Dempster.

A lanky, four-legged creature steps out of the forest and into the ditch. The eyes peering through the tall fireweed lock on mine; they're golden, the colour of cloudberries. I straddle the bike, barely breathing. Its paws are unusually large, its legs longer than a dog's and its shaggy coat the colour of cedar bark. The wolf steps onto the highway, stops, and calmly looks both ways down the Dempster, as though it's a pedestrian in a city. It studies me curiously, then bows its head as though suddenly shy, and slowly saunters toward me. My heart beats to the wolf's gait. The wolf stops, raises its head, and gently tosses its nose into the air. It tilts its head, considering me, and then slinks into the ditch and into the forest from which it appeared. It pauses, half-hidden in the trees, and our eyes connect again. I remain still until I no longer see its cedar fur among the tamarack and spruce, and then glance in all directions, for a moment wishing Charlotte was here to bear witness to my sojourn into an implausibly wild world. I slide my journal from my pack. *June 21, sometime after midnight, Dempster Highway, Yukon: In this moment, I feel more wolf than human. I want to belong to what lies beyond the mountains, to all that my eyes will never see.*

The sound of a choppy motor cuts into and then drowns out the forest symphony. A helicopter flies overhead in the direction of the hotel.

I pedal back up the hill, barely moving on top of the shale, swaying from side to side like a metronome in tempo with the Beringian wild.

The helicopter's parked in the hotel parking lot and its occupant is sitting on the front steps of the hotel. Under moonlight, he would not know that I ride through the parking lot and park my bike along the side of the trailer. Under the midnight sun, he knows all. He slowly walks toward me with a sense of purpose that he's trying to disguise.

"I thought that was you on the bike," Leo calls.

"Yeah?"

"Not many locals take a bike ride at one a.m."

"Their loss. I saw a wolf. Is that the time—one?"

He looks at his watch. "Ten to two. A wolf? Just now?"

"Yeah—that was you in the chopper?"

"It was. It's great, the all-night sun doesn't last but while it does, we set our own working hours."

"Where were you working?"

"North of Tombstone. I brought you something." He hands me a bag of stems and little spiky leaves. "Labrador tea. Boil a little in hot water about five minutes—when the water turns brown, it's ready. I collect a little each time I find it. Thought you might want to try it. It's good, relaxing." He stands awkwardly for half a minute. "It's an ancient brew—one of the few plants that survived the ice age."

I take the bag of dried greens. "Thank you."

"I'll see you at breakfast?" He slips his hands into the front pockets of his jeans and takes a step back.

"Maybe—if you're lucky enough to be served by one of the waitresses from hell."

"I look forward to it."

I watch him walk away—quickly but controlled—as though his legs want to break into a run but he won't let them.

VII

The doorknob rattles. "Let me in!" Charlotte kicks the door. I ignore her shouts and kicks. My watch says six-thirty. I slept for four and a half hours. I sit up at the faint sound of tinkering with the door lock. Charlotte bursts into the room, a bobby pin in her clutch.

Charlotte plugs in her hair iron and then unscrews a mascara lid and applies several coats in front of the mirror with her mouth hanging open. Her side of the room is a pigsty. I shoved her dirty underwear pile, empty aerosol cans, and all her grimy, used kitchen dishes under her bed so I won't have to look at them. She broke a glass last week and never bothered to pick it up. I swept that under her bed too, so I won't accidentally step on the shards.

"I saw a wolf last night."

"Where?"

"South of here."

"Why were you there? Who were you with?"

I don't bother to reply. I open my journal. *June 21, Living the trailer trash life. The bitch is back. Charlotte doesn't care about anything outside of herself. She could care less that I saw a wild wolf. All she's worried about is the thought I might be having fun with someone from the hotel without her. It's a ceaseless competition with her and I am sick of it!*

"Are you writing about me?"

I scoff. "You wish."

She picks up the hair iron. "Are you going to the summer solstice party?"

"At the Arctic Circle?"

"That's the only summer solstice party happening, so yeah."

"Doubt it. It's too far to bike."

"We can give you a ride."

"In Tom's Jeep? I don't think so."

She sprays herself with perfume. "You should come."

I cough. "Why?"

She studies me, in my bed. I consider my men's undershirt and no doubt scabby face from the late-night, clogged-pore search session. If her expression of practised pity is designed to make me feel pathetic, it works. "If you're coming meet at Tom's by nine." She fills the room with a noxious mist of hairspray and then leaves for her morning shift.

"No, not this year. I'm getting too old for all that partying, and who will watch Seb?"

Age really is what you decide it to be. I suspect Eugenie has been middle-aged since she was a kid. I can't imagine her ever being young and carefree.

"Seb would be fine on his own. He's double digits and he seems mature to me—besides, everyone here watches out for him," I say.

"I'm not going." Eugenie lowers her voice, "You could try Louise, but she's not one to leave the hotel in the evenings."

I glance at Louise as she pours oil into a large, blackened frying pan. Images of purple-faced, hacking Larry pollute my mind. "Can I leave a little early tonight? I'll need to get ready in case I find a ride."

"Louise, do you think you and Susan can manage any latecomers tonight?" Eugenie says loudly.

Louise looks at Eugenie and then at me. I can't tell if it's her bored face or her pissed face. She lowers her eyelids and shrugs.

"Right. Rumer, see to the dishes early. You can leave at 8:45."

Eugenie takes a bag of popcorn from the shelf and then says, "Good night, then," with firm conviction, as though all problems have been successfully resolved. She leaves through the outside loading door.

My problem remains. Eugenie was my only sane hope of getting to the party.

"Those plates aren't going to get to the tables on their own." Louise nods toward the two orders cooling in the order window.

I knock on Maxine's door. It opens almost instantly. "I don't got all day." She sounds more bored than irritated by my intrusion.

"I was wondering if you're going to go to the summer solstice party?"

"I'm thinking about it." She's wearing blood-red lipstick, huge hoop earrings and smells like a perfumery. She's done thinking.

"If you go, can I catch a ride with you?"

She looks me over, as though debating whether I'm worth the effort.

"Ask Sera. She's driving tonight."

"Okay, I will do that." Maxine shuts the door before I say, "Thanks."

If Eugenie was born middle-aged, Maxine was born a slick centenarian, currently trapped in a nineteen-year-old's body.

"Which room is Seraphina's?" I ask George.

"Who?"

"Seraphina, your daughter."

"Down that hall, behind you," he says. The hands of the grandfather clock are positioned at thirty-five minutes after nine.

"Do you know the room number?"

"I don't."

I walk toward the staff rooms. The hallway is lined with photographs of early Arctic oil exploration. I wonder which of the rigs is the one that claimed George's memory? I am eager for a peek inside the staff rooms—the rooms we were promised in the March interview—curious to see how they compare to trailer living. I have no clue which room might be Seraphina's. I pause at each staff door and listen. Anxiety constricts my chest. The hotel seems empty. Everyone must already be at the party.

It is pure desperation that leads me toward Tom's room. I've never been to his room, though I walked by it with Charlotte when we were newbies, wondering where the singing cowboy lay his hat. I hesitate at his door, my stomach in a tight knot. Charlotte and Tom never want to hang out with me for the sake of my charming company. I knock once. They have probably already left for the party. I knock twice. I worry I'm overdressed for the outdoor occasion in my black knit mini dress. However, the daypack slung over one shoulder and Dempster-dusted sneakers ground the look in Arctic-casual. The door opens.

"Hello . . . Rumer," Tom says slowly but obviously surprised, almost pleased to see me. His breath smells of whisky. He's wearing blue jeans and a thin, white, short-sleeved T-shirt, the type he wears beneath his flannel shirts.

"Come in," he says, gesturing with his arm.

"Where's Charlotte?"

"Inside. Come on in—visit with her."

It looks like a typical three-star motel room with mustard-coloured drapes, floral bedspread, and carpet. Charlotte lies on top of the ruffled spread, dressed in cut-offs and an off-the-shoulder black T-shirt. She smiles at Tom but deliberately avoids looking my way.

"When are you heading to the party?" I ask.

Tom stands at the laminated dresser and fills a glass of ice with whisky. "Sit down, have a drink with us."

"I'm okay."

Charlotte lies completely still, except for the turning of her head, as her gaze follows Tom. He stops inches from me. "We'll go when your sister's ready. Talk to your sister, relax," he says with boozy-cigarette breath. He walks to the bathroom and returns with an empty glass.

"How long does it take to drive to the Circle?"

"Fifteen minutes—have a drink," he says as he drops ice into the glass and then pours in whisky.

"Have a drink," Charlotte echoes. Her voice is surprisingly irritated in contrast to her lazy body language and vacant smile.

"I'm ready to go. I already picked up a cooler from Ode—it's in my pack." Tom thrusts a glass of amber liquid at me. "No, thanks. I don't like whisky."

"Try it," Tom commands, pushing the whisky glass into my chest. I take a step back. He forces a smile. "Fine. You don't like whisky. What do you want? I'll get it. Talk to your sister. You owe her that."

"So, talk Charlotte! What are you waiting for?" I say, controlling the urge to scream. Charlotte lies on the bed with a detached grin, seemingly directed at the wall behind me. "Fine. I'll catch a ride with someone else."

"Hold on!" Tom slams the glass on the dresser and then grabs my backpack strap and tries to pull it from my shoulder. "Sit down on the bed with your sister." He continues to pull on my pack as I hold it tight to my body.

"Would you stop!" I shout. He releases his grip. I adjust the pack and give him a stern look. "I'm not taking off my pack and I'm not having a drink with you. Got it?"

He leaps in front of me, blocking the way to the door.

"Your sister wants you to stay. I asked you to sit down and relax with us, for a couple of minutes." The words roll off his tongue like little balls of mercury, smooth and dangerous.

I glance at Charlotte, reclining on the bed. Her vacant smile has turned to one of sneaky pleasure—this is a game to her.

"I want to leave. You're blocking my way, excuse me," I say too fast. I no longer sound calm. He grabs my upper arm as I try to push past him.

"I said, sit down." His sinewy muscles bulge beneath the T-shirt.

I try to push past him. He places his hands on my shoulders and pushes me back into the room.

"What are you doing? Let go of me!" I glance at Charlotte, but my sister doesn't exist, and Charlie refuses to meet my eyes. She watches Tom with nervous delight.

"Tell your fucking geriatric boyfriend to let me go!" I scream as I struggle against him. He grips my forearm with the pressure of a jungle snake and twists it behind me. I try to spin away but he's too strong. I stomp my heel into his bare foot. He wrenches my arm tighter against my back and then pushes me, chest-first, toward the bed. My shins connect with the hard box spring.

"Let her go." Charlotte sounds bored.

"Fuck off!" I kick my heel up and back, trying to hammer his crotch.

"Christ—you cunt." He can hardly get the words out.

I run for the door, sprint past the photographs of oil wells sinking into the tundra, past George in the lobby, through the parking lot, and keep running along the highway, toward the Eagle River, where the trees are tall enough to get lost in.

I run until I skid on shale and hit the highway with my knees. The shock of falling triggers tears. I sit cross-legged on the side of the Dempster, among the fireweed, and pick out the flakes of shale that are embedded in my knees. Sobbing starts a chain reaction of coughing and heaving until my cardiovascular and gastric systems threaten to turn inside-out. A grey, fox-sized creature emerges from the ditch and then freezes, startled by the noise. It darts across the highway and into the ditch on the other side. Another follows closely behind, and then another. Their grey fur is fluffy yet fine. They cannot be anything but wolf pups. I dust my dress off and creep to where the pups entered the ditch. About six feet into the sparse forest, two pups lie snuggled together under a tree. One pup stands behind them, half-hidden by the tree, only its fluffy grey tail visible. The pups watch me with sleepy yet curious grey-blue eyes. One pup yawns, leans forward, and wraps its neck around its sibling. I do not see any adult wolves in the vicinity, though their mother must be close. That lone wolf I encountered the other day was about ten K south of here. He might be their father.

The pack has been patient with me. I won't tempt nature. I walk slowly along the highway, not turning my back on the wolves until the trees seem to close around them, as though they've been swallowed by a supernatural force.

I walked toward wild and was invited inside.

A vehicle approaches from the direction of the hotel. It's too late to jump in the ditch. I take my sunglasses from my backpack and put them on. If it's Tom and Charlotte, I will sprint across the sacred tundra—running like I've never run before. It's Rob's black truck. He stops and unrolls the passenger side window.

"Need a lift?"

"Are you heading to the Arctic Circle?"

"You know it—I'm the last ride outta here." He leans over and then opens the passenger door. I glance down the highway in both directions. Rob is one of the last people I want to catch a ride with. However, as of this evening, he is not dead last. I climb inside the truck that smells like generic aftershave. Rob's ditched the garage coveralls for pleated khakis and a short-sleeved polo shirt. If I didn't already know what type of guy he is, I might fall for the John Junior façade.

"I said to Susan, I'd take Rumer over her sister, any day—she disagreed. She likes your sister more."

"I'm going to have to agree with Susan on that one. Charlotte's probably more your type."

"Yeah?" His eyes leave the highway and rest upon my legs for too long.

My breath tastes like vomit. "Do you have anything to drink in there?"

He reaches for the glove box but instead of opening it, he places his hand on my thigh. Before I can dig my nails into his sweaty hand, he lifts it off my leg, opens the glove box, and rummages inside. He shuts the compartment and hands me a flask.

"What is this?"

"A little Southern Comfort and the good Doctor." His southern accent is so convincing, I wonder if his Canadian accent is the fake one. I unscrew the flask and take a swig. It's sweet and strong.

"Do you have anything else?"

"Take it or leave it. Where's your sister tonight?"

"Don't know." I take another sip from the flask. It tastes surprisingly better than the first swig. "Where's Susan?

"Already at the Circle."

"How soon until we get there?"

"Five minutes—give or take."

I hold onto my building nausea until a generous bubble of trapped air forces its way up my throat. My stomach spasms. "Pull over. I feel sick."

"Don't get sick in my truck." Rob pulls to the side of the highway and brakes abruptly. "Get out."

I jump from the truck, shut the door behind me, and then breathe in the tundra-infused air. Instantly, I feel a little better. I motion him to go on ahead. He revs the truck as though insulted and speeds off. My thigh itches where his hand touched my leg. I wait for the dust to settle and then walk north along the highway toward the parked cars that dot the sides of the Dempster.

I wander into the small crowd standing in the Arctic Circle rest area, not caring who or what I find inside. Pulsating drumbeats roll through me and onto the tundra. The acoustic music is like nothing I've heard before. I close my eyes, and let the smooth rhythms flow in waves, sinking and rising over the wet tundra like oceans of caribou. The dark cello strings are storm clouds, ripped open by the wind. I open my eyes. The lead singer holds onto a high note for a remarkably long time. Her bare arms, the colour of pale tea, seem unusually long, yet elegant. The cellist, drummer and two guitarists are all women.

A YTG face that has no name offers me a joint. I decline, though pleasantly surprised that he doesn't seem to hold my waitressing persona against me. A hot guy, possessing a set of finely sculpted biceps and long hair that looks like shiny black licorice, stands beside the stage. If he were YTG, I'd smile at him, might even refill his coffee. All the men at Hotel Beringia are over thirty, most over forty, except for Ilya—who, if I believe Ode, is older KGB with facial reconstruction.

Susan's big, giggling head appears suddenly. She looks like she's been getting make-up tips from Charlotte; her dark-lined eyes dart apprehensively into the crowd. "Have you seen Rob?"

The drive replays in my mind. "No." Her painted face scrunches into a pinched scowl—considering the hesitation in my answer—before she pushes her way through the partygoers. The scent of cheap Hotel Beringia shampoo floats in the air. Ilya stands on the edge of the crowd. His hair is combed smooth and must be freshly washed as it's still wet. "The band is amazing!" I shout. He nods in his usual polite yet morose way. "The lead singer's really talented."

"Valerie."

"You know her?"

"She lived at the hotel last summer. Seraphina's sister."

I follow Ilya's gaze beyond the party. I take off my sunglasses. This is why I have come. Beyond the Beringian valley, faraway mountains roll across Earth to infinity. The view is ethereal and untouchable, as though the Arctic Circle might be a painted backdrop inside a fairy tale. The vista is so vast that some mountains are shrouded in full sunlight, while others are blurred by misty rain, and still others are half-hidden under dark storm clouds. The Arctic Circle is not a destination, it is an entity. I turn and glance at the cluster of humans on the gravel. In contrast to the vista, we are a blight on the tundra.

"Where are you from, Ilya? Where did you grow up?" He doesn't answer even though he had to have heard me.

Then, "Russia."

"When did you come to Canada?"

"I came from Germany—over the Berlin wall."

"Seriously?"

"You doubt?"

"No, it's an expression."

A family of birds, the size of small chickens—two adults and four fuzzy, spotted chicks—work their way along the edge of the gravel. The birds seem unfazed by the crowd and the noise. The mother bird hoists herself into a ground nest. She fluffs her white-fanned tail repeatedly and calls her chicks. The chicks scurry to her and into the safety of the nest.

Fuzzy legs and Birkenstocks enter my field of vision.

"You found ptarmigans," Leo says.

"Ptarmigans. I was wondering what type of birds they were. They seem so relaxed, unfazed by humans."

"Makes them easy to catch for dinner."

"Where'd the dad go? He was right there, just behind where you're standing."

"I swear, I didn't eat him—behind you, he's heading for the nest." The ptarmigan dad struts around the nest as the momma tosses branches about, scratching with her feet and flashing her white tail feathers.

"I didn't know you were coming to the party."

"Last minute decision. Caught a ride up with Caroline."

"A double rainbow. This place is too beautiful—is it even real?"

"The weather system's constantly changing. One minute your back is baking in the sun and the next you're shivering in cold rain—where there's sun, there's rain, where there's rain, there's a rainbow. At any given moment in the summer, somewhere over the Arctic, there's a rainbow."

"I like that. At any given moment, somewhere, there's a rainbow."

Leo sits down on the gravel. "Do you mind?" he asks, as though the gravel pad is my living room.

"Feel free." I sit next to him. His legs are very tanned and covered in blond hairs. His feet are substantial: wide, long, and decently manicured. Not the disgusting feet that I imagined at the restaurant, when I told him to put on his muddy sandals.

"What were you talking to him about?" Leo says.

I turn to try and see where Ilya disappeared to. I can't find him in the crowd. "You mean Ilya?"

"The YTG kid," Leo says in a tone of scoffing disapproval.

"He's not a kid. What's wrong with Ilya?"

Leo sighs in agitation, as he gazes at the expansive view. "He's always watching. Never says anything."

"He's a little odd but seems harmless."

Leo takes in what I've said without reacting. The band is back on the stage. "What do you think of the Cloud Berries?" he says.

"That's the name of the band? I love it! They're good—Valerie and her sisters look so much alike."

"Everyone is in love with the Stanley sisters. Beringian royalty—good old King George.

He's the poster boy for never-trust-a-white-man."

"That sounds racist."

"Oil is colour blind—only sees the colour of money. Big Oil lured him in, chewed him up and spit him out."

"That's harsh."

"Ask around. You'd be surprised how many people think George got what he deserved."

"Why?"

"Oil and gas industry hired him to promote the Mackenzie Valley pipeline in the seventies. Gas pipeline was to run from Alberta to Inuvik, cut through Dene territory. He was gullible enough—or desperate enough—to believe the oil company propaganda. George was hired to make it look like his people were on board. His people, the Dene, were never consulted. He was a hired clown." Leo stands up slowly and holds out one hand for me to take. "Do you want to dance?" He raises his eyebrows playfully. "I just brushed my teeth."

Some people cringe at the memory of things they've done while drunk. I cringe at the memory of things I've said while sober. I take his hand. Fantasy fades in an instant. His hand is real, and touching it feels intense—like I've agreed to something, but don't know what it is yet.

"What are you drinking?" he asks.

"I'm good."

"Come on, what do you want?"

"I'm fine."

"You don't drink?"

"I have a cooler. It's somewhere—wherever I put my backpack."

Leo reaches under the stage and pulls out a beer and hands it to me. "My treat."

"Thanks," I take it but don't open it.

He leans down and says with peppermint breath, "Let's dance."

He moves with oblivious confidence, despite dancing like a Sasquatch. My gaze is diverted to Ode. I hardly recognize her in the great outdoors. The wind blows her auburn-streaked hair to the side. Her numerous earrings sparkle in the sun. She's smiling. She never smiles. Caroline leans in toward Ode, close enough to share a kiss.

Susan's aggressive arm gesturing at the side of the stage intrigues me. Her cheeks are flushed with emotion as she swings her hands in the air in front of Maxine. The youngest Stanley sister seems to take it all in with cool detachment. Susan abruptly turns her gaze to the dance floor and surveys the crowd. She catches my gaze. Her eyes bore into mine. I spin around and dance with my back to her. I can tell by Leo's perplexed expression that she still has her laser eyes locked on me. I clasp Leo's forearm, stand on tiptoes, and shout, "Is Susan still watching us?"

"The British waitress? What's her problem?" Leo shouts into my ear.

"No idea."

The song ends. "Rumer, get over here!" Maxine shouts as she holds her arm straight up and beckons me toward her with her hand.

"You go ahead. I'll be around," Leo says. I can't read him. Sometimes it seems obvious he's interested and other times, it's like he's doing me a favour, being kind to the lonely waitress.

Before I reach Maxine, Susan's head suddenly pops into view. Her face is scarlet. "Susan," I say, surprised and slightly frightened.

"You're a liar."

"What are you talking about?"

"Maxine saw you getting out of Rob's truck."

I fight the urge to laugh at the absurdity of the day.

"Stay away from my husband." Her tone is murderous. Her tubular curls bounce erratically, as she kicks up dust, stomping away in low-heeled pumps.

Maxine's face is frozen still for a moment and then anger slides across it. "Crazy bitch—she wants to play house with Rob, but Rob doesn't play by the rules—fucks everything but her."

I study Maxine's face, unsure if I should be thankful for her surprising support, or if I've been betrayed by her—she told Susan I was in Rob's truck. "For the record, I would *never* fuck Rob!" I shout to Maxine as she pushes her way into the dancing crowd.

A low, arctic wind, cooled by the active tundra layer, floats up my dress and I break out in goosebumps. I glance at my watch.

"Waiting for someone?" Leo asks.

"More like avoiding everyone."

"The British waitress?"

All at once, I'm too tired to repeat any of the insanity of the day. "Forget it—this day is the longest of the year and the longest of my life. I'm ready to bring on the night."

Leo nods, considering what has been said and unsaid, and then he hands me my unopened beer. "Here's to bringing on the night."

"To the night!" We clink our bottles together.

"Where did all these people come from? They didn't all come from the Beringia."

"Fort MacPherson. Circle party's a big deal up here."

"Isn't that like a couple hours' drive from here?"

"A couple hours' drive is nothing in the Yukon. Where's your sister tonight?"

I straighten my spine and take a step forward as if to avoid Tom's hot whisky breath, as though it exists, beyond the cerebral, despite time and distance. "Far away, I hope." I crack open the beer.

"Sorry—forget all." He swings his beer against mine.

"Forget all." I take a swing of beer.

I am too tired to be standing on the Arctic Circle after midnight. I place the beer on the ground, slip on my backpack, and then cross my arms over my chest and shiver.

"You taking off?" Despite his attempt to make the question seem casual, I sense a hint of distress at the prospect.

"I'm just trying to get warm."

"You're cold?"

I nod. "I thought there was supposed to be a hot tub. I brought a bathing suit for nothing."

"I want to show you something." I follow Leo toward the highway and a YTG truck.

"Oh, my God! Who's tub is it?"

"Caroline's."

"How did she get it up there?"

"It wasn't easy."

"You helped her?"

"Yeah." Leo unbuckles his belt. His shorts fall and nearly take his boxers with them. He lifts his T-shirt over his head. He's big-boned, so he appears boxy when dressed, but underneath he's surprisingly thin and muscular. He hoists himself onto the open back of the truck and then holds out his hand to help me up. I decline the hand as I struggle to climb onto the flatbed. "You're coming in," Leo says. He jumps into the water in his boxers and soaks all the tub occupants. Their grumpy faces remind me of pioneer children, gathered for their weekly bath.

I inadvertently lock eyes with Cup-Thumper. He smiles as though all that happens at Hotel Beringia, stays at Hotel Beringia—all is forgiven under the midnight sun. Leo smirks, as though proud that he's presented me with a hot tub filled with hairy men and Cup-Thumper in wet Jockeys. I spot Charlotte's white shoulders in the dancing crowd and Tom's cowboy hat bobbing next to her. I jump from the truck. My tribe is not here. I left them in the forest, under a tree. I duck under the tourist sign, slip past Tom's jeep, and don't exhale until both feet hit the Dempster.

VIII

The Arctic Circle is nearly twenty kilometres north of the hotel. I can run ten K in less than an hour; though, I estimate it will take me at least four hours to walk at my current pace. I don't work until the afternoon—or is this the day I agreed to switch shifts with Maxine? I'm too tired to think. Worst case scenario, I'll get two hours of sleep and then get up for work. I can always take an afternoon nap.

The walk is quiet but not lonely. The sunlit landscape feels more like home than the hotel. Fluffy, white heads of cotton grass are less threatening than human heads. I scan the tundra for a grizzly. With the sparse forests of waist-high spruce trees, I should be able to spot one at least a kilometre in advance. "…and then I don't feel sooo bad…" I sing "My Favorite Things" at the top of my lungs, telling all bears to avoid the Dempster—crazy woman walking. Charlotte and I memorized the entire *The Sound of Music* soundtrack album when we were little. For a moment, a hopeful feeling of familiarity passes through me, a longing to meet my sister again, the Charlotte who took turns with me in singing all the roles of the Von Trapp children in "So Long, Farewell." The memory of Tom constricts my throat. I choke out the lyrics as tears burn my eyes. I will never know that girl, that Charlotte, ever again.

Fast footsteps sound in the gravel behind me. Leo's out of breath. His hair is wet. "Why didn't you tell me you were walking?"

"I like to walk—you dunked your head in that crowded tub?"

"I got tsunamied." He slows to my pace and follows behind me, almost silently, except for the occasional rattle of shale.

"It's an empty tundra tonight."

"That's the norm at this hour."

I stop for a moment to allow him to catch up to me. "Are you usually up this late?"

"No—and yes. If I'm at the hotel, I'm in bed, editing my dissertation, listening to Malik snore from the next bed."

I laugh. "Seriously? You bunk with Malik?"

"Government budgets aren't as generous as you think."

"So, what does Malik do? Is he just your pilot?"

"His official title is 'Natural Resource Technician.'"

"What's your official title?"

"I was a full-time hydrologist before I started my PhD. Kept it up in the summers. The government is interested in measurements, stats. I'm interested in ice."

"Ice science. I never knew there was such a field."

"The Canadian Arctic holds the world's largest source of freshwater—it's blue gold."

"What does the government want stats on?"

"Permafrost. We look at the inactive layer—the permafrost that never melts."

"How does it look?"

"It's looking thin."

"Is that a problem?"

"Maybe. A growing active layer causes Arctic lakes and streams to dry up."

I glance behind us. A dust cloud is gaining toward us. "Is most of your work in northern Yukon?"

"Most Arctic oil and gas is located under the Beaufort Sea but the majority of the land deposits are here, under Beringia—truthfully though, I like the service up here. World's friendliest waitresses."

"It's true. We are the worst."

Leo laughs.

"Truth—who comes across as more horrible, my sister, Charlotte, or me?"

"Is this a trick question?"

"Are we both terrible?"

"No—I saw you the first day we came up here this summer. You were standing in the lobby reading. You were wearing a blue tie-dyed T-shirt."

"You have a good memory." I'm both flattered and flustered that he remembers what I was wearing. In my internal chaos, I shift the conversation back to a safer topic. "I don't get it, as a hydrologist, are you interested in water or oil? Larry mentioned that Big Oil used to be up here, that's what built the hotel."

"They need water to drill. I'm one of the water guys. Water keeps the rigs cool, and they need ice roads to access the wells. About sixty wells have been drilled up here. Most of them right here near Beringia—only a few are currently functioning, but it's only a matter of time. The whole world is eyeing the Canadian Arctic."

"So, you do work for Big Oil?"

A billowing dust cloud, from exiting party traffic, edges closer. "Hit the ditch!" I scramble to the side of the Dempster and duck into the fireweed. Leo remains standing on the highway, watching the approaching traffic. Rob's truck is leading the pack. "Get down! If you want to walk with me, hit the ditch! I'm serious."

Leo looks confused as he lumbers into the ditch and then throws himself down beside me. "Am I allowed to ask why we are hiding?"

"No."

A warm hand squeezes my bare arm gently. "You know, it's okay, you can hitch a ride with one of them, if you want to," Leo says in a throaty, low voice—a failed attempt at whispering.

"Does it look like I want to?" I peek through the purple flowers.

Tom's jeep flies past. I wait for silence to return to the tundra. "Coast is clear." I shake the morning dampness from my dress and step onto the highway. "I can't believe you work for Big Oil. After the hard time you gave George."

"Hey, believe me, I'm on George's side—I work for the government. My stats are used by the government to negotiate with Big Oil. Do I work for Big Oil? That depends on who you talk to. Stats can support whatever you want them to if you know how to spin them."

"What do your stats tell you?"

"Off the record, oil and gas are warm. The generators burn diesel. The amount of energy it requires to keep things cool enough to extract them, without melting the permafrost, is insane. You can't put a pipeline on tundra for the same reason you can't put a railroad on tundra. When you disrupt the tundra, plants die and then the permafrost melts—things get messy."

"As in diseases are released?"

Leo laughs softly. I'm not sure if he finds my input amusing or if he's pleased that I remembered our first official conversation that didn't involve burnt food.

"That, and the infrastructure sinks."

"Hopefully it will never happen."

"It will happen."

"I don't believe that. What about the Mackenzie pipeline? That got axed."

"The death of the Mackenzie bought the Arctic time. The feds are up here with a mission: to sell the Arctic."

"It's a fucked-up world when lives are commodities."

"It's a capitalist reality. Heard of Petro-Canada? In the early seventies, ninety percent of all Canadian oil and gas revenue went to foreign investors. Trudeau created Petro-Canada to try and keep at least half of Canadian oil revenue in the country. Big Oil is fighting it. It's only a matter of time before it's sold off to foreign investors. Canadians won't profit from Arctic oil drilling. At best, it will offer a few blue-collar jobs—all the profits will go out of the country again."

"This is pretty deep shit for two a.m."

"Sorry. I'm a night owl. I get my best ideas after midnight. I forget that not everyone's awake at this hour."

"Are you and your supervisor's—Basoalto—research funded by Big Oil?"

"Universities are run on a capitalist model. If you don't do research, you don't have a job. Scientists depend on grants to do their research. It's competitive. If you don't take the money, your competition will. When Big Oil offers to pay for your research, you take it. Obviously, they hope to see stats, something, they can work with."

"So, you're saying that I shouldn't necessarily believe a study, even when it's from a prestigious university and a big-shot researcher?"

"All I'm saying is that it's worth checking to see who's funding the study. That's where the truth lies."

"So, when do you graduate—get your PhD?"

"I defend this fall—there's a good job opening up in environmental studies. Tenure track."

"At UBC?"

"Yeah. Right now, at this stage of my life, it's my dream job."

"Cool. I'd love to even have an inkling of what my dream job might look like—maybe we crossed paths on campus. I took my first three years at UBC."

"I don't think so—I'd remember crossing paths with you."

"Yeah, I'd probably remember you too."

"Right. My dirty feet and bad breath are hard to miss."

"Stop. I was in Ottawa this year, studying journalism."

"Journalism?"

"Yeah, but I'm not sure it's my destiny after all."

"No? What is?"

"That is the question—school sucked all the joy out of writing."

"You might feel different by September."

"Maybe. Leo, I like the name. Is it short for anything?"

"Leonard in English. The Swedish name's better."

"How do the Swedes say it?

"Leonartt."

It sounds exactly the same to me, except he put on a Swedish accent the second time. "You've been to Sweden?"

"Born there, raised in Toronto."

"Is Leo your astrological sign?"

"It is. I would show you the constellation . . . we should be able to still see it now, we're quite far west. Leo is easiest to spot in late spring, that is, if we were further south. Stop." He puts his arm in front of me and holds it there. "Grizzly." It takes me a few moments to spot the bear, grazing about thirty metres from the highway. Its coat is the same colour as the tundra. "We're upwind from her. She knows we're here. Keep walking—slowly."

We creep past the grizzly, not speaking for another half a kilometre.

"Is she getting enough to eat on the tundra?" I say quietly.

"Looked like it to me."

"How long will she have, the grizzly, to fatten her belly? Winter comes early up here, doesn't it?"

"Tundra is active for about two months. But it's a solid couple of months of growth. Twenty-four hours of sunlight and constant water beneath the roots—that grizzly belly will be full."

"Nature's hydroponics. So, where is all this growth?" I glance at the flat tundra dotted with the odd tamarack tree.

"Wind keeps things low. Growth is horizontal."

"I feel shorter and wider already. How many years will it take for the wind to flatten us?"

"I was six-five when I started working up here. I think I'm down to six-four."

I pick up the pace, speed walking, and then break into a jog. Leo trots behind me, unenthusiastically. "Why are we running?" He says and then picks up speed and passes me. I go full out, the kind of run that makes you puke if it's longer than one hundred metres, but I can't catch him. He obviously does a little more than sit in the chopper all day. He stops suddenly and turns around, runs toward me, and then picks me up in his arms. I scream in surprise as he twists me behind his shoulders, spins around and then places me, feet first, back onto the Dempster.

His presence feels new, promising, as though we met for the first time tonight and the mountain man was someone else from my distant past. My steps feel lighter. We walk in shale-crunching silence.

"Does anyone ever call you Rumi?"

"Like the poet?"

"Yeah."

"Not so far."

The dust cloud that's been gaining on us has caught up. The YTG truck stops. Ode unrolls the passenger window. "Need a lift? Hop on." The driver, Caroline, squints ahead on the Dempster, like an uninterested chauffeur.

"Is there still water in the tub?" I tease.

"Of course. We're not going to dump chemicals on the tundra," Ode says abruptly.

"I'm good, really—but thanks. I like walking the Dempster and I can practically see the hotel from here."

Ode tightens her mouth and lowers her eyebrows, as though she's not buying it. She leans her head a little further out the window to look behind me. "How about you? Are you good, Leo?" Her question sounds like a challenge.

He nods slowly once. "I'm good."

Ode shakes her head, scoffs, and then stares straight ahead. Caroline finally glances our way as Ode bends over to get something off the floor of the truck. Ode hands me a can of Coke. "Take it." Her eyes focused ahead, out the truck windshield.

"Thanks. Coke, straight up."

She holds out another can, a club soda. She won't look my way. "Take it."

"World's best service. Bartender on wheels."

"Go!" Ode instructs Caroline in a commanding tone. Caroline obeys and they leave us in shale dust.

I hand Leo the soda water. "I need the caffeine to keep going."

"You a friend of hers, Ode?"

I slurp up the frothy mess exploding from the spout of the Cola can. "I guess so. Never thought about it before but yeah, she's cool."

Ode's brief interruption reminds me that we are no longer inside the Arctic Circle, the mystical place where reality and fantasy intermingle and ugly truths fade in the sunshine and evaporate into rainbow mist. Hotel Beringia, with all its desperados, is getting closer. With each step we return to our beautifully ugly selves: Hell's Waitress and Yukon Cornelius.

Leo walks over to the opposite side of the road. He's peeing. Could he not excuse himself first or stagger onward and go in the hotel?

He trots across the road and keeps pace beside me. The pee ruined the moment. I ignore him until I start to feel like the mean waitress from hell. "You're shivering," I say, in an accusatory tone.

"My clothes got a little wet. They're draining my body temperature."

I reach over and squeeze his baggy T-shirt. "A little wet? You're soaked! You should take it off."

"Are you trying to seduce me?" He struggles out of the T-shirt. Every muscle in his torso constricts with cold. He is an impossibly perfect V—wide shoulders that taper to a skinny waist and narrow hips.

"No. It's the Beringia ambulance assistant talking." I want to stare at each crevice of his abdomen, but I force my gaze onto the tundra, looking for movement along the smooth, rippled mountains. All those times in the restaurant, I dismissed him as average under all that flannel.

"Who is that?"

"Yours truly."

"Ha! Seriously?"

"Why is that amusing?"

"I guess it's not." He laughs again. "Let us hope EMT Rumer is more compassionate than waitress Rumer."

"She's not. I'd avoid all catastrophes if I were you."

Leo finds that hilarious. He clutches his skinny gut as though in pain. He finally stops laughing and gazes into the midnight sky. "Shit. I'm seriously scared."

"You should be."

"Is your hair naturally blond?"

"Ah—if that's a line, I suggest you get a new one."

"I was just wondering."

"Wonder no more. This is me. I had highlights put in last winter, but they've grown out." I hold up a bleached end of the hair that frames my face. "This is what's left. What about you? Is all this natural? Your beard's lighter than your hair." I make a sweeping gesture in the direction of his head.

"It is what it is."

Social pleasantries continue to drop like tired dogs along the Dempster, soon followed by all conversation between us. We walk in silence for long enough that it no longer feels awkward or maybe I'm too tired to care if it is. The hotel appears, sitting high on its bedrock perch.

"Is that a mirage?" I say.

"I don't think so. No palm trees."

I walk across the parking lot toward the trailer. Leo stays with me. "How long are you up here for this time?"

"We fly back to Whitehorse tomorrow, but we're up again next week." He has the same look on his face as he had as he grabbed me and flung me in the air. He leans down to kiss my mouth. His breath is no longer peppermint but delicious in a way that I don't want it to be. The pause afterward is long—our lips millimetres apart. The single kiss relaxes me into a euphoric state that is more asleep than awake. The twenty-kilometre walk has made exhaustion my only intimate friend tonight, and not even a kiss from a celestial lion will rouse me.

"Good night, Rumi." He walks backward, toward the hotel.

"Good morning." I open the screen door.

Charlotte's side of the room is tidier than usual. The bed remains unmade, but her clothes are no longer scattered all over the floor. All her things are gone. Charlotte is gone. My collage is gone, only the ripped corners remain, attached to thumbtacks. A crumpled poster lies partially visible under Charlotte's bed, among the broken glass and dirty dishes. I pull the wrinkled paper toward me and attempt to smooth out my collage. A dried, muddy footprint bisects the collage diagonally—a men's work boot. Someone must have ripped it off the wall, and asshole Tom stepped on it as he helped her move out. The pictures are ruined.

Ironically, the crumpled mess is a more accurate reflection of my current existence. My toiletry and make-up bags are open on my bed. My fingers sort through them in a panic and then I dump the contents on my bed. My grey eye shadow palette is missing and a black eyeliner. I pull my backpack from underneath my bed and fumble with the zipper. I dump the sock into my shaking palm, and with trembling fingers, reach inside and pull out the goddess. I wipe the paltry trickle of tears from my cheeks. I am too dehydrated to cry.

I fall asleep in my dress and fill the empty room with dreams, an all-night movie marathon: pirate and Viking ships sail on an ancient sea, and I am the lone human living on a tiny island, in an orange trailer with a family of wolves.

Doris and Seraphina sit side by side behind the front desk. Doris is a mirror of what Seraphina will look like in twenty-five years: the same small, thin build, a few strands of grey hair, a face hardly lined, and eyes that are softer, perhaps from gained wisdom. I pause at the bookcase. "What are you looking for?" Doris says.

"Just looking to replenish my stash . . . books about the Yukon."

"There are a few Jack Londons, and a Farley Mowat in there."

"I'm thinking more non-fiction."

I pull out a book on the Beringian land bridge, and another on human geography of the Americas.

"Found a few. Thanks," I say and then glance down the hall of guest rooms on my way to the saloon, to see if I can catch a glimpse of Charlotte, coming or going from Tom's room. The hall's deserted.

The saloon is empty. I dash to a club chair, throw myself into it and then peruse the book on the Beringian land bridge, making notations in my journal: *Grizzlies crossed the Beringian land bridge from North Asia. They're relatively new to North America. No surprise that we North Americans have been unkind to the grizzly. They're nearly extinct in their new home, except for dwindling populations in the northwest. They're no doubt waiting for a new land bridge to appear, one that leads to a human-free continent.*

I leaf through the book to find the chapter on human migration. A photograph catches my eye. I turn back a few pages and press open the book. There, in black and white, is a photograph of a female sculpture that looks remarkably similar to the Bluefish goddess. I write feverishly, as though the photograph might vanish before I've penned the information: *female goddess figurine, mammoth tusk, Siberia, Russia, 23,000 BCE.*

Ode's voice startles me. "Taking it easy, are we?"

"It's peaceful in here during the day," I say warmly, despite her arrival feeling like an intrusion. I use a saloon napkin as a bookmark and then close the book.

I flip through my journal to my first entries. The interesting observations are few and far between, with rants about Charlotte taking over page after page of my Arctic journal—*my* journal. It stopped being my journal after page six. It evolved into a boring chronicle of my responses to Charlotte's ass-holic behaviour. If it were a legit assignment, I'd call it *The Summer of the Rant.* I tear page after page of my depressing ramblings from the leather-bound journal. The remaining Arctic facts, hidden truths, and covert personal observations remain precariously tethered inside the book. I rip each discarded page into little pieces, then walk to the bar and dump the confetti in the trash.

Ode shrugs. "The way I see it, Charlie's done you a favour. Let her go."

I stop. There's no way she could know about the attack. She must be referring to Charlotte moving in with Tom. "News travels fast in this hotel."

"I've seen it my whole life, blood or no blood."

"Seen what?"

"Women turn on women."

"Yeah?"

"So, what do you do when family turn on each other?"

"I love them from a safe distance—seven thousand kilometres, in my case."

"We live at Hotel Beringia. It's not exactly Caesar's Palace. You have to love–hate people from an unsafe distance up here."

"Have you talked to Eugenie today?"

"No. Why?"

"Go talk to her."

"Why? What's going on?"

"Tom's RV is gone and the jeep. He took his dog, and I assume your sister, with him."

"Where'd they go?"

"That I cannot tell you."

What if it's true, that Charlotte has left Beringia? It never occurred to me that Charlotte would stray farther than the hotel. She loves a familial audience and Tom's camper is hardly big enough to stage her dramas. She has to be hiding out in Tom's room, lying on his bed with a hedonistic smirk on her face.

I open the door to our room, *my* room. That explains the stomped-on collage—a parting gift from the psycho-couple, a final fuck-you. I pull out the toiletry box from the end of my bed. Charlotte left behind all the boxes of tampons we brought, enough to last the entire summer. I race to the bathroom to see if she took her body wash and shampoo. The shower is bare except for an empty bottle of conditioner. I glance under the long vanity and into the trash can for clues of her departure: a pregnancy test box and a used wand with a double-line result. I grab the box and scan the directions—two lines is positive. It could belong to Charlotte or Maxine.

Shit, I left my journal in the saloon. If anyone gets a hold of it, I am doomed: floppy-mouthed Larry, Clint Eastwood with ovaries, jolie-laide Ilya, and the recent addition of Leo's provocatively ripped abs will mortify me to eternity. I race across the parking lot and sprint through the front doors and into the saloon. The shutter-style doors swing wildly, announcing my entrance.

Caroline is the only new addition to the quiet room. It must be her day off. She sits across the bar from Ode. My dramatic entrance has gone unnoticed by them both. The journal is still on the back table where I left it. I stash it under my arm and walk to the bar. Ode briefly glances at me—standing at the bar, waiting to ask her something—but chooses not to engage. Caroline looks my way and holds her gaze. Ode finally acknowledges my presence, only because Caroline is no longer gazing at her with exclusive captivation. "What can I do you for?"

Caroline laughs. "You said that like a local."

"Did I? I have been practising." Ode laughs self-consciously.

The rapport of the lovebirds is a little annoying. "Caroline, I was wondering if you have any idea at all where Tom might have gone?"

"Tom's on holiday. He had these two weeks booked since January," Caroline says.

"Do you know where he went?"

"I assume he's in Whitehorse."

"Do you know for sure that Charlotte went with him?".

"I don't," Caroline says.

"I told you to ask Eugenie. Maybe Charlie booked some time off," Ode says.

"Yeah, okay." I step away from the bar, about to leave.

"You worry too much. You are not Charlie's mother," Ode says.

"Maybe, but my parents will blame me if anything happens to her. How many kids did you say Tom has?"

"Four—why?" Ode says.

"Four kids is a lot. Isn't it?"

"That depends. I have eleven sisters and brothers. Two sets of twins—all home births. In northern Quebec there weren't many hospitals."

"She has a twin brother," Caroline says.

"Really? You're a twin?"

"I am, and he's almost as handsome as I am." Ode laughs.

"It's true. I've seen a photo," Caroline says.

"Four kids would be hard to support on Tom's income," I say.

Ode stops laughing. "Why are you thinking about that?"

"No reason."

"What if the roles were reversed? Would your parents blame Charlie if you went astray?"

"No. That would be my fault. I'd be blamed for abandoning my sister."

"There you go. There is no glory in being a martyr."

"I'm not a martyr!" I snap. Ode raises her eyebrows, surprised by my tone. "I'm just . . . I don't know what I am." I turn to leave as Ode swiftly clasps hold of my wrist.

"Rumer, you do know he's married, right?" she whispers.

"Yeah, we've established that—but he's obviously separated, if only by distance." I shake my wrist loose, confused as to why she brought up Tom again, after insisting that Charlotte is not my business. I don't know which bartender dictum to take and which to toss.

IX

I carry a basket of dirty laundry across the parking lot. I've wrecked all my pretty bras and panties using the hotel laundry detergent; throwing them in with my darks hasn't helped either. The flesh-pink transparent bra has turned corpse grey. I shift the basket under one arm and pull open the lobby door. Leo is on the pay phone. A rush of adrenalin hits my brain. He speaks quietly, yet it's obvious whoever is on the other end of the line is not happy with him. His muffled tone is apologetic, pleading. He hangs up the phone and turns around. His expression is tense, the call did not go well. His eyes are as turquoise as ever, but his face is hairless.

"What happened to the beard?"

He strokes his bald face. "I'm not used to it yet. It feels weird."

I study his lips. I've never truly seen them before, so pink and plump—pretty lips for a mountain man.

"You don't like it?"

"I do . . . like it. You look a lot younger."

"I'm not sure that's a compliment."

"It is. How old are you, anyway?"

"Twenty-eight," he says.

"Seriously? You don't look that old."

"How old are you?"

"Twenty-two."

"I would have guessed you'd be older."

"Thanks?"

"I'm heading to Tombstone. There's time for a hike. You free?"

"I work a lot this week. With Charlotte temporarily gone, I have no days off until the undetermined day of her return."

"Where'd she go?"

"She left with Tom. She told Eugenie she had a doctor's appointment in Whitehorse but that she'd be back in four days. It's been nearly a week. No one's heard from them."

"Most people take two days to drive from Beringia to Whitehorse—I wouldn't sweat it."

"When are you going on the hike . . . to Tombstone?"

"As soon as you can get ready. I'll have you back by midnight."

This is, no doubt, another business trip. I shift the basket to under my other arm. A whiff of skanky laundry assaults my nostrils. "Is Malik coming?"

"He's got business in Dawson."

"You're the pilot now?"

"I'm in my truck. I have some work to do on the North Klondike."

"How far is Tombstone from here?"

"About three hundred K."

"At home, driving three hundred kilometres for a day hike would never happen, but up here, it seems like nothing."

"Is that a yes?" He raises his eyebrows with exaggerated optimism.

"Okay."

"As in, you'll come?"

"Yeah—should I pack a picnic?"

"I've got the food situation covered."

There is a handwritten note duct-taped to the dusty truck dashboard: *Live like the lotus, at ease in muddy water.*

"Did you write that?"

He shakes his head. "Buddha."

Dark clouds chase the truck as we speed along the highway through the valley. The mountains look easy to climb but there are no trees, no man-made landmarks, to use as a scale to guess their height. "Where are we? Looks like another planet."

"The beginning of the Ogilvies."

"They look purple—I'm calling them 'the lavender hills.'"

"They look more pewter to me—could you look beside that cooler at your feet and hand me the Thermos?" I locate a beaten-up Thermos behind the small steel cooler that my feet rest on and hand it to him. He puts it between his legs and unscrews the lid. "You don't have much room there, sorry. Remind me to put the cooler in back for the trip home."

"I'm okay. Why'd you shave your beard?"

"Got tired of it. I have enough hair. Facial hair, pubic hair, pit hair . . . it's all the same."

I nod slowly, as though pubic hair talk is weather talk, and then pick up the cooler and place it on the seat between us. I play with the truck's radio as a scratchy newscast fades in and out.

Leo finally pulls over to the edge of the highway and then starts to unload water equipment from the back of the truck. "Follow the North Klondike with your eye. See the tallest peak? Tombstone. First climbed in the seventies."

Tombstone lives up to its macabre name. Slate-hued, sharp pinnacles cut through a rain cloud floating halfway up its water-blackened base. Adrenalin pains shoot down my legs simply imagining my limbs clinging to its vertical walls. "Have you climbed it?"

"No. Not yet."

"You want to climb *that*?"

"I'd like to try. Possibly later this summer."

"Seriously? You can climb that?"

"I've been climbing for over ten years."

I follow Leo along the river's edge, through the valley, toward the tall, jagged mountains. Leo wades into the water carrying the metal rod with a propeller attached to it.

"What are you measuring?" I shout.

"Discharge." I don't bother to ask what discharge means. I wade into the cold water, stepping on river rocks in a full spectrum of colours.

Leo splashes through the shallow water with a roguish smile. "Hold this. Right here. Don't move. Hold it steady." He places the end of a cord in my hand. "Stay there." He crosses the stream to the opposite bank. I hold the cord for what seems like ten minutes. Leo wades toward me and pulls the cord from my hand.

"Discharge measured?"

He smiles but does not answer the question.

I slide onto a warm boulder and take my journal out of my pack. *June 28, Tombstone: The afternoon passes slowly, with storms of misty rain and fierce, cold winds that swoop like ravens, from mountain peak to mountain peak, through the valley and then, as fast as they fly, they leave, and the hot arctic sun bakes my skin.*

Watching shirtless Leo measure discharge—with the formidable Tombstone and its serrated peaks in the distance—feels surreal, as though I'm a privileged guest at a fantastical party, a party that I will not be invited to again.

"Finished, for today. Let's get out of here." He stretches his arms wide and then over his head. I yawn instinctively.

Leo stashes his equipment in the back of the truck.

"Are we dining in the truck?"

"Supper in the truck?" He holds his chest as though wounded. "I'm taking you out to dine," he says as he unloads the gear. "Where I'm taking you . . . you won't believe me if I tell you. Let's go. I'm hungry."

We cross the highway, leaving the dark and mysterious for the light and whimsical. The round mountains on the opposite side of the Dempster are illuminated under the evening sun, like giant, golden orbs. We step on the spongy carpet of wildflowers, steadily climbing the chartreuse hills.

"These four flowers always grow close to each other. I saw them along the trail and in the forests near Hotel Beringia. They're the quintessential arctic bouquet to me: purple monkshood, wild rose, bluebells, and this small white flower."

"Dogwood," Leo says.

"Bonsai dogwood, I love it—I feel cruel walking on all this life."

"It's a legit hiking trail. Don't sweat it. We hit rock soon."

"What is this trail called?"

"Goldensides." He points to a branch with tiny leaves, flush with the tundra. "Dwarf raspberries."

I pick one and plop it in my mouth. "A basket of deliciousness packed into a single berry. How is it that the most exquisite food exists as a tiny morsel in the most remote location?"

"It's not remote to those who live here."

We reach the end of the trail. The rocky summit drops abruptly, falling to the base of a neighbouring mountain, and then another. It is a land of tors with no room for valley.

"So much wild."

"I guess it can be a little overwhelming—from where you're standing, you're looking at the Seven Million Dollar, behind us the Tombstone, North Klondike, and two . . . three . . . at least five different ranges," Leo says.

"I'm in awe-shock Arctic love."

"What?"

"I have never experienced so much beauty all at once."

"Awe-shock love," he repeats and then chuckles in amusement.

I sit next to him on the flat rock at the summit's peak. Our legs dangle into the deep void. He hands me his thermos of water and then reaches into the backpack and takes out two brown bags—YTG lunches. The cuisine is disappointing, especially in contrast to the grandeur of the venue. "These look familiar," I say, my tone unable to hide my true feelings.

"I hope this is okay—Eugenie recommended the turkey."

"Yeah, turkey is fine. The safest choice."

"Safest?"

"Never trust a sandwich with the word 'salad' in it—chicken salad, tuna salad, egg salad. Especially if Louise is on sandwich duty."

His eyebrows shoot up.

I laugh. "Your face is so expressive sometimes—there's got to be a story tied to those eyebrows."

"I ate an egg salad sandwich from Beringia about a week ago, barely lived to tell the tale."

"What day of the week did you eat the sandwich?"

"Does it matter?"

"Yes, it matters. Big time. Every sandwich matters at Hotel Beringia—who makes them, who eats them, who takes one, who takes two."

"We had the chopper. It was early in the week. We were up near the Beaufort Sea. Malik couldn't land the damn machine in time."

"What happened?"

"I shit my pants."

"I am sorry." My attempt at empathy is blindsided by laughter.

"You don't sound sorry."

"I am sorry that you shit your pants—it's just, Louise made the YTG lunch on a Sunday and left them on the counter overnight. Eugenie found them on Monday morning and freaked out. She made me go through all the bags and throw out the sandwiches. Maxine said she sold one to a guy as soon as the restaurant opened. I can't believe that was you!"

"Pleased my misfortune is so entertaining. And here I thought their burgers— charcoal briquettes—were the biggest risk."

"I was hoping you'd forgotten about that. I tried, I really did, but Louise is like the devil in hell's kitchen—she burns everything and then roars and bares her fangs if I request a redo."

A marmot scurries from rock to rock, edging its way toward us. It pauses on the ledge above to watch us eat.

"I don't remember the burger as much as I remember the waitress."

I pass the Thermos to Leo and then watch his Adam's apple move as he swallows. He passes the Thermos back to me.

"Sorry. I guess it's fitting that hell's waitress works in hell's kitchen." I take a sip, not bothering to wipe the rim.

"No, believe it or not, that's not what I remember."

Whatever he remembers, it's probably mortifying. "That marmot might be the cutest animal ever."

"It is cute."

"It has no fear of humans."

"It's not likely to run into a lot of humans up here. The summers are short, not a lot of hikers this far north. Naivety is bliss."

"I don't know. Not knowing what assholes humans really are leaves it vulnerable."

"Probably. This asshole human brought dessert." Leo reaches into the backpack and pulls out two peanut butter marshmallow squares.

"Who told you?"

"Eugenie might have made a suggestion," he says and then adds, "What I remember is you made that ugly waitress uniform sexy as hell."

I watch Leo take a bite, suddenly aware that I've been smiling for some time, unbeknown to me until now. Leo stuffs the entire square in his mouth.

The space between us collapses. I hold my breath and then swallow. "Thank you for saying that, but no one looks sexy in Hotel Beringia polyester."

"I disagree."

His cold bare, thigh presses against mine. My legs feel metres long, as though I could step from one summit to the next. In the evening sun, everything is gold. Leo's hair is a halo of light. "I thought the Arctic has been mined of all the gold it could possibly hold but trust nature to show me I'm wrong."

"She has plenty of gold if you know where to look."

"I was speaking metaphorically about the colours tonight . . . the sun rays, the mountain, you."

"Me? I'm gold?"

"Tonight, on this mountain, you are."

He watches me as I speak. His expression reveals both pleasure and uncertainty. "I'm speaking mineral-phorically, about what's hidden in the water."

"You can take the man out of the water, but you can't take the water out of the man—where is this gold that you speak of?"

"There's still gold in the Yukon, a lot of gold. We are more like the rivers than we admit. Gold flows through rivers and our blood. It's what fires the brain."

"Is that true?"

"Truth. Gold is heavy. A single star's death doesn't make gold. It takes a kilonova to make gold."

"What exactly is a kilonova?

"Two stars collide and die."

"I like it. The universe is Rumpelstiltskin—gold gives life yet is born out of death."

"I can tell you're a writer."

"How?"

"The way you use words . . . I like your words."

I put my lips on his cheekbone. His beardless cheek is smooth and tastes like peanut butter.

"You smell good."

I believe him for a brief moment, until I remember that I am wearing dirty clothes that smell of mildew. "I smell like the hotel." I lift off my T-shirt.

Leo's gaze stops on the flesh-coloured bra that I wore for the German tour bus, the one tinted grey from Yukon life. The bra is suddenly revealed to me as what it is: hideous. I remove it and toss it. The wind catches the ruined bra and it sails off the cliff.

"You know your bra is history, but your breasts . . . wow," Leo says like he's fourteen. "You're even sexier out of uniform."

I crawl to the edge of the cliff.

"Careful. That's a long way down."

"I can't see the bottom." All at once I am overcome with vertigo. "Hold my hand, please!" I extend one arm behind me.

Leo grabs my wrist "What are you doing? Slide back a bit."

I sit back, my breath fast and deep, my heart racing. "I can't leave it down there, in all that wild—the polyester, spandex . . . chemical fabrics, polluting. . ."

"It's gone. Nothing you can do about it now. You'll never see that bra again," he says and then adds quietly, "I have protection," even though we are the only humans for as far as the eye can see.

"Bear spray?" I say even though I know what he means.

"Condoms." His expression is serious.

"How many condoms?"

"I don't know, a few."

"A few condoms and two Hotel Beringia sandwiches. You were feeling optimistic when you loaded your pack today." I don't want to care about him, but I'll allow myself to want him. My hand slides under the hem of his canvas shorts and up a firm quadricep. "Take off your shorts." I watch as he struggles to be free of them. As I suspected, he's not wearing underwear. "Don't toss them. I don't want you hiking back naked."

"I will if you will." He pulls his T-shirt over his head and throws it next to his shorts.

His mouth is on mine. I pull back, suddenly unsure if I'm prepared for what's about to happen. All my rationalizations that sex means nothing, it's just a physical act, dissipate in the thin mountain air. I know the truth: sex changes everything. He stops, trying to suss out my hesitancy. His eyes are less intense, more curious. All at once, he's just a beautiful man with eyes the colour of the sky, and smooth skin that smells like the mountain: musky vine bark and spiced spruce needles. *Walk toward wild.* I lean toward him and kiss his pretty-boy lips. The first kisses are gentle, almost cordial. The intensity builds rapidly. There is no shyness; everything feels easy, almost familiar, as though we're long-lost lovers, from another time. I draw my fingers along his smooth abdomen. His callused yet gentle hand slides up my thigh.

A swell of calm engulfs me; for a moment I am floating, observing the feverish dance of our mouths, torsos, and limbs. My back burns from the friction of rock, and what must be lichen, that brushes like fine sandpaper against my skin. I grasp onto his taut, round bum, as my spine is pushed into the cold mountain, and I lose myself in the pleasure, refusing to surrender to the pain. Leo pauses for a moment, straightens his arms, and smiles at me from above, as though he can't quite believe his luck with what has transpired.

"I warmed the rock for you," I say.

He lies where my back once was, and I climb on top of him. He gasps. "Warm is still . . . hard."

I gulp in cool alpine air as a riptide suddenly takes hold, pulling me into an all-consuming ocean of fire, water, earth, sweaty—organic—scents, and our feral calls. He ceases to be Leo and I am no longer me. We are the sun, the sky, and Goldensides. I hold him inside me as I fall onto his warm chest, seeking his body heat.

A cool gust sweeps through the summit peak and reminds me of our nakedness. I climb off Leo and snuggle in beside him, resting my head on his smooth chest. He wraps his arm over my back. We lie together, sharing the uncomfortableness of the brutal rock bed, our chests pressed together, legs entwined. "How did you get so tanned?"

"I'm outside all day. The hole in ozone helps."

"You've got the golden Yukon glow. I'm West Coast white," I say.

He gently drags his fingertip down my nose, over my chin, and along my throat. "I fucking love your freckles," he says with the satisfied grin of a stoner. The expression reminds me of George's sleepy smile when he's nodding off behind the front desk.

"You were right about one thing."

"What's that?"

"Your pubic hair and your facial hair, it is all the same."

He laughs. "So that's the reason you seduced me."

"Not really—do you ever wear underwear?"

"Yeah."

"Just not today?"

"You saw how wet I get in the river. Underwear stays wet. My shorts dry faster without it."

I reach over to the rock where they lie. "You're right, they're already dry."

"Rumi? What were you thinking about, before, on the edge of the rock, when you asked me to hold your hand?"

"The void was so beautiful and mysterious—in that moment, it felt right to surrender my body, to fall into it, but my mind wouldn't let me—it was pure terror."

We descend Goldensides, the mountain lit by the evening sun, with bursts of gold reflecting off the tundra's yellow and white anemones. We retrace our footsteps, leaving nothing but my bra behind. I skip along the path and shout, "This place makes me want to sing *The Sound of Music* soundtrack. If you were wearing shorts made out of curtains, I'd swear this was heaven. Come on, can't you skip?" He hauls his big feet from the tundra, lifting his knees awkwardly. He can't skip. I turn away quickly before he sees me laugh.

Across the highway, voluminous, dark clouds have formed over Tombstone. Streaks of grey rain fall down her face and blacken her gown. In the mist, her serrated top appears smoother, less formidable, and yet the mountain is no less menacing. "Why is the Tombstone range so tall and jagged compared to Goldensides?"

"Tombstone escaped glaciation. The last ice age left her alone."

"Climb her."

"What?" he shouts from the switch back above me.

"Climb Tombstone."

The lone truck is waiting for us, barn red, warmed by the sun, like a little cabin in the hinterland. I pause outside the driver's door. "Can I drive back?"

"I guess—actually, that would be great. You don't mind if I sleep?"

"What is that?" I point to a single, black wing lying on the engine hood.

"What the hell?" Leo scrambles to the front of the truck and picks up a wing. The blood on it looks fresh, as though it was ripped from the raven's back while in flight.

"It must have fallen from the sky."

"Looks like an eagle dropped its lunch." He tosses it into the ditch and then jumps inside the passenger side and shuts the door.

"Seatbelt," I sense him looking my way. I focus my eyes out the windshield and wait to hear the click. The red blood splotch remains on the engine's hood.

"You know, now that I think about it, I might have seen Tom's motorhome last week," Leo says after he snaps his belt.

"Where?"

"Dawson. It was heading toward the ferry."

"Was it towing Tom's jeep?"

"Don't remember the jeep, but a yellow motorhome got on that ferry."

"Where would they be going in that direction?"

"Alaska." He places his hand on my knee. "She'll be back. I'm sure she's okay. Tom seems all right."

"He's not!"

Leo's shocked expression makes me realize that I've already said too much. I start the truck and swing it around, too fast, unintentionally skidding dangerously close to the ditch. I smile weakly at Leo, pretending the skid was a calculated joyride. I straighten the truck with less vigour until I face north, and then drive toward wild.

X

After a four-hour sleep, I stumble to the trailer showers. The fluttering in my chest fuels my brain with manic optimism. I smell my bare arm and inhale a fistful of my hair and decide that I'm not yet ready to wash off Goldensides.

I cling to the golden thrill all morning. It fades as four hunters in head-to-toe camo enter the room. I boost my morale by checking the back windowsill for dead flies—knowing they're there for future meal sabotages is empowering.

Eugenie's head appears at the order window. She motions me toward her.

"Rumer, can I talk to you in the kitchen for a moment." Eugenie's tone makes me fear what's coming next. I can't cope with being bawled out for some waitressing infraction, as though it's my fault we're short-staffed because my sister went AWOL. Finally, I get it, what Ode's been trying to tell me: that my sister is not my business—pity the poor sucker who thinks that she is. I'm existing on four hours of sleep and the only thing keeping me going is the current of sex-hangover euphoria that occasionally floats down my spine.

"Tom called Caroline yesterday," Eugenie's sombre tone makes me too terrified to ask her to continue. "He's hurt his back and extended his time off. He won't be back until late August, at the earliest."

"Charlotte?"

"Tom said she won't be coming back to Hotel Beringia."

"Did Caroline ask where she is? If she's safe?"

"Caroline didn't get a chance to ask. The conversation was short."

I stroll past the table of hunters and keep walking until I reach Tom's door. I put my ear to the door. It's hard to hear anything except the sound from a loud television coming from the room across the hall. I pause and listen to see if I can recognize the program they're watching. It has to be a YTG room; guests are up here for such a short time, they never turn on the TV. I knock, three timid raps, so pathetic that it's doubtful human ears will detect them. I rehearse my lines in my head. The chain on the door rattles and the door opens a crack. Grey eyes focus on my face. I'm relieved it's Ilya and not a face with no name or worse, Cup-Thumper.

"Have you heard from Tom?" I struggle to see into the room behind him. Papers are strewn on a single queen bed. The place looks surprisingly neat and tidy.

"No."

"Charlotte?"

"No. Tom's RV is gone."

"Yeah, I know. Do you know where he was going on his time off?"

Ilya takes a step forward, pokes his head into the hall, glances in the direction of the hotel lobby and then steps back into his room. "No." He shuts the door. The television goes silent.

"Thanks!" I shout at the door.

"Rumer?" Leo's voice breaks the silence. In the artificial light, his presence is harsh and intimidating, like the mountain man I first met in the restaurant. He's not supposed to be here. He said he going to drive back to Dawson early this morning, stopping on route to finish his work. I'm flustered as he walks toward me, filled with conflicting thoughts and emotions: panic that his breath will be foul, his boorish ways will revolt, and that the golden man is a delusion, brought on by loneliness. I can't look at his face, terrified he'll be Yukon Cornelius with the beginnings of a beard.

He wraps his long arms around me. I stiffen. "What are you doing back here? What about your work?"

"Just finished. Had to take a detour to see you again." The sonorous sound of his voice and his musky, spiced-spruce scent take me back to the man from last night. I relax in his arms as he kisses my neck. He is Aurelian, perfectly golden.

"What are you looking at?" Leo bellows. The aggression in his voice is unexpected. Ilya's door slams shut.

"Let's get out of the hall." He leads me down the hall to a room and unlocks the door. One of the queen beds is dishevelled—the mustard-coloured floral bedspread shoved to the end of the bed.

"I thought you'd stay upstairs."

"What's the difference?"

"I don't know—better view. Who was on chambermaid duty today?"

"How would I know?"

"They suck at their job. No one made up your bed."

Leo sits on the messy bed that's closest to the door. I sit beside him. He stands suddenly and then strides toward the dresser and picks up one of the huge, beat-up, work boots on the floor. He reaches inside, pulls out a sock, holds it in his palm, as though testing its weight, and then slips it back in the boot and returns to the bed.

"What was that about?"

"Making sure everything is as it was."

"Translation please?"

He walks back over to the boot dumps the sock into his hand and holds up a goose egg sized gold rock.

"Is that what it looks like?" I walk over to get a closer look.

"My bloke. Biggest nugget I ever found."

"How much is that worth?"

"Some decent cash."

"Five figures?"

"A solid five."

"Why do you keep it here, in the hotel? Strangers clean your room."

"I keep it close. Would you stick your hand inside one of my boots?"

"You have a point."

"Anyway, it's temporary."

"Where did you find the gold?"

"In a pot at the end of a fucking rainbow."

His flippant remark feels rude. I turn from him, considering whether or not to leave.

"A ways from here. I have access to every river up here." He sounds surprisingly arrogant.

"What river?"

"You wouldn't know it . . . a tributary of the Peel."

"Is it your gold? You claimed it?" He is silent. "You never claimed it?"

"We've got a little placer mine. It's not a big deal," he says sounding defeated.

"It seems like a big fucking deal," I say, gesturing toward his "bloke," and then add, "Who is 'we'—you and Malik?" He doesn't answer. "You're hiding the gold from Malik, aren't you?"

"Does it matter?" Leo puts the gold back into the sock and slips it back inside his boot. "I leave tomorrow morning. This might be it for a while," he says.

"You're not coming back to Beringia?" I walk to the bed and sit on the edge.

"I want to. I'll try to get back in a couple of weeks for a night or two." Leo sits next to me. "We're heading further north. No field work near here in the foreseeable future."

"No more discharging?"

Leo laughs. "That doesn't sound right."

I laugh too and then process that this means no more Leo. "Charlotte's still gone," I say quietly.

"Isn't that a good thing in a way?"

"Why would it be a good thing?"

"At summer solstice you indicated that you two weren't getting along—sorry."

"You're right, but I have no idea where she is, and I don't trust Tom. Can you keep an eye out for Charlotte in Whitehorse, Dawson, Inuvik—all the places you might travel?"

"Of course—did you talk to Eugenie? Maybe Charlotte booked some more time off."

"I did talk to Eugenie. Caroline is such a clueless idiot. Tom called her to book more time off for some back injury. He said Charlotte wasn't coming back. That was it, and then he hung up. I would have asked to speak to Charlotte. She didn't even ask where Tom was."

"Doesn't sound like he gave Caroline the chance."

I glance around the messy room. It's as if as if there is an invisible wall dividing the dresser top. A photograph is strategically positioned on one side of the dresser: Malik in a pastel Lacoste polo shirt posing beside a woman with a commodious smile. "Is that Malik's girlfriend?"

"Wife."

"Malik's married?"

"That surprises you?"

"Sort of. Where does she live?"

"Lower mainland."

"Malik commutes?"

"He has a place in Dawson."

"Is his wife there?"

"No. I don't believe she's stepped a toe in the Yukon."

"Have you met her?"

"Yeah—If you think Malik's ambitious, she's something else."

"I don't know Malik," I say, annoyed that he thinks I do. Malik's a cold fish. "Where are your pictures?"

"I go home all the time. I don't have time to miss anyone."

"I noticed." His half of the dresser top is completely empty. "Is there anyone you miss at home?"

"The cat."

"You have a cat? Who looks after it when you're here?"

"A friend."

"How long have you lived in Whitehorse?"

"Since I got the government job—about six years. Winters I live in Kitsilano—the PhD."

"Kitsilano is where I grew up. My mom has a house there . . . Will you move there permanently once you defend your thesis?"

"Don't know. Depends. I'd take that position at UBC if it becomes an option."

He leans in and kisses my cheek, my ear lobe, and then my neck. I listen to the sound of his deep breaths. We are back on Goldensides' summit. My body ignites, recollecting the tundra and diffused sunlight. We fall back onto the bed.

"Will Malik walk in on us?"

"He's in Dawson."

"But what if he decides to fly up and surprise you?"

"That's not going to happen, but I'll lock the door for you."

"He doesn't have a key?"

"I'll use the chain."

I'd rather be out on the tundra. I place my finger on his lips. "I have something I want to show you—I too have a sock." Leo props himself up on one elbow and stares at the room door, as though he too is suddenly worried it will open. "I found something at Bluefish, down at the river. I didn't show it to you . . . I guess I was afraid you'd tell me to leave it be." Leo's gaze is fixed with a hyper-eagerness, like a vampire who's caught a whiff of human blood. I've already said too much. I sit up and swing my feet onto the floor.

"Hold on." Leo grabs my wrist. I shake it loose and bolt for the door. "You can't leave now."

"Yes, I can."

"We were talking . . . and so forth." He raises his eyebrows to emphasize the pertinence and privacy of our exchange.

"Follow me and behave yourself."

I open the trailer door and Leo follows me to my room. "Have a seat—on what used to be Charlotte's bed."

Leo lies down and stretches. His legs shoot out, a foot beyond the end of the bed.

"It's a good thing you're not a lowly waiter. You couldn't handle the servant's quarters."

"I've slept in worse." Leo's head rests on Charlotte's pillow. I pull my backpack from under the bunk bed and lift the heavy sports sock from the make-up case. I slip the sculpture from the sock and place it in Leo's hand. He turns it over in his hand and sits up. "You found this at Bluefish?"

"Yeah."

"Where?"

"In the river. Actually, inside a big rock on the riverbank."

"Inside?"

"I was sitting on top of this flat-topped boulder that had a crack down the front. It was lodged inside."

"Did it look like it was intentionally placed in there? Like someone stashed it and was going to come back for it?"

"No. It was hard to get out. It was a fluke I even found it. It was lodged in there with a bunch of river debris. Do you know what it is? Is it old?"

"It's old."

"I thought of you, since you said you find things in the water and ice sometimes."

"You found it in the Bluefish River . . . it possibly could have been frozen in Lake Old Crow and washed downriver as the glacier melted."

"I've been reading a little about the Beringian land bridge. The only thing I found, remotely like it, was a fertility symbol from Siberia. Similar figurines date from twenty to thirty thousand years old. From what I've read, there's evidence of trade, back and forth, between the old world and new world by boat."

He holds the Beringian goddess in a gentle hand embrace and gazes upon her like a besotted lover. I have never been on the receiving end of such an expression. His Adam's apple bobs as he swallows air excitedly before he speaks in a low, scratchy voice that would seduce the sculpture if she were alive. "I don't know, not my expertise, but she is ancient. Look at that ass."

I sit beside him on Charlotte's bed. "She does have a nice bum."

He slowly and gently turns the sculpture over and over in his hand. "Even if Lempicka is right, finding a twenty, thirty-thousand-year-old, intact artifact in the Yukon is . . . impossible."

"Mischa Lempicka, the archeologist?"

"You know her?" he says, surprised.

"I served her in the restaurant once. She was nice, polite, treated me—the lowly waitress—decently."

"Sounds like Mischa."

"And what do you mean, 'if Lempicka was right?' Right about what?"

"She dates human settlement in the Yukon at approximately

twenty-four thousand years ago. It's not a theory that's shared by her peers."

"When do they think humans first reached Beringia?"

"Tony Jones says thirteen thousand years tops. The theory's referred to as the 'Clovis first model.' Tony and the majority of their peers are united in the belief that the first immigrants were the Clovis. If this artifact is as old as I think it might be, this could change what we know about human history in North America. This could prove Lempicka's been right all along." He looks up from the sculpture. "Let me show it to my supervisor, Ana—Dr. Basoalto."

"Why? Isn't she a water scientist like you?"

"Yeah, and we work closely with archeologists. We find things in the water and ice all the time. If it looks like ancient organic matter or an artifact, we involve them. It works both ways. If they notice significant water or ice changes, they alert us."

"I don't know. She's married to that Fat Fuck, Tony Jones. I don't want him anywhere near her. Maybe I'll just hold onto her and show her to Mischa Lempicka, next time she comes through."

"She might not come through until fall. Will you still be here?"

"No."

"I'm heading down to Vancouver next week. Short trip to meet with my committee. I could head over to SFU and see Professor Lempicka."

"Seriously? You'd do that?

"I can try. If she's on campus, I'll go talk to her. But if I can't find her, I think you should let me show it to Ana. She'll know whether it's something of interest."

"No Ana. Only Mischa Lempicka. No one is to know about her except Dr. Lempicka—you got it?"

Leo nods. I stand. He embraces me from behind and then quietly says into my ear, "Do you want to fuck?" I stiffen. His touch feels like a violation, maybe my body reacting to the memory of Tom. I spin around inside his embrace and then lean back, away from his body.

"The pubic hair talk was the real you, wasn't it?" I say. Leo's expression is blank; he's already forgotten the Tombstone truck-ride conversation. "Is it the waitressing uniform? It's such a turn-on that you've forgotten the art of seduction."

"I'll seduce you if that's what you want."

"How are you so perky? What time did you get up this morning?"

"Six."

"You never came for breakfast."

"No time. I wanted to get working early, so I'd have time to stop for an extra night. I'll take the sculpture now, so I don't forget. I'll lock her in the truck."

"Ana is not to know about her. You can only show her to Lempicka. Got it?"

He nods. "I got it."

The cheap two-by-four bedframe wobbles dangerously. Shh . . . the walls are like paper."

"Who's going to hear us out here?"

I spotted Maxine in the saloon playing pool with Doris when I left shift. "No one."

The bag of Labrador tea on the milk crate beside the bed falls and opens. Neither of us acknowledges the event. The dried needles spill onto the floor, in a slow but steady stream, watching it is meditative, like sand seeping through an hourglass. Something snaps. The rickety bed falls silent as the foot of the bed loses altitude. The foam mattress slides toward the floor. Leo's feet stop us from sliding any further. "What just happened?"

"The bed broke. Are you okay?" One of the rear leg supports has left the bed and the other has split into dagger blades.

"Unsure." Leo lies flat on his back, as though paralyzed. His shiny penis stands alert, rising from its dark blond crotch beard, pathetically unaware of the recent calamity. I hold onto the sides of the bed as I manoeuvre myself onto the floor.

"Charlotte's bed. We killed it."

"Don't say that—I'll fix it."

"There's no fixing this."

He rolls off the side of the bed and then pulls the foam mattress onto the floor.

"What is this?" I say, tracing a small deep indigo tattoo on the side of his groin area with my finger.

"Tyr, a Norse God."

"God of what?"

"War."

"What happened to his hand?"

Leo scoops up the dried Labrador tea, holding it in his palm. "Sacrificed it to a wolf."

I eye his fist of Labrador needles "There could be broken glass in there."

Leo releases the needles, and they fall slowly onto the floor in unison with the muted wails of a woman. Leo and I exchange a quizzical look. I wrap a sheet around myself and open the door.

Maxine is standing with Ilya at the far end of the hall. "Max?" I call, surprising myself, as I've never called anyone up here a nickname that I'd repeat in public. She turns sideways. Her belly is huge. It's not Maxine, it's Seraphina.

A voice, whom I assume belongs to the real Maxine, shouts a harsh, "Shh!" at me from behind the bedroom door.

"*You* shush!" I go back inside my room, lock the door, and snuggle into Leo.

We fall asleep on the foam mattress, his warm skin permeates my entire body, like a blanket of Zen.

Leo swings his long, tanned legs over the edge of the narrow mattress, sits up, shakes sleep from his brain, and then rubs his hands down an invisible beard.

"Stay another day."

"I have to get back to Dawson. We fly out of there tomorrow. I'm working in the far north all week." He stands.

"Will you come to the restaurant for breakfast?"

"I'll save you the extra work—might stop by to pick up something to go."

"I'll tell Louise to prepare her finest egg salad sandwich for you."

"You're a cruel woman."

I touch his fingertips that hang above me. "Loneliness stops when I'm with you."

He smiles sleepily. "In your darkest of days remember, you are made of stardust . . . Carl Sagan." He kisses my hand before reaching for his shorts.

"And your mind's emblazoned with gold dust . . . Rumer Rantanen."

I wait for him to ask me to get up, pack up my things and come with him, check out of Hotel Beringia for good, but he doesn't. He leaves to gather his things from his hotel room. I fall back asleep, in my own bed, waking momentarily at the sound of a truck door slamming and the engine starting. He's gone.

XI

July 14: I've heard nothing from Crotch Beard, as I have now trained my mind to refer to him. It's been two weeks to be exact. That buffoon of a mountain man, with giant clodhoppers, and vulgar manners is ignoring ME! Though, in the first instant on waking each day, it's his turquoise eyes that are imprinted on my mind. The hotel feels deserted without him, without Charlotte. Good energy and bad energy serve the same purpose: they fill up space. My languid mood refuses to rise, as though it's been run over by the Expedition and dragged for several kilometres down the wet Dempster.

The trailer door opens, and someone knocks frantically on my bedroom door. The urgency of the rapping squashes my hope that it's Sebastian with a board game.

"What is it?"

"Larry needs you," Susan says, out of breath.

I open the door. "Seriously? I don't work for half an hour."

"It's an emergency."

A jolt of fear shoots through my body, terrified something's happened to Charlotte. I'm too afraid to ask what the emergency is. "Okay. I'll be there in a minute."

"Hey, Rumer, would you be interested in doing a little housekeeping work on your days off?" Doris asks as I stride past the front desk.

"Maybe—are you hiring?"

"Seraphina's getting too big to do the restocking. I'll need to help her more in the shop."

"Sure. Not much else to do on my day off. Might as well be making money."

"That's what I thought—right, George?"

Moaning and then whimpering sounds from the wall behind the lobby, in the vicinity where Larry's office is located.

"He doesn't sound too good . . . screeching like a banshee," George says.

"He's begging for stronger drugs. All we got is Tylenol 3s," Doris says.

"He's had two Tylenol. He's cut off," George says.

"You're one of our first aid people, aren't cha?" Doris says.

"We're waiting for him to pee," George says.

Larry walks out of the men's room looking strained, as though he battled long and hard in that dank room and lost. "I need to talk to you. Follow me," he says and then shuffles down the hall.

I cannot be sure that the pasty grey-faced man lying on a roll-away in the room next to Larry's office is Cup-Thumper. The man is bald, but his eyes are closed, and any tattoos are hidden under a long T-shirt.

"Pain came on suddenly. He was fifty K from here, working with Ilya—Louise tried to get him comfortable. Chopper is on the way to lift him to hospital," Larry says.

"Where is the pain?"

"Groin. We're thinking kidney stone."

Whoever he is, he's not up to arguing with me this morning. Lying on his side with closed eyes, he looks old and vulnerable. He was once somebody's baby, the epicentre of someone's hope and love; yet here he lies with me as his first line of health care, and I don't even know which YTG he is . . . a face with no name. I put my fingers on his wrist to check his pulse. He opens his eyes. It is Cup-Thumper. I smile at him reassuringly. I focus on my watch as I count the beats. "Heart rate is ninety-four—high end of normal," I whisper to Larry.

"Call me if things change," Larry says and walks out the door.

I follow him. "What am I supposed to do with him?"

Larry stops but doesn't turn around. "Nothing. Just watch him."

"Where will you be?"

He turns to stare me down, as though I've crossed an invisible employee–employer line. "I'll be in the garage if you need me." He turns and walks down the hall toward the exit.

"Eugenie needs me in the restaurant in like eight minutes. Is it all right if I just check on him periodically?" I call.

"Suit yourself."

I stay near the till and watch Ilya eat oatmeal at two in the afternoon. He adds a fresh, heaping spoonful of brown sugar to it after every slow swallow. It's basically a bowl of brown sugar with an oatmeal crust. He pushes his chair from the table and then slowly weaves his way between tables, to the till. He takes a toothpick from the ceramic holder. Despite his stringy hair and wrinkled shirt, he smells refreshingly clean, like a soap-scrubbed child. "Good day," he says, looking directly into my eyes. He walks to the dining room entrance, pauses, and then turns. He half smiles and nods his head to me—a gentleman's farewell.

I push open the kitchen door.

"Why was he in here so late?" Eugenie says as she peers out the order window.

"He was working with the YTG guy that's in the first aid room. Ilya's the one who brought him in."

Eugenie relaxes her tiptoe stance, wipes her hands on her apron, and then points to the pan of sliced Nanaimo bars on the counter. "Will you kindly find a place for those in the dessert cabinet?"

"Sure."

Cigarette smoke billows into the kitchen through the loading door. Louise's attempt to spare us her second-hand smoke is futile since she's chosen to park herself right outside the open door.

"Did my Sebastian come into the restaurant? He's supposed to help me bake a cake for George's birthday," Eugenie says.

I shake my head. "No." I look through the serving window. The restaurant is empty. Frank suddenly appears at the entrance and heads for his favourite table. "There's just Frank out there now."

"Frank? I haven't seen him in weeks."

"He's the only one out there."

I check the kitchen schedule. Charlotte's name is blackened out with a felt pen.

"Did you call your folks like I suggested?" Eugenie asks.

"I did."

"And?"

"She's definitely not there. They think she's still working up here with me."

"You didn't tell them?"

"No."

"Why not?"

"What am I going to say? Charlotte ran off in a life-sized version of her Barbie camper, with a married druggie who abandoned his four kids, and is the same age as you, Dad?" Eugenie keeps her rubber spatula still as I rant. "And I didn't mention it to you until now because I thought she'd be back any day, but it's been three weeks, and she and her singing cowboy seem to have vanished off the face of the earth."

Eugenie rapidly stirs whatever's in the steel baking bowl. She pauses and then says, "Yes, something like that. I'd want to know."

Louise walks into the kitchen, having finished her smoke break.

Guilt percolates from my subconscious. The relief that Charlotte is out of my life could be misinterpreted by the universe. What if something terrible has happened to her, a tragically ironic scenario? It happened to George. "Eugenie, I heard that some people believe George got what he deserved. Do you believe that?"

"Who told you that?"

"Leo said that a lot of people thought George sold out his people, that he was a puppet for Big Oil and the Mackenzie Delta pipeline, and that he talked it up to the media as a good thing for the First Nations, even though they were never consulted."

Eugenie stops stirring.

"George was trying to help the northern economy. We'd be sitting pretty right now if the left-wingers hadn't gone crying to the press. Feds were forced to hire some big-shot lawyer to go poking around. Pipeline fell through and the oil company dumped George. Tell me, how is that fair?" Louise interjects.

Eugenie shakes her head, as though dismissing Louise's commentary. "Leo said that?" She sounds both annoyed and surprised. She wipes away the hair that's fallen across her forehead and then turns her gaze to me. "Show me a young man with debt, another baby on the way, and the promise of easy money who wouldn't take it."

"Used and abused," Louise says as she smacks burgers onto the grill.

I place Frank's burger in front of him.

"Is this Arctic honey?" he says, holding up one of the breakfast condiments that have been on the table since breakfast shift. They should have been cleared off hours ago; Susan is slipping.

"No idea. Is that even a thing?"

"You bet it is. The Bombus Polaris—its honey would be a magic elixir. Come to think of it, the Bombus Polaris is a bumblebee, so I suppose they don't make enough for commercial honey."

"The Bombus Polaris is a real bee?"

"She is. One of the toughest on the planet."

"How does she survive the winter?"

"Like we do—with a thick fur coat."

A sweet, chocolate scent wafts through the order window. I peer into the kitchen. Eugenie's holding the bowl steady as Sebastian scoops batter into a round cake pan; he must have slipped into the kitchen through the loading door. "Seb, what kind of cake are you making George?"

"Triple layer chocolate." He smiles with both pride and excitement.

"How does it already smell delicious?"

"We melted four big chocolate bars," Seb says as though he can hardly believe it himself.

Eugenie glances up at me and winks.

I give them a thumbs up.

Frank sips his coffee in slow motion as he reads the *Whitehorse Daily Star*—no hurry, no worry. "Hey, Frank?" he looks up, curious and with the same expression as the Frank I asked a favour of when Hotel Beringia felt new, and my Arctic adventure still held promise. "Did Seraphina catch a ride with you up to Tuktoyaktuk last winter?"

Frank lowers his eyebrows, seriously considering the question. "She did. That seems like a long time ago."

"Why would she want to go up there in the winter?"

"Best time to go, only time there's a road—to tell you the truth, I don't rightly know. She seemed to be in a hurry to get away from here." Frank leans toward me and lowers his voice. "She was upset, and what have you." He sits up and resumes his normal voice. "Never dreamt a truck would go through the ice and we'd be stranded there."

"Thank God it wasn't the Expedition."

"That's how we felt. Why do you ask?"

"Just thinking about where to go on my long weekend off."

"Hard to get there this time of year without wings. I take it there's still no word from your sister?"

I shake my head. "No, nothing."

"Tom and I share a mutual acquaintance in Whitehorse. Tom used to live on his property, rented space to park his RV. I could check with him to see if Tom's moved back. If that is something that interests you."

"That would be great!" I say with embarrassing, childlike enthusiasm.

"Will do. I'll keep you posted."

"Thank you, Frank." I press my palms together in a prayer gesture.

The unmistakable reverberating beat of a helicopter cuts our conversation short. Larry walks past the dining entrance, as straight-backed and fast-footed as I've ever seen him move. I forgot about Cup-Thumper, and it appears as though Larry did too. Doris leads two medical personnel toward the first-aid room. I follow them, stopping outside the open door. White spots take over my field of vision. I slide down the wall and rest my head on my knees.

"Donald, I'm going to start an IV. You might feel a little pinch," a woman says.

Larry grumbles something indistinguishable.

"He goes by Donny," Doris says.

Donny, formerly known as Cup-Thumper, lives.

The birthday boy sleep-smiles from behind the desk. The dinner party in the restaurant must have tired him out.

I'm distracted by the unmistakable gait and long legs that lope down the hall of guest rooms.

I pause at Leo's door. Cold sweat drips inside my sweater. My throat is too dry to speak. I slowly try the door handle, expecting it to be locked. It opens easily. The curtains are drawn and the room dark. Leo flips on a bedside lamp. "It is you," I say.

"Rumi?" Leo's deep voice resonates through the room. He steps toward the door. His eyes remain unchanged despite my revolving perception of him; their sincerity causes me to revert to the shyness they once incited in me. He attempts to put his arms around me.

I back away. The sweater stinks more than it usually does. In my melancholy, I haven't bothered to wash my uniform for at least a week. It's not who I am, and I instantly hate myself for it.

He backs away. "What's wrong?"

"I stink."

"I like the way you smell."

"No one could like this."

"Try me." I hold up my arm. He obliges and stupidly sniffs my armpit. He steps back quickly. "Shit! You weren't kidding. What happened to the sweater?"

"I happened to it. Why are you here?

"To see you."

I want to believe him. "The only helicopter that landed today was the medevac. It left hours ago."

He shakes his head. "Drove up—just now."

"From Whitehorse?"

"From Dawson," he says, seeming unsure if he should admit to it. "What time is it?"

"Nine-thirty. Why are you really here?"

I expect him to be defensive but instead, he laughs and then crosses his arms behind his head and leans into them. He slowly inhales and exhales. His expression calms. "I came up for you. That's the truth—please, Rumi?"

"You vanished after Tombstone. Seeing me hasn't seemed like a top priority."

"I have other responsibilities. I've been working around the clock on something with Malik, south of here. We flew back to Dawson, and then I drove straight up here to see you." Leo sighs loudly and then sits on his bed. "I'm tired. It was a big day."

"Where is my artifact, the Bluefish goddess?"

"Safe. I promise you that."

"Where?"

"She's in Vancouver under lock and key."

"Did you show her to Mischa?"

"Not yet.

"Ana?"

"Yeah."

"I told you not to!"

"I had to—she's my boss and a scientist. I didn't want to go behind her back and take something to Lempicka that I wasn't convinced was legit. I'd look like a traitor and an idiot."

I shake my head in disbelief, trying to comprehend what he's said. My curiosity momentarily quells the visceral sense that he's hiding something. "What does Ana think?"

"She was intrigued but it's not her field."

All at once, I recall a conversation we had at the Bluefish Caves. Leo mentioned that they were some of the oldest, human-inhabited caves in North America. "That was Mischa Lempicka's site we visited at Bluefish, wasn't it?" Leo hesitates, as though he's considering whether or not to deny it. "I remember what Louise said about Tony Jones . . . " Leo squints, as though he doesn't want to hear what's coming next. "Tony has a court order against him. He's supposed to stay away from another archeologist's site."

Leo scoffs. "Louise doesn't know what she's talking about."

"Mischa has a court order against Tony Jones and Bluefish are the caves he's not allowed to visit. I'm right, aren't I?"

"He's banned—doesn't have a permit."

"What did he do to get banned?"

"He wanted to collaborate with her. She wasn't interested. He's not one to take no for an answer. Ultimately, he had to settle for publicly discrediting her work."

"How?"

"He pushes the Clovis first model as though it's a scientific truth, and anyone disputing it is a radical."

"Isn't that a good thing for a scientist? To be thought of as cutting edge?"

"That's a myth. Academia is about kowtowing to the status quo—*and* Jones insinuates Lempicka's data is skewed."

"He is a Fat Fuck. How is it that Ana and Mischa can have any kind of relationship, if Mischa has a restraining order against Ana's husband?"

"I assume they're trying to keep things professional. They're women in science; Basoalto and Lempicka supported each other's work before Tony's antics got between them. They've collaborated on a few science papers."

"But they're not in the same field."

"We find things in the ice. If they've got any archeological connection, they collaborate—I suppose what they have in common is ambition. They're both looking for the same thing. A big paper in *Nature*, that one discovery that will make them academic stars."

"So, what's next? How do I get the sculpture to Mischa?"

"I'll hang onto it until I see her next."

"When is that?"

"She's in Montreal until early August. I'll track her down as soon as she gets back."

"Will you take the goddess straight to Lempicka as soon as she gets back to Vancouver? Maybe you should just bring her back to me and I'll take her to SFU in late August myself."

"I will take her to Lempicka. She's safe in Vancouver, I promise. Don't worry." He draws me toward the bed and onto his lap. I shift from his lap and sit beside him instead, wondering whether we could get into legal trouble for landing at Bluefish without Mischa's permission. I glance at the open cardboard box on his bedside table. "Research articles," he says.

I stand and select a journal from the stack of magazines inside the box. "What's this?"

"I meant to give that to you," Leo says. I sit on the bed and flip to the article on the Bluefish Caves. "I brought that one up for you," he adds.

"It's about Mischa Lempicka's work! Why didn't you mention you had this?"

"I forgot it was there."

I skim-read the article and then close the archeological journal. He shifts his focus from the magazine to me. His eyebrows are high. He either believes his own innocence or he's a crack manipulator. The goofy expression is the same one he had when I told him to take off his muddy shoes. I'm unable to stifle my laughter.

Warm breath touches the back of my neck moments before his hand brushes aside my hair and lips touch the skin below my ear. His touch is a slow, easy tranquillizer. I crave the love-drunk waves that ambush my body for days after sex with him. His hair is soft and smells fresh-washed, and his neck is warm and lightly scented with vetiver. For one night, my first night as a guest at Hotel Beringia, I delay hating him.

I wake to silence: no rattle of a reefer truck, no banging trailer doors, no stench of gasoline drifting through the window. Leo's breaths are inaudible. I poke his round, bare bum with my toes. Without lifting his head from the bed, he reaches one arm behind, pats my stomach and then settles his hand on my breast.

"You never did tell me what you were working on yesterday, south of here. Water stuff?"

"You could say that." He lifts his arm, stretches, and then rolls over.

"Does it have anything to do with gold?"

Leo yawns. "Yeah. We were working at the mine."

"Malik and you?"

"Yeah."

"How much gold is there?"

Leo runs his hands down his face. "It's a lucrative placer, but time is not on our side."

"What do you mean?"

Leo yawns and then sits up. "The recent agreement between the government and the First Nations fell apart. As of right now, no one's in charge—it's a shitshow out there."

"Why did it fall apart?"

"Gave the First Nations cash but severed the rights to their traditional lands. Territories, Feds, First Nations, they're battling out a new agreement as we speak. We're moving as fast as we can to get as much gold out of the river before any rulings come down."

I sit up. "Oh my god, the gold is on First Nations' land! You're cleaning them out while they're embroiled in land claim negotiations . . . Whose gold is it, really?"

"Mine—and Malik's. It's a legit claim."

"Then what's the panic?"

Leo lowers his voice, "Environmental laws could come into effect and the Band could get mineral rights on settlement lands."

"Who? The Gwich'in?"

"Yeah."

"Because it's on their territorial lands?"

"That, and there's concern that our operation is damaging the watershed."

"Is it?"

Leo shrugs. "I work hard for that gold. You have no idea."

"I don't doubt it, but it doesn't make it right—all that talk about Big Oil, raping the Arctic with no conscience—you were talking about yourself."

"Do I look rich to you? Do you think I'd care about finishing school if I were anything like Big Oil? Anyway, I'm not the one calling the shots."

"Who is? Malik?"

He reaches for my hand. I shake him off and then say, "Of course, it's Malik. Your gold mining *partner*." I emphasize "partner" to let Leo know that I'm on to his duplicity, and then add, "The one you're hiding your bloke from."

Silence and then he says, "I'm sorry. I shouldn't involve you in all this." He sounds sorry that he's involved me but not that he's duping Malik.

I lie back down and then roll out of bed. I pick up Leo's Ron Jon T-shirt from the floor, slip it on, and put on yesterday's underwear.

"Where are you going?" Leo says as I pull on my socks and waitressing shoes.

I open the door and step into the hall. "I'll be right back," I say and then shut the door.

The smattering of YTG look more forlorn than usual. Susan stands at the till. Her eyes follow me with the hopeless gaze of a wild creature in a zoo. I grab a tray, plate, cutlery, orange juice, and a cup of coffee, then load the plate with pancakes and sausages. I follow the cinnamon aroma into the kitchen to see if the sticky buns are ready for taking.

"What sort of outfit is that?" Eugenie says while staring disapprovingly at Leo's T-shirt.

I glance down at the long T-shirt. "A new mini dress." Eugenie raises her eyebrows. "What happened to the YTG? Everyone seems so woebegone out there."

"They haven't hired any replacements yet. With Tom, Donny, and now Ilya gone, they're most likely struggling to manage the workload," Eugenie says.

"Where's Ilya?"

"He quit," Eugenie says, sounding as surprised as I feel. "Left a note for Caroline, saying he resigned, effective immediately. Gave no indication of where he was going or why he left. I talked to Doris this morning—she said he cleaned out his room. He must have left yesterday, sometime after he brought in Donny with the kidney stone."

"I saw Ilya eating his breakfast at lunch. Oatmeal, remember?"

"That's right."

"Where would he go and how would he get there?"

Eugenie shrugs. "Probably caught a ride south."

"Hitchhiked?"

Eugenie nods once. "It's the Greyhound of the north. Everyone does it."

"What's with Susan?"

"Men troubles," Eugenie says so quietly, I can hardly hear her.

"Rob?" Eugenie nods. I slide in close to her and whisper, "Why doesn't she leave him—get away from here?"

Eugenie lengthens her neck to take a quick visual scan of the kitchen, and then whispers, "Her visa's expired. Legally, she shouldn't even be working in Canada."

"Does Larry know he's employing an illegal alien?" I say quietly.

"Louise is the one who informed me of the situation. Though I see his point. We can't afford to lose her right now."

I pull off two sticky buns from the dozens cooling on the counter and add them to my tray.

"Are you going to eat all that yourself?" Eugenie says, staring at my loaded tray.

I flash a guilty grin and use my shoulder to push open the kitchen door.

Leo follows me into the hall. He shuts his room door and then turns the knob a few times to make sure that it's locked. I spot Seraphina at the far end of the hall, waddling her way toward the YTG and staff rooms. She stops outside a room, opens the door, and then disappears inside. "Did she just go into Ilya's room?"

"Looks like it. Ilya's been sniffing around the Stanley girls for a while, long before you got up here," Leo says.

"Ilya's gone. He quit his job. His room should be empty. Sera sometimes cleans the rooms, but I doubt that's what she's doing today. She's huge! The baby must be due sooner than everyone thinks."

Leo follows me to Ilya's room. The door is partially ajar. Leo motions, with a head jerk, for me to go inside. I knock and then step into the room. Seraphina sits on Ilya's bed, holding a fragile-looking, yellowed newspaper clipping. "You okay?" I ask.

"He left this," she says.

"What is it?" I ask.

"It's Ilya, when he was a kid, in the orphanage." It's a photo of eight boys, dressed in identical shirts, gathered around a large rectangular table, set for a meal, with Russian script underneath.

"Where was it taken?"

"Russia. Leningrad. He said it was Christmas 'cause everyone has an orange by their plate, see." I follow her finger with my eyes. Among the nearly shaved heads, Ilya's thin, cautious face is unmistakable. He'd be about six—maybe his story about escaping over the Berlin Wall is true.

"Why are you in here?" I ask.

"It's my right to be here. Why are you in here?"

I glance at Leo. He widens his eyes, clueless.

"I saw the open door. Thought I'd check to see if Ilya was back." Sera winces. "What's wrong? Are you in pain?" I say.

"A little." Her plump lips look taut.

"Should I get your mom?"

"No."

"Maxine?"

She shakes her head.

"George?"

"Are you joking?"

"You can't just sit here. If you're in pain, you need a doctor to check you out, to make sure the baby's okay."

"My baby is no one's business."

"You must have seen someone when you first found out you were pregnant. A doctor?"

"No."

"Okay. You rest here. Leo will keep you company. I'll bring you some ice water."

"No! You stay."

"Okay. Leo, can you bring her a glass of ice water?"

"Bring me a Coke. A cold can from the store fridge—hold on." She tosses Leo a set of keys. "It's the one with the red dot."

Leo shuts Ilya's door. Seraphina exhales loudly. There's a fresh stream of tears on her cheeks.

"You're not in labour, are you?"

"No, I'm good." She wipes her eyes.

"Do you have any pain?"

She shrugs and then leans back, bracing herself with her arms, to stretch out her torso. "A little."

I sit on the bed beside Seraphina. Her hair is long, thick, and smells of floral conditioner. It's the kind of silky, clean hair that you long to stroke. "Are you scared?"

"No."

"Why don't you want your mom or sister?"

"They'll harass me about the baby's father."

I'm curious too. "You don't want him to know?"

"He doesn't care."

"I'm sorry."

"It might not be his anyway."

"Ilya's?"

"Yeah." She lowers her back onto the bed and then rolls to the side, facing the window. "I made a mistake. It was only one time." She shakes her head. "It was after a night drinking in the saloon. Rob followed me to my room. He wouldn't leave me alone. I barely remember it."

I have no idea what to say. Her silence makes me think she's waiting for a reply. "I am sorry that happened to you."

"I felt safe with Ilya. He's quiet, but no one messes with him. Even though no one knew that we were together, somehow, Rob knew to stay away."

"Did Ilya know about . . . Rob?"

"I told him." She gives a long mournful wail, long enough for me to be worried that she's ready to start pushing the baby out, and then she pauses and gasps for air. "Then he buggered off." Tears stream down her face.

"Do you know where he went?"

"No." Seraphina shakes her head.

A small crowd of Beringian staff watch from the parking lot as the medevac helicopter, with Sera and Doris on board, rises in a puff of shale. Susan stands just inside the lobby doors; she's as glammed up in red polyester as she's ever been, sausage curls sprayed tight. I almost allow myself to indulge the sympathy that threatens to soften my convictions about her.

"Will your mom stay in Whitehorse until the baby's born?" I ask Maxine.

"That's her plan."

"Who's going to look after your dad?"

"Me. I'm moving in with him."

"Oh," I say with conflicted feelings about me living in the trailer without the cold comfort of Maxine's presence.

"Is Seraphina's in labour?" George asks.

"No, but the baby could come early. She needs to be near a

hospital. She'll stay in Whitehorse, on bed rest until then," Louise says.

"What about my grandchild?"

"She'll be back with the baby once it's born, Dad," Maxine says.

As the helicopter's motor grows fainter, I notice Rob, standing away from the crowd, at the far side of the parking lot, nearest the garage. His face is a black-and-blue mess. He pulls down the brim of his ball cap, as though sensing my gaze.

XII

A rap on the door startles me. "Charlotte?" I surprise myself by calling out her name.

"It's Maxine. I have to talk to you." Her voice is clear and loud, as though she's in the room with me. "Hello?" Maxine says loudly.

"Just a minute." I drag the chair that I wedged under the knob, away from the door and then open it.

Maxine's gaze takes in the foam mattress on the floor. She shakes her head slowly, in theatrical pity. "Your sister's gone. Leo's gone. Looks like you got no plans."

"What do you want?"

"Hotel needs you to cover a chambermaid shift. You're off, right?"

"Where's Crystal?"

"She's sick." She folds her arms over her chest and looks bored.

"I guess I can. Will I be finished in time for my afternoon waitressing sift?" Maxine doesn't acknowledge the question. "What time do I start?"

"Eight."

"I'll do it for Doris."

There's a helicopter in the lot. I never heard it land. It must have arrived in the night. The brief elation wanes when I realize it doesn't look like it belongs to the mountain men. As I drag myself toward the hotel, I'm hit with a pain of nostalgia for the magic of Ilya lighting a cigarette in the Arctic wind. I pull open the front doors and savour George's sunshine greeting, one of the few remaining Beringia pleasantries.

Louise walks out of the women's washroom with the mop and bucket. Her eyes bore into me, as though I'm responsible for the staff shortages.

"Good morning," I say, even though it obviously isn't. "I'm supposed to clean guest rooms. How do I get in to clean the rooms?"

"Master keys hang on the back of the front desk." Her tone humourless, possibly hungover. "Do you know what you're doing?"

I shrug. "I guess. Maxine filled me in on the basics."

"Today's Monday—all the lifers get new towels and bed linens," Louise says.

"Lifers?"

"Permanent guests. YTG."

"Got it."

In the back of the laundry room, I find the linen cupboard with folded white towels, sheets, and the dated polyester bed coverings. It suddenly occurs to me that I will have to pull off all the dirty YTG towels and sheets before I put on the clean ones. I throw a pair of rubber gloves onto the chambermaid's wagon that's already loaded with a bounty of toxic chemicals.

The cart squeaks in front of me in the dark hall. I stop outside Leo and Malik's room, slide in the key and step inside before I talk myself out of it. The bedroom is a dark cave, heavy with pheromones of the resident beasts. I cannot find Leo among the sultry aromas. I shut the door and stand in darkness for a moment. The room smells foreign, slightly feminine, mixed with fresh human sweat. Someone has recently been here. I flip on the bathroom light and lean over to examine the tub: a scant selection of black pubic hairs that must be Malik's. The vanity drawer contains a filthy-looking razor, several trays of used blades, three identical, used deodorant sticks, and a toothbrush, so old the bristles fan out to the sides. I take the cap off one of the deodorants and smell the fresh, woodsy scent that is Leo's armpits.

I cross the room and pull open the drapes. Malik's bed is in disarray. The rest of the room is quite civilized. Leo's bedspread is pulled tightly across the bed with a few loose papers scattered on top. I open the bedside table drawer: two condoms, and an assortment of pens, loose change, and a rolled joint. The papers on his bed are maps of Arctic water systems with handwritten notes in the margins. I recognize Leo's scratchy handwriting from his signature on a credit card receipt.

I open the top drawer on Leo's side of the dresser: an old UBC hoodie, two pairs of work socks and boxers that cannot be unseen—the blue is faded, and the crotch area ripped and stained pale green. Nothing in the bottom drawer except a photograph: Malik and Leo, bare-chested on a tropical beach with two women. Leo still has his beard. Malik's wife holds a tropical cocktail. A woman in Leo's oversized Ron Jon's Surf Shop T-shirt has her arm around Leo's waist. She's a lot shorter than he is, shorter than all of them, and pretty, in a curly, wild-haired, outdoorsy way—"Maui, February '88" is written on the back. I met Leo in May, three months after the picture.

The door handle rattles, and the door opens. "What are you doing in here?" Malik holds a mug of Beringian coffee in his hand. Defined biceps and dark chest hair bulge from his sleeveless T-shirt. He's wearing loose, cotton pants that could be pajama bottoms.

"Ah, sorry, I thought no one was in here. Just bringing fresh towels and soaps."

"Get the fuck out of this room." His tone is controlled but heavy with rancour, like I am fresh dog shit that he's scraped from the bottom of his designer loafers. I walk quickly to the door. He doesn't step aside to let me pass. I turn sideways to avoid brushing against him. I take the wagon, squeak my way back up the hall, and then duck into the linen closet. I'd rather waitress all day than have to finish cleaning the rooms. I need caffeine—a lot of it—for the heinous work ahead. I pull off the chambermaid smock and throw it on the cart.

"You're early. Your shift doesn't start for another five hours," Eugenie says.

"Just passing through, looking for caffeine."

Susan struts into the kitchen. "The contessa is back."

Eugenie stands on tiptoe to peek out the order window. I manoeuvre in next to her. The woman has strong facial bones and an elegant Roman nose. Her long, glossy hair is knotted loosely behind the nape of her neck; it reminds me of raven feathers. She is dressed casually in jeans and a loose linen blouse, though she has the majestic presence I imagine that Frida Kahlo possessed.

Eugenie gives me a tired look. "She's a scientist from UBC. Dr. Basoalto."

"That's Ana Basoalto—Leo's PhD supervisor? I've never seen her up here before."

"She's been coming up here for a few years now."

"*She's* married to Fact Fuck Tony . . . Dr. Jones?"

"Yes, and please watch the language. They're paying guests." Eugenie widens her eyes, as though to say: *Anything else*?

I hover behind the buffet bar, waiting for Susan to take a tray of dirty dishes into the kitchen. As soon as the kitchen door swings shut, I grab a pot of coffee and head for Ana's table.

"Oh, no more, thank you." Ana places her hand over her coffee mug and then she goes back to her book. Up close, she looks about twenty years older than me.

"You're Leo's supervisor."

She glances up. "Yes?" She furrows her brow, as though trying to place me. "Have we met?"

"No—Rumer." I extend my hand.

She places her open book page-down on the table and then shakes my hand with a strong grip, and a confused expression on her face. She smells of cultivated flowers that cannot be found on the tundra. "You're a waitress here?"

"For the summer, yes. Leo mentioned that you're a friend, an acquaintance, of Professor Lempicka, the Bluefish archeologist."

Ana raises her eyebrow and gazes at me with practised pretention. "Did he?" Her tone is a face slap; the dismissal of me as someone not worth her time is familiar since I started waitressing, yet always disappointing. "So, you know Leo . . . do you also know Mischa Lempicka?" she says with the same condescending tone. I am a Klondike geisha.

"No. I've read a little about her work though—I've recently become fascinated with all things Beringia."

She narrows her eyes with cautious consideration and then straightens her posture, pressing her back into the chair. "What do you know of Beringia?"

"It's amazing to consider how the first humans may have arrived here, crossing over the land bridge over twenty thousand years ago."

"The amazing thing is that so much has been preserved—the ice holds stories. Hopefully, we won't know the deepest stories anytime soon. We need those stories to stay buried."

Maybe she's talking metaphorically, and she's telling me that the Bluefish goddess shouldn't have been taken from her boulder tomb. "Why? Isn't it important that some stories are told?"

"My research indicates the earth's atmospheric temperature is increasing steadily. If we reach a point where the permafrost melts, the carbon that is stored in the ice will cause the planet to heat up. It will become an inferno—but don't look so worried. We are safe, for now."

The fact that I am relieved that she is talking about her water research and the impending climate disasters, and not the goddess, might make me slightly worthy of her initial dismissal after all. "When do you believe the first people arrived in North America? Do you agree with Dr. Lempicka—that it might have been twenty thousand years ago or more? Or are you a proponent of the Clovis first model?"

"You *are* interested in all things Beringia." She sounds surprised. "I believe that some humans crossed the land bridge. Did some cross earlier, by way of the sea? When did the first wave cross? That is up for debate." She takes a noisy sip of her coffee, which I assume has turned cold by the unsatisfied grimace she makes before putting the mug down on the table. I don't refill it.

"I was wondering about the sculpture that Leo showed you. I don't know if he told you, but I'm the one who found it."

"What sort of figure is it?" She says, as though thousands of ancient artifacts cross her desk each day.

"According to what I've read, it looks like it could be made of mammoth ivory or woolly rhino horn. It's oblong, about this big." I make a long, narrow oval with my fingers. "A female form."

She shakes her head. "Woolly rhinos never made it to North America. Their remains are found in Siberia. They never crossed the land bridge."

"Okay, it's most likely mammoth then. Leo said he showed it to you—I could be confused. He's waiting to show it to Dr. Lempicka. Maybe I should write to her."

"I do recall that Leo brought in an artifact that he found in the Porcupine River, near Antony's camp."

"No. *I* found the sculpture in the Bluefish River. Leo and Malik were about half a kilometre away, looking through the Bluefish Caves."

"That is impossible. We do not have a permit to land at Bluefish Caves."

"Well, regardless, they did. I found the sculpture on my own. I only showed it to Leo because I wanted help to date it, to understand its significance. He said he would show it to Dr. Lempicka, since I found it so close to her site."

"It has been dated by an expert—my husband, Dr. Antony Jones. Leo discovered it while conducting research for me near Antony's camp, close to Old Crow Flats."

"That is not true. I found it in the Bluefish River below the Bluefish Caves."

"Pardon me, but who would believe that a waitress would have the permission—and could afford the permit—to land a helicopter at Bluefish? Not to mention, miraculously stumble upon the oldest human artifact ever found in the New World."

"The oldest?"

"I'm not at liberty to divulge information on artifacts without the consent of the other researchers involved."

"Malik landed the helicopter at Bluefish, not me. Ask him. He's in his room."

A startled look crosses over her face and then anger. "I authorize all flights linked to our research. There is no record of a Bluefish landing."

"I found the Bluefish River artifact on Gwich'in territory. She is not Leo's—or yours—to claim."

Ana leans back in the chair, takes a visibly deep breath and then, with regained composure, she leans toward me, lowering her voice, "The artifact will lead us closer to the truth about human migration. What does it matter how it was found or who found it? Can we agree that the scientific truths that the artifact will help us to uncover are far more valuable?" Suddenly she is my comrade, speaking in encouraging tones, like a teacher trying to convince a failing pupil that repeating the year is actually a good thing.

I stare out the back window at the smooth mountains. They remind me of the goddess' plump bottom. I do not know how to respond to this wicked woman. All I know is that she has claimed the goddess. Suddenly, I remember her scent. I smelled her earlier; she lingered, like chemical fumes, on the sheets in Malik's room.

"I'm all for scientific truth. Though, truth is based on fact, and the fact remains that I found the goddess sculpture—the artifact—in the Bluefish River, beneath the Bluefish Caves."

"Is the truth worth it to you? Should truth be sought, regardless of the consequences?"

"I think so."

"Your truth may not be a simple one. Allow me to use the permafrost as a metaphor: if the ice melts and reveals truths that we are unprepared for, the truth may destroy us all. You and Leo will not be spared."

"Maybe things that can be destroyed by the truth should be."

"This has very little to do with me. Leo found the artifact while conducting our research and passed it along to experts in Beringian archeology. It's out of my hands, and you should be relieved that it's out of yours. You are young. A conviction for trespassing and tampering with ancient Arctic artifacts would limit your future. Travel bans are not fun—imagine if you could never leave Canada?"

I pause, considering her threat. I have no idea what the legal consequences are for removing an ancient artifact. "Where is Leo?"

"I'm his PhD supervisor, *dear*. Not his mother." She stands up and closes her book. "I'm ready for the bill."

I place the coffee pot down on top of her book and then stride through the lobby, steady and fierce. Chambermaiding can wait. All at once, my legs feel wobbly. Leo gave the goddess to the Fat Fucks. He never planned on showing her to Lempicka. A guttural howl threatens to escape from my throat. Once my feet hit the parking lot, I run full speed toward the trailer, crouch on my bedroom floor, snatch a pillow from my bed, and sob into it.

The flowers that Leo brought me on the morning of the Bluefish Caves have petrified in drooped positions, except for a single shooting star. It stands, crisp, brown, and delicate. I place my palm over the little star and form a fist. When I open my hand, it is stardust.

A helicopter starts up. I watch them leave through the window on the trailer screen door. They head northwest: the brigand queen the beast.

George's voice hits me before I even open the hotel doors. He sounds wonderfully optimistic. It makes me realize how foreign optimism has become—it is not something I experience in my day-to-day life at the hotel. We're pretty much a pessimistic bunch, me included.

"Oh, Niki, you're so fine, you blow my mind, hey Niki!" George's singing voice is a surprisingly on-pitch rendition of Toni Basil's pop song "Hey Mickey."

"You got it, babe!" Doris says and slaps him on the bum. "Oh, Georgie, you're so fine, you're so fine, you blow my mind!" she sings.

"Doris, you're back! Did Seraphina have the baby?"

"She sure did."

"A girl! And what do we call her?" George says.

"Nika."

"Congratulations! That is so exciting. How is Seraphina doing?"

"She's all right," Doris says in a quiet way that makes me think maybe she's not.

"The baby's doing well?

"Yes! She was a big eight-pounder."

"When did she have her?"

"On Monday, July twenty-fifth, a little after four in the afternoon. She was on bed rest for a week. On the way to the toilet, her water broke. Contractions never came. Waited until noon, and then the doctor gave her something to speed things along."

"We never had a blond in the family," George says.

"The blond will fall out. She'll be dark like her mama. Her eyebrows are dark," Doris says.

"Goddamn Russian!"

"That's enough out of you, George," Doris says.

"When do we get to meet her, Nika? When will Seraphina be back?"

Doris looks at George and then says, "She's not coming back for a while—the father stepped up and is trying to be there for Sera and the baby."

"By father, do you mean . . ."

"Sera's marrying the goddamn Russian!" George shouts.

"Shh, George. Keep your voice down! She's not marrying anyone. Sera and the baby are staying in Whitehorse with Valerie. She has a house in town. We bought her a stroller, the kind that reclines so newborns can lie flat. Sera will be able to get out more with the baby in Whitehorse, meet other new moms," Doris, says.

"That sounds like a good idea, for Sera and the baby. So, now that you're back, do you still need me to chambermaid?"

Doris hunches her shoulders and winces, "I'm a little tuckered from the trip, but I should be okay by tomorrow."

I sigh internally with relief. I am not up to scrubbing YTG pubic hairs from tubs. "Sounds good—and congratulations again on your first grandchild. Do you have a picture of little Nika?"

Doris lifts a framed baby portrait from the desk. It's the kind that professional photographers take of the baby while they're in the hospital. Nika's eyes are almond-shaped, and the front of her nearly bald head is covered with blond fuzz. She is Ilya's. For reasons unknown, emotion overwhelms me. I bolt out the front doors before anyone notices my glassy eyes.

July 29, Nika of Beringia: I inhale the savoury autumn air, which smells not as sweet, yet just as delicious, as spring Arctic air. The tundra is flecked with ruby, umber, and gold. She's created a gem-coloured robe to amuse herself before the polar winds cover her in a heavy, monochrome cloak.

My eyes fill with tears, thinking of Nika's precious little face. May she never know the ugliness of those who have raped this land, its creatures, and its women.

XIII

Maxine and Eugenie hover over the front desk. Eugenie's eyebrows are raised high enough to tuck under her hairline. George sits rigidly behind the desk as though he's had a shock. Doris paces, gesticulating dramatically with her hands. Something must have happened to call them together so early in the day and in such a state. I'm not psychologically ready for whatever it is that they're discussing. I try to slip by unnoticed.

"Good morning, Rumer!" George says.

I stop in my tracks. He's never said my name before. "Good morning, George!" I say, matching his enthusiasm.

"Mary invited us down," he says.

I glance at Doris for clarification. "George's sister—we haven't heard from her in over ten years," Doris says.

"Sounds promising," I say.

"Mary is involved in the new treaty negotiations," Eugenie says.

"They stole our land. Then our children!" George shouts.

Eugenie's brows disappear under her hairline. Doris wraps her arm around the back of George's shoulders.

"The Yukon has never had treaties with the First Nations. We're cautiously optimistic," Eugenie says.

"I hope things go well with the . . . your negotiations," I say.

I sit at the bar beside Caroline, feeling like a colonial idiot, as Ode unpacks boxes fresh off an eighteen-wheeler. Caroline gives me a side glance. "You seem like a happier person since your sister left," Caroline says. She has never said anything to me that could even remotely be considered intimate. In truth, she never really says anything to anyone. Since Ilya left, she's been awarded the title of Hotel Beringia's most mysterious resident.

"Do I?"

"Yes, Caroline and I were just discussing that," Ode says.

"If this is a happier version of myself, I'm a walking tragedy."

"Drama's dead weight. Don't make someone's drama your business," Ode says.

"That's how I stay sane," Caroline says.

"Me too," Ode says.

"Well, forgive me for leading you astray but, it sounds like things might be looking up for the Stanleys."

"Seraphina. She's the one they should thank," Caroline says.

"The baby brought George and his sister together?" I ask.

"They're not interested in the baby. His sister's a big chief. Land claims. That's what the family reunion is about," Ode says.

Caroline spins around in her seat, suddenly come to life, as though she could not sit through another minute of Ode's version of Beringian truths. "Of course, they're interested in the baby. They're family. And how is any of this 'minding your own business?'"

Ode falls silent. I wait for her to roar from across the bar and tear into Caroline. "I'm the bartender. Everyone up here is my business," she says with confidence. Caroline leans her elbow on the bar and rests her chin in her palm, surrendering to Ode's authority.

"Speaking of my business, Ilya is one dark horse, *oui*?"

"You've had news of Ilya?" I ask.

"News! Hell, he came out of nowhere, showed up at the hospital in Whitehorse, looking all cleaned-up and professional."

"He'd cut his hair," Caroline interjects.

"That's not all. He came back to Whitehorse, showed up at Valerie's place, and took Seraphina and the baby away with him."

"When did this happen?"

"Doris got a phone call from Seraphina this morning. She's on her way to Anchorage. Ilya got a job on a ship. He's found a place for Seraphina and the baby to live while he's at sea."

"Seraphina would be in no position to make a decision like that. Moving a new mom and her newborn is disruptive" Carolina says.

Ode and I are stunned into silence by Caroline's random opinion. Ode quickly fills the silence with enthusiastic camaraderie, "I agree. She'd be better off staying with Valerie."

"Does anyone even know what nationality Ilya is? Does he have an American passport? How can he work in Alaska?" I say.

Ode stares at Caroline, "Well? You employed him."

"I was his forewoman. I didn't hire him. I assume he's a landed immigrant. He had Canadian ID—a social insurance number—and a Yukon driver's license."

"He is a mystery man," I say.

"KGB," Ode says.

"You watch too many movies," Caroline says.

"Maybe, maybe not," Ode says, challenging Caroline.

"Maybe Ode's right. He could be working for Russia, not as KGB—sorry Ode—but on a Russian ship."

"I like the way you think." Ode taps her temple with her finger. "Any decisions about when you're leaving us?"

"Larry said he would book my flight home on August 22. That will give me just over a week at home before I should go back to Ottawa."

"Should?" Ode says and raises an eyebrow.

"Working on that," I say.

"Any news about your sister?" Caroline asks.

"No, nothing."

"Tom's an arrogant ass but he's not going to let anything happen to her," Ode says.

"I don't know about that. He has violent tendencies. He nearly ripped my arm from its socket for no reason except that I wanted to leave his room."

"I know what that's like. I was married to a prick for nearly twenty years," Ode says. Caroline looks up. Ode's confession has taken her by surprise. "Eleven years ago. I freed myself."

There are so many unseeable chains. I think of the shackles that bind me to Charlotte and the darker shackles that I cannot admit to Ode: a handsome Viking distracted me with stardust for just long enough to steal the Bluefish goddess.

Susan strides into the saloon with purpose, wearing heeled pumps with jeans, full makeup, and curls. She stops beside me at the bar. The lack of physical space between us feels wrong. "What are we talking about? I love a good natter," she says with manic exuberance. If I flip her hair over, there will be another face on the back of her head: Susan's real face; the hopelessness, frightened face of a woman trapped in her own mess of a life.

Ode gives Susan a bored, bartender stare. Caroline focuses on the steaming contents in her coffee mug. "Sorry to hear about Leo, love," Susan says.

She can't possibly know anything about Leo, the gold, or the goddess. I try to sound cool, uninterested. "What about Leo?"

"The accident."

"What accident?"

"Mountain climbing."

"What?"

"I can't believe you don't know. Why would anyone be stupid enough to try and climb Tombstone?" Susan says.

Ode shoots Susan an impatient glare and then says to me, "He's in the hospital in Whitehorse. I thought you knew."

I stand quickly and accidentally bump Caroline's arm. Her drink splashes on the bar. Ode reaches across the counter with a dish towel to mop up the spill. "Sorry," I say to Caroline.

"No worries."

"When did it happen? Will he be okay?"

Susan shrugs her shoulders. She has the same satisfied expression on her face as when she marched into the saloon with her girls' night groupies.

"I don't think it was that serious. I heard he broke his arm, maybe a few ribs," Ode says.

"I hope he recovers before his wife has the baby," Susan says, with the innocence of a sweet, young au pair. Then she turns to me and with a twitching, raised eyebrow, "You know Leo's married, right?" Ode and Caroline exchange glances. They know. Susan walks toward the saloon doors, stops and spins around. The chatty voice cracks and the real Susan says, "May God forgive you," and then struts her sanctimonious ass out of the saloon.

The bar is quiet, nervous energy stirred and not yet settled.

"Never pegged her for religious," Ode says. Caroline nudges her head in my direction, signally Ode to shut up. "Don't worry. Jesus is no fool. If he's going to stage a second coming, he won't be booking an all-inclusive at Hotel Beringia to do it," Ode blurts. No one laughs.

I hammer frantically on Eugenie's door. Sebastian peeks through the curtains. A few moments later, the front door opens. "We're moving," Sebastian says before inviting me in.

"Moving? Where?"

"BC."

"That's where I'm from. Vancouver?'

"Prince Rupert."

"Is your mom home?

He nods.

"In here!" Eugenie shouts from the tiny kitchen.

I weave my way around cardboard boxes to get to her.

"You make sticky buns at home too?"

"I confess, I do. Sebastian likes the way they make the place smell."

"When's the big move?

"I gave Larry notice that I'd be gone by the first of September. School starts for Sebastian after Labour Day."

"Prince Rupert?"

"I have a cousin there. We grew up together. She said we can stay with her until we're settled."

"Any job leads?"

"Not yet, but I'm not too worried. Everyone needs a cook. Who knows, it's always been a dream of mine to open a coffee shop and bakery."

"You'd be good at running your own business, 'I say and then, unexpectedly, burst into tears.

"What's happened?" Eugenie says in a hushed tone.

"I had some news today. Shocking to me, everyone else seemed to already know." Tears form in my eyes, a sadness deeper than I expected, as though my subconscious has known that this day would come.

Eugenie puts her hand on my shoulder. "What's happened? —It won't go further than this kitchen."

I toss my face toward the ceiling, shake the tears from my eyes, and then look into Eugenie's dark eyes. "Leo's married."

"I don't know if he's actually married. Though I'm pretty sure he's been living with the same woman for a few years."

"You too? How is it that everyone knew he was married but me?"

"It's no secret. He's been coming up here for years."

"Why didn't you say anything? Why didn't *anyone* say *anything*?"

"I thought you knew. Besides, it's none of my business who befriends who up here."

"Has he 'befriended' other waitresses?"

"No. You were the first. Leo's one of the good ones. I was surprised he took such an intense interest in you."

"Why?"

"He's a pretty straight-up guy and his girlfriend is pregnant."

"He's not that straight-up," I say.

"Yeah, he's not that straight-up," Sebastian says from the living room.

"Well, I never thought he was the type to cheat on his wife. I figured it must be the real thing with you." She pauses to wash her hands in the sink and dries them on the dish towel. She raises her eyebrows and delicately adds, "When it comes to true love, I try not to judge."

"True love—when the truth is so cloudy, can it be love?"

Sebastian walks to the kitchen entrance and says, "Mom says three things cannot long remain hidden: the sun, the moon, and the truth."

Eugenie pauses to smile with maternal adoration.

"Is that Old Crow wisdom?" I ask.

"I think the Buddha said it," Eugenie says, and then flicks her hand, shooing Sebastian back into the living room. "Arctic truth is a little different. The moon and the sun share the day less frequently."

"So Arctic truths won't be revealed until the sun and moon share the same day—equal day and night?"

"The truth moves a little more slowly up here."

"Fall equinox? I can't wait that long."

"Be patient, Rumer—the clouds will pass eventually, and the truth will be revealed. Have you decided how long are you staying?"

"Supposedly until the twentieth. I fly out on the twenty-second—but I don't know."

"You're considering staying the winter?" She sounds shocked.

"Doubt it. I couldn't survive up here without you and Seb."

Eugenie nods. "You'd be fine, though. You're stronger than you think."

"I don't feel it."

"You took me by surprise. A sophisticated, city girl, in a place like this? No one expected you to last a week."

"Seriously?"

"But you did."

"You took me by surprise too!" Sebastian shouts from the living room sofa.

I laugh, aware that Sebastian has been my truest friend since I arrived in Beringia. Eugenie and I share the same wonderstruck smile: maternal adoration is contagious in the cramped apartment.

"Sebastian wrote a poem about you, you know," Eugenie says quietly and then with more volume she says, "Seb, what was it you said about Rumer, in your poem?"

"Mom, no!" Sebastian shouts.

Eugenie takes my arm. "I had it on the fridge, but he took it and hid it somewhere. It went something like, 'Rumer always cares, she likes Shorty Bear, Rumer always cares . . .' It went on like that."

"A poem about me? That is the most wonderful compliment I've ever had." I swallow a slobbering cry, too dramatic to inflict on a child. "I love that kid."

"Me too." Eugenie places a warm bun on a plate and hands it to me. "Have one, they're cool enough."

I hold it up to my nose and inhale the delicious cinnamon scent. "The hotel will crumble without your sticky buns. I think they are what's holding this place together, seriously."

"You might be right."

"Have you met her? His wife—common-law or otherwise?"

"Once, last summer. I was in Whitehorse. Sebastian was having surgery—he had to get his appendix out. I ran into them downtown."

"What's she like?"

"I don't know . . . pleasant, pretty, older than Leo. She's a physiotherapist, I think."

"How much older?"

"I'd say she has to be at least thirty-five."

"Does she work in Whitehorse or Vancouver?"

"Whitehorse. I know Leo commutes back to the Yukon, as often as he can, in the winter."

I slump down the wall and sit on the kitchen floor. "Thank God the summer's nearly over—why do I want to drive down to the hospital to make sure he's okay? Why do I give a shit?"

"Because you care about people, even shitty people."

"Do you think Seraphina will come back to Beringia—with the baby?"

"Eventually, for a visit. Time will tell."

"It's all a little crazy. Suddenly she's with Ilya, and they're a cozy little family in Alaska."

Eugenie rips off a corner sticky bun and stuffs it in her mouth as she slides down the wall and plants her butt on the floor, next to mine. "Real life is crazier than fiction."

The midnight sun dips and hovers along the horizon, teasing twilight. George assured me, though, that darkness won't officially arrive until the end of September. I'll be long gone by then.

Maxine cashes out; she takes all the American bills from the tip jar, and leaves me the Canadian, once again. For the first time, I have no hard feelings; she's mistaken me for the patriarchal posse that stole her ancestors' land and created a culture of Klondike greed.

The saloon is reasonably full for a Saturday night: a few travellers passing through, a scattering of YTG, and a table of international trophy hunters. Larry sits at the bar next to Louise. They are loud and pink with drink. I stand at the far end of the bar, nearest the exit. I came in wanting something strong to slide down my throat and make me fall asleep with ease, but seeing Larry and Louise's faces, ugly in animated intoxication, changes my mind.

Ode makes her way down the bar toward me. "Restaurant empty?"

"Yeah, just need a drink before I tackle the clean-up."

"What can I get you?"

"Ginger ale and soda please."

She leans over and whispers. "I'm sorry about Leo. I did warn you."

"When? Your rants about the patriarchy—you could have been talking about any man."

"And I was." Ode has a quizzical, slightly indignant expression on her face, as though deciding whether to be offended by my referring to her talks as rants. "No, when you first started getting involved with him. I told you he was married."

I try to remember my early conversations with Ode, but I don't remember Leo ever being mentioned. "You told me Tom was married, not Leo."

"I was talking about Leo, perhaps you chose to hear otherwise?" She hands me a beer stein filled with ice, soda, and a shot of ginger ale.

"I was duped, Ode. How did I not see it coming? My eyes were open."

"Not wide enough. We're taught to wear blinders, eyes open just a little, enough to see the beautiful boy, with the blue eyes, megawatt smile. We believe all that romantic crap—and we do why? Because we don't have an agenda and we don't want to believe that he might. But he does. He always has an agenda. It's the patriarchal way: schmoozing, wheeling, and dealing, to get what he wants."

My stein is nearly empty except for the ice. I place it on the bar. "He had an agenda. He had a fucking agenda. I need an agenda."

I take out the vacuum and start near the back windows. The sill is ripe with dead flies. If only Tom or the Fat Fucks, or—especially—if Crotch Beard, were here, I'd have some use for them. I'd serve Leo a meal he'd never forget. Louise's egg salad sandwiches would be an epicurean delight next to a Rumer special.

Vacuuming becomes an obstacle that prevents me from hearing all the comings and goings of the hotel. I'm on high alert for one of the many missing Hotel Beringia people to suddenly appear, despite knowing their reappearance would probably traumatize me even further at this point. Though I'll risk the trauma to ease my curious mind, which has concocted the darkest scenario for each person's possible disappearance: Donny—aka Cup-Thumper—dead; Ilya—KGB called him home; Tom—too dark to think about; Leo—can't think about; Charlotte My mind stops with Charlotte . . . Despite all, she is my sister. Every scenario that I allow myself to explore ends in light.

The kitchen lights go out and Maxine leaves the restaurant for, what I imagine, will be a quiet night in her new hotel room; she moved from her parents' apartment directly into Seraphina's old hotel room.

Larry saunters stomach first into the dining room with an unlit cigarette hanging from the corner of his floppy lips. His eyes are red and his steps clumsy. His mouth flaps at me but the cigarette doesn't fall. I keep the vacuum on. I don't want to hear his inebriated ramblings. His mouth won't stop flapping. The vacuum motor slows to a relieved sigh. Larry's ripped the vacuum cord from the wall.

"Why in the hell are you vacuuming at this hour? I want a cold beer and five minutes' peace—is that too much to ask, for Christ's sake?"

I glance up from the patterned carpet, controlling the rage within. "It's my job to vacuum the dining room after closing. I don't make the rules, I only follow them, sir." I say "sir" with the same inflection as if I'd said "asshole."

"Lippy little . . . I should'a fired you when I fired your sister," he says. His cigarette drops to the carpet. I stare at it, commanding his eyes to follow. He finally looks down and grinds it into the carpet with his tattered faux-leather moccasin.

"Thanks!" I say, sarcastically. "It wasn't even lit. You wasted a cigarette."

"You!" he shouts, pointing an unsteadying finger, "Need to be quiet."

I drop the vacuum hose, step over it, and meet his angry gaze. "A man like you has no right to talk to me like that. I will not work in these conditions. I want to go home. Send me home."

Louise emerges from the saloon in intoxicated bliss, her smile fades when the dining room energy hits her. "What is going on?"

"Ask the manager," I say.

Larry's anger deflates, like a child caught being a bully by his mother. He mumbles something indecipherable.

"And for the record, you never fired Charlotte, she quit."

"Hell, she did. I fired her."

I glance at Louise for confirmation. "She disrespected authority. Called Larry, looking to add an extra week on to her doctor's visit. Larry told her no and that she better get her butt back here. She got all belligerent and called Larry an asshole."

"Didn't want to have to do it, but she left me no choice," Larry says.

"Belligerent?" I say and then shake my head. The irony is lost on them both.

Charlotte was never coming back, and they knew it all along. I leave the vacuum where it sits and stomp from the dining room—as best as I can in soft-soled sneakers—stopping to grind Larry's cigarette further into the carpet.

The trailer vibrates in the night. I step into the hall and look out the screen door. It's not a helicopter, it's the north wind. The realization hits me like a punch in the stomach—Leo's not coming back.

In the morning, I pull on a hoodie and cross the parking lot as the wind blows fresh alpine air from the glacial summits down to Hotel Beringia. I inhale, expanding my rib cage, nourishing the deepest recesses of my being with minute Arctic particles. Louise stands behind the front desk, holding a lit cigarette. She must be feeling entitled today, staff isn't permitted to smoke in the lobby.

"Larry wants to see you in his office," she says in a taciturn manner.

All the blood leaves my head and pools in my feet. I lift them, like heavy bricks over the polished, wide-plank wooden floor, and down the hall that leads to his office.

"Come in," Larry says from his office chair. He abruptly stands and turns his back to me to gaze into the parking lot. "Your ticket is waiting at the airport. One way to Vancouver, Wednesday, the seventeenth. The cost will be deducted from your final paycheck."

"No, it won't. You owe me the flight back."

He turns to face me. "Contract says if you quit, you pay for your own flight home."

"I didn't quit. I was forced to leave due to abusive working conditions."

He looks surprised but says nothing, probably wildly searching through his boozy memories.

"Good day to you," I say.

XIV

The morning wind is polar—a generous warning to those who might have forgotten that winter is near. The heater in Frank's cab blows heavenly warmth onto my legs. I glance at the passenger side mirror. A bike pedals through the shale, chasing the Expedition.

"You forget something?" Franks asks.

"It's Sebastian. Can you honk your horn a few times, to say goodbye?"

Frank sounds the horn, two long blasts, too loud to be comforting, but startling enough to be a celebratory goodbye. Sebastian stops on the hilltop and waves with one arm extended, until the road dips and I can no longer see him. True love is so much better than romantic love. I hold in my hands the comic he made for me, *Shorty Bear and the Wolf*. Shorty Bear falls in love with a wolf, but the wolf's pack doesn't trust him because he's half-dog. My eyes are a blurry mess and the lump in my throat presses against my esophagus. I scan the trees for a glimpse of my wolf family—my golden-eyed beauties. I never got to say goodbye.

The cab smells of maple-soaked tobacco but Frank—in his leather cowboy hat and fancy, three-inch-heel cowboy boots—has the courtesy of a gentleman and does not even attempt a chew.

"It's relaxing in here and the view is perfect—maybe I should become a trucker."

"Nah, can't see it. You're going to be someone important. You'll make us proud."

"Thanks, Frank, that's very kind of you to say. I hope you're right."

"I am. You'll see."

"I don't know. I'm no Arctic bee. I survive, develop a thicker skin, an insulated heart, but I don't make honey. I'm more of a parasite." I focus my gaze out the window at the roadside splendour that I may not see again, the fuchsia fireweed ribbon with yarrow lace trim.

"Balderdash." I sense Frank glancing my way. He taps my journal that lies on the seat between us. "What's in there?"

"Summer project, a journal about my Arctic adventures. It's mainly filled with rants, heavily scrolled swear words, and multiple exclamation points."

Frank laughs. "That's your honey right there. Do something good with those words."

"What good can I do with my words?"

"Tell the truth. Use those words, your voice, to inspire action."

"What truth?"

"The truth is in there. Your truth. Tell it wisely. Tell it with compassion. Don't water it down."

"Eugenie says that Arctic truths will be known when the sun and moon share the same day."

"Horse feathers. Does Eugenie know of something happening this fall that the rest of us don't?"

"Doubt it. She's heading south, moving to Prince Rupert. The hotel . . . so many have left or are leaving."

"One journey ends, another begins . . . Take our Bombus Polaris, the queen won't allow drones to drain her resources. Come autumn, her loyal posse removes the useless from the hive, kicking and screaming, leaves them to die. She winters with only those she needs."

Frank's bees exist in a beautifully ugly, raw, and wild world with no innocent, no guilty. Whether I am the queen, a member of her loyal posse, or a useless drone, is of little consequence; beehives are nature's business.

"Until spring, and then she begins again," Frank adds. He sorts through a box of cassette tapes with one hand and then shoves in a tape. "The end of a journey is as important as its beginning." Willy Nelson's "Always on My Mind" plays on the truck's stereo system.

Tombstone is hidden under heavy cloud. The craggy, ominous pinnacle, frosted in a fresh dusting of snow, is the only thing visible above the clouds. She silently thunders: stay away, your greasy human hands will stain my granite gown. She could have killed someone I once loved, but she showed mercy, crushing his ego and not his life.

"Three things cannot remain hidden," I say aloud.

"What was that?"

"Sorry, I was thinking out loud."

'Don't leave me in suspense—what are the three things?"

"The sun, the moon, and the truth." Goldensides is no longer golden. She is sienna, amaranthine. The *Sound of Music* memories of mountain-man Leo are blown from the ochre hilltops, onto the wet Dempster, where they lie, drowning in mud, until the Expedition's eighteen wheels put an end to them. "So many things are not as they appear. It's hard to know the truth."

"Go with your gut. Trust yourself. You always know the truth, deep inside. Don't let anyone talk you out of it, not even yourself," Frank says.

We pass the area where I remember Larry telling me the Dempster was made of shale. It seems like a decade ago, when I was still a girl. The truth has hardened me. I open a small bag of Old Dutch ripple chips.

"No snack food," Frank says.

"I'm not allowed to eat?"

"No," he says, seriously, without glancing from the Dempster. "Nothing that makes crumbs. I have to sleep in here."

I crumple the bag shut and put it back inside my daypack pocket. My hand hits cold aluminum. "Pop allowed?"

"As long as you don't spill it."

Cracking open the diet soda is disturbingly loud. It fizzes out of the top. I slurp it up in a panic, afraid it will dribble on the cab's upholstery.

I wake on the Klondike Highway just outside of Dawson City. The landscape is ugly and unidentifiable. Never-ending mounds of gravel and rock line the highway. A creek meanders clumsily through the random-sized rocks, and an occasional green plant emerges from the rubble in search of the Arctic sun. "What is this place? It doesn't look real."

"Gold mine tailings."

"They're allowed to dump all that rock in the river and forests?"

"Yup."

"How? Doesn't the government have any environmental laws?"

"No—It's the Klondike mentality. The earth is only worth the gold that you can take from it. How and where you get the gold—liquid, solid—don't matter—as long as you get the gold. The money doesn't even stay here. It feeds the fat cats in the mining companies, and they live nowhere near the Yukon, nowhere near Canada, in most cases. They don't give bupkis what happens to the Yukon. First Nations, wildlife—they're commodities or obstacles, and they don't bother figuring out which is which. They go in guns loaded."

"Why do we let it happen?"

"Most of us are oblivious to what's happening right under our noses and the rest of us—too darn lazy to care. Take the Dempster, the entire highway, only road access to the northern Yukon, cuts through the entire territory, all the way to the Beaufort Sea. No environmental assessment, not before, not after it was built. They carve an over seven-hundred-kilometre highway through virgin Arctic tundra with no environmental assessment." Before I have time to respond, he adds, "I make my living off this highway—but still, it doesn't make it right. I'd gladly take a longer route if it meant I'm not ploughing through a wildlife corridor."

Dawson City appears, like a fairy-tale Victorian town juxtaposed against a backdrop of pure Yukon wild. After three months on the tundra, cruising into Dawson feels as though I'm pulling into New York City.

"Is there a bus from Dawson to Whitehorse?"

"There is. What are you thinking?" Frank says.

"I'm thinking I might stay a night in Dawson. Look around. I might never get up here again."

"It is the Klondike experience. I agree it would be a shame to miss it."

Frank pulls the semi to the side of the highway. "I'm going to pull over, get something to eat and then rest for a bit. If you change your mind about taking the bus, you know where I'll be—oh, before I forget." He reaches into his shirt pocket for a folded piece of paper and hands it to me.

I open the paper. There's a Whitehorse address written on it. "What is this?"

"Address belongs to that mutual acquaintance I told you about . . . used to work with Tom, lived at the Beringia. I think you'll find some answers there."

"Thank you, Frank—for everything."

"Take care of yourself, Rumer . . . there's still a lot of Klondike left in Dawson. Remember, I'm pulling out for Whitehorse early, no later than six a.m."

"Noted." I open the door to a flood of heat from off the truck and jump down to slightly cooler air, warmed by the evening sun. I strap on the heavy backpack and then attach the smaller daypack to my chest to balance the weight.

Dawson City is more than a little Klondike. The roads are dirt, the sidewalks wooden, and there are no traffic lights. The Victorian buildings have been restored, making the streets complicit in Dawson's deception of time: modest, brightly painted, clapboard hotels and stores hold their own alongside austere colonial buildings. Human beings are scarce and yet it feels bustling. I turn onto Princess Avenue and then onto Second and stop outside a red clapboard hotel of a style that reminds me a little of Hotel Beringia. I walk through to the saloon, slide off my packs, and sit at the polished wood bar, aware, that this is not something I would have ever done before Hotel Beringia. I used to be too insecure to go into a bar alone. The bartender's wearing a 54-40 T-shirt. Instantly, I am brought into the modern world—a place where twenty-somethings go out to clubs, listen to bands, and have a life. It's a culture shock from Beringia, where twenty-somethings walk the highway alone in the wee morning hours and seek out the companionship of wild wolves.

"What's really in the Sour Toe cocktail?" I ask, after reading the painted sign above the bar.

"A human toe."

"Seriously?"

"If you drink a shot and the toe touches your lips, you're in the sour toe club."

"Whose toe is it?"

He shrugs. "People donate a toe when they die." Despite his hip T-shirt, with his scruffy shadow beard, French-Canadian accent, and eager green eyes, it's easy to picture him in a prospector's hat.

No one in the bar is trying the toe. They're all drinking beer. A bottle of liquor, on the shelf behind the bar, seduces me with its moss colour. It's nearly eight. I didn't get to eat the chips I brought—Frank and his rules. I order a Nouvelle-Orléans Absinthe Frappé from the Klondike classics list. The drink is the same shade as the mountain that looms over the town like a wise ancestor, wearing its life wounds without shame. The mountain's been slashed open, a gash of raw earth exposed among the coniferous trees. I compare the window view to a black-and-white photograph on the wall behind the bar: the hotel in 1898, ninety years ago. The treeless chasm was on the mountain a century ago; nothing has changed except the crowds of pedestrians on the street and their fashions.

"Why were the streets so crowded? Was it Victoria Day or something?" I say.

"Dawson was a real city back then. Thirty thousand lived here during the gold rush."

"Wow! What's the population now?"

"Maybe one thousand. Grows a little in the summer."

"If only the rest of the world was becoming less crowded with people. What's a must-see in Dawson?"

"Diamond Tooth Gerties—you gotta check that out. Dancing girls, gambling—it's the Klondike experience."

I sip the frappé slowly, slipping in and out of any notion of time. Boots clap along the wooden sidewalk outside the saloon and then stop at the door. I imagine that it's Charlotte. She sits beside me at the bar, and the bartender hands her an absinthe. Tom and Leo are historical figures that we read about on the saloon walls. Their crimes captured in black-and-white photographs, like Albert, the Mad Trapper. We laugh at the absurdity of our Arctic adventure, the two of us, Klondike geishas. The only thing that spoils my fantasy is the small television on the bar, spewing news. Even with the sound off, it's annoying.

"Where's a good place to stay?"

"Here, of course," he says in a throaty French accent and then winks.

Fat Fuck Tony's face takes over the small TV screen.

"What the hell? Can you turn up the TV for a minute."

" . . . the artifact has been dated as approximately twenty-five thousand years old. UBC PhD candidate, Leo Stromberg . . .

conducting research in the Yukon, near the community of Old Crow. . ." the reporter says. My heart races. The screen fills with Leo's face. His hair is a little longer, parted on the side, smooth and wavy. He looks professional in a pressed cerulean blue shirt. His matching eyes penetrate beyond the screen.

"Liar!" I shout, startling the bartender.

"You know that guy?"

"I wish I didn't."

I wander the downtown area until the boardwalk vanishes from beneath my feet, and then kick up dust along the dirt road. I leave the brightly painted town centre and wander into an entire street block in decay. Time has stripped the paint from the buildings that slump and sag into the ground. Somehow the derelict buildings feel more alive to me than the Klondike restorations. There is a beauty in old. Their histories are no longer contained within their decaying frames; their stories spill onto the streets, seep into the earth and surrounding atmosphere, and into my consciousness. I walk slowly along the street—open to their stories—experiencing the odd, fleeting moments of joy, and then arduous pain.

Loud music streams from within a quaint Victorian on the street corner. A familiar song by The Cure entices me through the door and down a claustrophobic hall that leads to a windowless room. Dancing people in dreadlocks pound the room's dirt floor. I have stumbled upon an attempt at nightlife in a nightless land. Judging by their age and skinny bodies, my guess is most of them are tree planters. The flashing lights and suffocating, skunky stench of weed, patchouli, and sweaty armpits, strikes me as garish on a pristine Arctic night. Even after three months at Hotel Beringia, or maybe because of it, I feel too immaculate—my hair too shiny and my lungs too pink—for the grungy den.

I advance to Queen Street and then head north toward Diamond

Tooth Gerties Gambling Hall. I never pictured Gerties as looking so humble: without the signage, it could pass as the town's curling rink. I check my packs and then give the woman behind the ticket window a ten-dollar bill for the dancing show that starts in five minutes. I climb a narrow staircase that leads to a second-storey balcony and stand next to the railing, surveying the crowd below. A low-voiced, middle-aged woman in an off-the-shoulder, floor-length evening gown walks to stage centre. "What's six inches long, has a head on it, and is desired by women around the globe?" The crowd hesitates and then the odd laugh grows into a rumble. She pulls something from her cleavage and waves it in the air. "Sorry, fellas—it's a one-hundred-dollar bill."

Long velvet curtains open as a wolf whistle erupts in the crowd. Four twenty-something women line the stage dressed in black corsets, multicoloured layered skirts, and high heels. Their hair is pulled into French chignons, topped with feathers. A man in a black top hat pounds the piano next to the stage and the dancers kick their gartered legs into the air in sequence. I shift my gaze from the dancers to the card tables below. A blond man plays cards awkwardly with one hand. Instant vertigo: the balcony railing is too low, meant for smaller people in the Victorian era—I could easily lean forward and tumble over. A waitress in a corset and fishnet stockings stops beside me, "Can I get you something?"

"I'm just leaving, but thanks."

I descend the staircase. His hair looks darker in the dim dance hall lights. Leo, the star that doesn't shine for me anymore. And yet he is Goldensides in the sun. I don't want to know the real Leo. I'm too fond of fake Leo.

I creep in behind him. "Hey, bright star," I say in a controlled voice.

"Rumi!" His eyes are wide with shock. His voice is formal, distant, despite calling me by the nickname he gave me. His gaze leaves me quickly, as he scans the room erratically. I glance around, to find who or what he seems to be afraid of. No one seems to have noticed that either of us exists. Even the dealer can't be bothered to glance up. Leo leans back. "What are you doing here?"

I speak into his ear; suddenly aware I have absinthe breath. "I caught a ride with Frank. Wanted to experience the Klondike mecca for myself."

He turns his face to look at mine. "You got time off?"

"You could say that."

He squints his eyes, as though knowing that there's more to my story but unsure if he wants to hear it. Then, "This is crazy! I can't believe you're here," he says into the hair that covers my right ear. He smells of spicy tundra shrubs, sweat, and beer. His wide, unselfconscious smile is reassuring. The real Leo likes me as much as, maybe even more, than fake Leo.

"Maybe I'm not. I'm a Dempster mirage. I don't exist once you leave the highway." I speak in a low voice designed to inform him that I never was, and never will ever be, his Klondike geisha.

A look of pain briefly passes over his face. He runs his good hand over my hair and down my cheek. "This is good." He gently clasps my hand with his.

His touch is like a drug. I close my heavy eyes and fall into him. Under the midnight sun, everything sparkles like gold—villains and heroes intermingle; it is difficult to distinguish between them. I touch his cast lightly, "What happened to you?"

"Snapped an arm bone."

"Will it be okay?"

"Should be. I'll have rehab to look forward to when this comes off." He waves his good hand, palm down, over the table. The dealer excludes him from the round. He stands and steps away from the table. I think of his wife, the physiotherapist, and begrudgingly, that he'll likely have the best therapy available.

"How'd you hurt it? Where?" I want to hear him say it.

"Tombstone." He said the magic word. I witness the memories pass through his eyes, like a grade-school film strip on rewind. "She got the best of me."

"Tombstone." I nod. I told him to do it and knowing that he did, regardless of whether he would have done it on his own, returns to me, a fraction of what he stole.

"After the ball . . ." The woman who told the money joke belts out the song in a throaty voice.

"I'm sorry," Leo says as the woman's voice falls quiet.

"What for?" I shout over the piano.

He leans down. "Let's get out of here."

We stop to retrieve my packs. "Let me take this."

I glance at his broken arm.

"No, I'm okay. You can take the small one."

We leave the dark dance hall, into the bright night, almost like lovers. The fingers of his casted limb gently brush against my arm. In the light, I see the scruffy beginnings of a new beard on his chin.

"I'm sorry I didn't get back up to the hotel. The job offer threw me."

I stop walking. "Job?"

"I was offered a job at UBC—a faculty position, assistant professor."

"Seriously? You're going to teach? What?"

"I'm in the Department of Earth and Environmental Studies. Two semesters of first-year courses no one else wants."

"Is Ana the head of that department?"

He nods. "She is." He quickly shifts his gaze to watch a sled-type dog trot down the middle of the road and pass us, without so much as a slide glance.

My eyes start to fill with tears. I can't pull off the charade. My mouth won't turn up into the Mona Lisa smile that I need it to. I walk in haste, turn onto King Street, toward the river, as though I'm in a surreal, Victorian dream. My only thought is to escape into some sort of wilderness near the river, to breathe. Fast feet scuff through gravel behind, a thrill runs through me along with the memory of fast feet on the Dempster, on summer solstice. I stop. "You haven't even defended your thesis," I say, trying to steady my voice.

"I will. Ana's arranged it."

The goddess was the exaction. She secured Leo's future. Real Leo stabs inside me, a needle-thin knife, slipping under my ribs. My desire leaves, like a silk kimono falling onto the dirt road.

"So, you're moving to Vancouver," I say, as though waking from a dream and struggling to fully grasp reality. "When?"

"Next week," he says quietly.

All at once, the ugliness of reality slaps me fully awake. "What the hell are you doing in Dawson? Don't you have to pack?"

"I've got some things I have to pick up here before I fly to Vancouver to look for a bigger place."

"How small *is* the place you crash at in Vancouver?"

"Small—a room in Malik's basement."

"Well, congratulations!" I say congratulations like a fuck-you. "Vancouver is perfect—I'll be there." The colour fades from his face. I loosen the dirt on the road and kick it over the big, greasy toes sticking from his Birkenstocks.

"Stop," he says and takes a step backward.

"I shouldn't have tried absinthe."

"You're drunk?" He bends over and dusts off his sasquatch feet.

"Fuck off." I glance inside the restaurant we've stopped in front of Belinda's Beanery and then laugh.

"What's funny?"

"I like the name of this place." I pull my small pack from his shoulder and step up onto the boardwalk and inside Belinda's. The restaurant is nearly full—English and French voices intermingling over burgers and beer. I order poutine to go and a can of pop.

I'm not up for small talk and neither is he. We cross the street and walk in silence. I spot what looks like Leo's red truck up ahead, on a deserted block of aging shops. It hurts to see it; Goldensides feels close yet unreachable. The handwritten note is still duct-taped to the dash: *Live like the lotus, at ease in muddy water.* Leo has personified the quote perfectly. "Is it legal for you to drive with one arm?"

"No one cares up here. Guess what that building used to be?"

I turn to look at a two-storey white clapboard the truck's parked in front of. Its façade is straight and solid, all it needs is fresh paint. "No idea, what?"

"A brothel."

"Fitting that you'd be parked in front of it."

He lowers his brow, trying to figure out my remark but is too cowardly to ask me to explain. I peer in the front window, between the narrow space where the lace curtains almost meet. The room is empty, with scratched wooden floors, cracks in the plaster walls and faded patches of floral print wallpaper. Abandoned, perhaps since the Gold Rush. "Is that your backpack in there?"

"It is."

"Why?"

"Malik owns the building. Our Dawson office. It's been empty since the forties. It was run by a French madam, known for handing out sweets to the town children."

"Like the witch in Hansel and Gretel."

Leo opens the door of a mangy-looking fridge. There is nothing in it except beer and mould. He takes a beer. "Want one?" I shake my head. I wander into a large room at the front of the house. Faded patterned wallpaper is hidden behind modern maps. A worn, upholstered antique chair sits in the corner next to a fireplace that probably hasn't been used since this place was a brothel.

"What's with the maps?"

"It's easy to get lost in the Arctic."

"Is that Malik's office?"

"Our office," he corrects.

I sit at the neatly organized wooden desk. I open the poutine. "There better be a fork in here."

"I can get you one."

I recall the mouldy fridge. "No, I found a plastic one in here." The poutine is barely warm and the fries floppy, but they've been generous with the cheese. I spoon the mess into my mouth and then crack open the pop which cascades over my wrist and onto the wooden floor.

"Watch—" Leo takes a step in my direction, about to scoop up my pop can and then, catching my warning glare, he aborts his mission and runs his hand down the side of his head instead.

"Don't worry, I saved Malik's desk. It only dripped a little on the floor." I take a slurp of the remaining foam to further vex him.

"Malik's looking at expanding our little venture."

"What kind of expansion? Is it legal, or should I say, ethical?"

He runs his good hand over his bristly chin, his eyes unfocused, distracted by some internal monologue. "I don't care. I'm out—I have the job at UBC . . . that's why I'm here in Dawson, picking up the last of my gear."

I spot the sled dog that I saw a few minutes ago, running down the street in front of the brothel. "I would guess she's lost but she seems to have a purpose."

"Dogs roam free up here. Some are stray, most aren't. Seasonal workers will adopt a pup for the summer and then abandon it when they leave for the winter."

"What kind of asshole would abandon a dog?"

"Same kind that would abandon their kid," he says.

Perhaps this is his way of explaining the truth that will come.

Leo will abandon a woman but not his spawn. He's right, only the deranged abandon a dog or their own kid. Tom would but not Leo.

I follow Leo up a narrow staircase, down a long hall, and past a bathroom with a claw-foot tub. We stop at a large bedroom, with a fireplace, that overlooks the street. The room is nearly empty except for a mattress, sleeping bag, pillow, a half-filled glass of murky water, and Leo's work boots. The wallpaper's ornate design is peeling and faded, though stunning, with drooping flowers in gold, pink, scarlet, and white. Leo throws himself on the mattress on the floor. He inhales loudly. His eyes narrow and his mouth turns up in pain. "I shouldn't have done that." He slowly manoeuvres his broken arm onto his chest. "Could you open the beer for me—please?"

I wait until I've turned from him to roll my eyes. I snap the aluminum ring open and then hand him back the beer. He takes a swig, and another, and then lies back, seemingly content. He kicks off his Birkenstocks. His long, tanned legs, hang over the end of the mattress. I inhale his scent as I trace my finger over his smooth mouth and then, with the lightness of cotton grass, I touch each swollen fingertip that protrudes from the sweat-soaked cast.

"Looks like your lucky star got a little tired of your ego and decided to shake things up a bit."

He enjoys my touch too much to contradict me. I run my hands along his muscular calves and then up his thighs and under his canvas shorts. If I had had hope for any sort of future with him, I would be repulsed touching him. His warm skin, crinkly pubic hairs, and thickening penis would be an assault to my fingertips and yet, the ease with which I touch his body tells me that I've accepted the truth. This is the last time I will be in possession of his beauty; after this moment, his ugliness will keep me far away.

"Do you want to have sex?"

He struggles to sit up and then kisses my mouth. I push him back onto the mattress.

"Do you want to have sex?"

He squints, confused. "Yes?"

I am impatient, aggressive, removed, observing my own physical sensations as Leo lies underneath, sighing, groaning, blissfully ignorant and seemingly happily lost. I am an Arctic queen bee, and he is my drone. I hate him and yet the sex is still good. Maybe I've become addicted to the raw beauty in him, the same unrefined grace that used to abhor me. Or maybe I've accepted that truth, whether revealed or not, is always muddy. I create a map of his body in my mind. His near-perfect masculine form will exist in my possession forever.

It's four-fifty. The flowers in the wallpaper hang heavy, closed. Leo hovers between bliss and sleep. I let go of his warm hand, get up from the mattress, and peer out the screen window. The quiet Victorian streets and the Yukon River are resplendent in the pre-dawn light, full of promise. I fill my chest with the slightly cool, thin air. I will never forget this moment of pure air, celestial sun, quiet dirt roads, aging Victorian beauties, and Leo, naked on the bed.

I study my reflection in the armoire mirror and hold my long hair up, in a loose, Gibson-girl bun. I wonder how many women have looked in this mirror before me, after having sex with a hideous man.

I slide my hand one of the work boots, and then the other, and pull out a very heavy work sock: Leo's precious bloke, the biggest nugget he ever found.

I slip on the same flowy mini dress that I put on yesterday morning at Hotel Beringia. I tiptoe toward Leo and squat beside him. "What news do you have of the Bluefish goddess?" I whisper in his ear. His chest pauses midrise. His eyes remain closed and then he slowly exhales, pretending to be asleep.

His face tightens. "What time is it?"

"It's morning—where's the goddess?"

"Right—I forgot about that—I've been busy," Leo says with eyes closed.

"Have you showed her to Lempicka yet?"

He opens his eyes. "I tried."

"What does that mean?"

He exhales loudly. "Ana discussed it with experts in the field and they decided it was probably old."

"Probably old? I thought they were experts."

He sits up and runs his hand through his hair. "It *is* old, possibly significant."

"What experts did she discuss it with?"

"Dr. Jones is looking into it."

"Fat Fuck Tony Jones? You showed it to him?"

His eyes are open so wide that it looks forced, almost painful. "Well, he is Ana's husband."

"Impressive, being a professor has already elevated your language. Last month he was Fat Fuck, today he's Dr. Jones. You've involved every scientist that I specifically asked you not to. You promised me you'd take the goddess to Lempicka. I trusted you with the artifact. I trusted you . . ." I turn away quickly, before my eyes tear.

"Ana would have discussed it with Lempicka, absolutely."

I turn around in an instant and shout "Liar!" loud enough to incite the street dogs into a barking frenzy. Leo's eyes expand and then shut tight, like dying stars spiralling into black holes.

"I *know* it's the oldest artifact ever found in North America. I *know* you never planned on showing it to Lempicka. You gave it to the Fat Fucks so Jones will be a star archeologist and Ana would make you an instant professor. The goddess wasn't yours to give away!" My eyes fill with tears, but I don't look away.

"Technically it's not yours, it belongs to the Gwich'in—you found it on their land."

"Like the bloke in your shoe?" I wipe the tears from my cheeks as I step my dusty-bottomed runner onto the mattress, leaving a patterned print. "How can you go along with this? You are the one who told me how Lempicka's been bullied by Jones and her research undermined. That asshole is trying to take credit for the very research he's mocked! The goddess proves that Lempicka discovered the truth first, not that blowhard! How can you be complicit in this? Have you no morals, ethics . . . basic human decency?"

"Wake up. Science, academia, it's brutal. Truth is—artifacts? They're secondary to egos."

"You've certainly made that clear."

"Not clear enough." He glances up at me but says nothing.

I nudge his thigh with my foot. "What does that mean?"

"Did you stop and think that maybe it's *your* ego that's getting in the way of science. Isn't the artifact where it should be, available to the scientific world at large?"

"Fuck off," I say, cold as permafrost. "It may be impossible for you to understand, but I wanted Professor Lempicka to research the goddess because she's interested in the truth. She's been working her ass off in those caves to prove that the First Peoples have been in North America far longer than the colonial pricks want the world to believe."

"You can relax. Jones isn't going to get any glory from it. Lempicka's twenty-four-thousand-years, first-people theory will continue to be rejected by archeologists. Their egos will hold onto the Clovis first model, even if the science contradicts it."

"You can cut the crap. Do you think I'm an idiot? You're a star! Jones will be a star."

"Not a star. I get to co-author a paper in *Nature,* that's it."

"That's it? Do not pretend that is a small thing. I'm a journalism major, remember? I know what a paper in *Nature* means. Oh, and for the record, Mr. Fake, I saw your lying face on CBC." Leo attempts to rub his eyes with both hands, but the cast stops him. "I know about your wife—everything is a lie."

He freezes. His breath becomes laboured, and he swallows in gulps like he's trying to shut down a crying jag. "Not everything," he says with regained composure.

"Shut up!"

He shakes his head. "I'm going to be a dad."

"I know."

"We're not married."

"Do you live with her, in Whitehorse?" Leo remains silent. "You're married. It's called common-law, idiot."

"I've got to do what's right by my kid—I'd love to be free, like you. I have to face the fact that I'm tied down at twenty-eight."

"Balderdash!" I fight the urge to laugh at another perfect word that I recycled from Frank. Anger refuels me. "I don't see the ropes. You do whatever you want."

"I'm sorry, *really*—she's my best friend, and it hurts that she loves more—someone always loves more."

"You're right. I loved the fake you more than the real you."

"I've never been fake." He chokes back a man-cry.

"Lying isn't done with words, it's done with silence too."

His emotional display, if it's meant to manipulate me, is working. I place my hand gently on his head and pat his smooth hair, as though he's a worried dog. "You don't lie to someone you truly love."

"I wish that were true. Fuck, I know it's not. I'm trapped. Fucking trapped—and I don't even want to say that because I love my kid already."

His hand follows my legs under my skirt. I am aware of the strength of his hand despite his gentleness. I stop breathing, in a subconscious moment, wanting him, despite all. I suck in air and then let it flow from my lips in a controlled, slow stream. I bend at the waist to smell his stale hair and savour the gentle hand on my thigh, and then press my mouth to his ear. "I don't feel sorry for you." I straighten to standing. "Trust me, she doesn't love you as much as you think she does. She finds out about what you've been up to, about me? Show me the love then." I pull my daypack from the floor and put it on my chest.

His hand grasps my calf and then slides up my leg. "Don't Rumi. Not like this."

I reach under my skirt and pry his hand off my thigh, then grab my day pack from the floor and put it on my chest while I run through the long hall and down the stairs. I stop in the front hall to pull on my big backpack with clumsy, feverish arms. The weight causes me to sway and stumble out the front door.

The red truck gleams in the dawn, devoid of Dempster mud and the memories of Goldensides. Leo stands naked at the open brothel window, his crotch hidden behind the sill. "Rumi!" he shouts onto the desolate street.

It ends as it began: no shirt, no shoes, no service.

"Rumi, wait—please!"

"Think of our relationship as a kilonova, two stars collide, make gold, and die."

"Rumer, seriously, come back inside." He leaves the window.

Heat permeates through the pack, as though the gold's become a fireball. I run like I've never run before.

Behind me, in the distance, I hear his booming voice, like Marlon Brando in a northern adaptation of *A Streetcar Named Desire*, "Rumer!"

The Expedition sits near where Frank dropped me, pulled off the highway onto a gravel rest area. I knock on the window. Frank struggles from his bunk and into the front seat. He unrolls the driver's window.

"You're back!"

I nod, solemnly. “I know. I’m sorry, I didn’t know where else to go.”

“What happened?”

“I happened upon Leo.” I stare at my dusty feet, to hide my burning eyes.

“I take it things did not go well.” I shake my head but cannot speak.

“Get in.”

The familiar hum and vibrations of the Expedition lull me to sleep before we’re even out of the mine tailings.

XV

The Expedition's long wipers slosh the heavy rain back and forth across the windshield. We've stopped at an intersection with traffic lights. "Where are we?"

"Whitehorse."

"Already?"

"You slept the entire way."

"Light's green."

Frank ignores my prod. "Can't let you off any closer. The Expedition is limited to what streets he can travel on. Go two blocks up and turn to the right. The street curves, Lloyd's place is three properties up, on the left, down a long drive. Flip over the paper, you'll find the address to the Edgewater on back. It's a hotel across from White Pass Station."

"Okay, thanks. Where are you off to?"

"Home."

"Where is home?"

"Atlin, another two hours south. Did you bring an umbrella with you?"

"Sadly no. Hang on—I'll put on something warmer." I open my backpack and then pull jeans on under my dress, and an oversized Carlton hoodie.

"Thank you, Frank. I don't think I would have survived the Arctic without the well-timed, heroic arrivals of Franklin and his Expedition."

"Ha!" Frank chuckles and then his cheeks flush pink. "Happy I could be of service."

The smooth flow of the large windshield wipers is comforting. I open the door reluctantly, not ready to leave the warm cab. "Watch the pipe. It'll burn your hand," Frank says and then adds, "Midnight sun's not gonna shine as bright on Beringia without you—I mean that. You take care, Rumer."

"Walk toward wild, Frank."

"You as well."

I jump from the truck into a tempestuous world and then blow Frank a kiss. The Expedition hums and grinds. I leap back to avoid getting splashed. My eyes fill with tears—I'm lost in water and wind, listening to the loud motor of the Expedition as it drives away. I already miss the beast and its awful hum. I never thought it possible.

I slog down unknown streets in the rain, my feet sloshing in wet runners, toward the house of a friend of my nemesis. I have never felt more alone in the Arctic than I do at this moment, in the largest city in northern Canada. I know no one in Whitehorse. Leo's wife is here, somewhere, at home, cuddling her belly in bed, waiting for her beautiful man to return. Blood drains from my head. His beauty returns to her as it leaves me. My face flushes in shame. He was never truly beautiful. He was beautifully ugly.

Lloyd's drive is shrouded in spruce and poplar trees. I enter cautiously, on alert for roaming dogs. Sebastian advised me to fear a wandering Arctic dog more than an Arctic wolf. Wolves are wise and fearless; they only attack an animal they intend to eat. Dogs tend to be foolish and fearful; they'll attack for no good reason. My caution is merited, and a giant dog lopes down the lane toward me. It jumps up, places its paws on my shoulders knocking me to the ground and licking my face. "Okay, boy, I'm happy to see you too, off! Off, Bear! Stay off. Good boy." I flounder on the wet ground like a walrus and then manage to stand and attempt to wipe the mud from my packs but only smear it.

Through the trees, I catch a glimpse of something big and yellow. I walk further down the lane with Bear by my side, toward a wood-shingled bungalow. The windows are dark behind the mid-century, faded drapery. Tom's camper is parked next to it, light shining from within. I'm afraid to approach the door—assuming Charlotte's been happily ensconced in a life with Tom is much better than finding out otherwise. I knock on the thin door. Bear barks from behind me, as though saying, you'll never guess who I found standing in the rain! The door jerks open. Tom stands, unshaven, bare-chested, in blue jeans, as sinewy as I remember.

"Woo-wee," Tom smirks. "Look what the dog dragged home . . . a drowned rat. A fat one at that." His lecherous smile makes me want to bolt. "How'd you find this place?" he asks, suspicious.

I suck in the cool, moist air, and breathe it out slowly. "I'm looking for Charlotte. Is she with you?"

"Charlie, you've got a visitor." He leaves the door wide open.

I stay in the rain with Shorty Bear. Charlotte appears behind Tom. She smiles in the first fleeting moment she sees me and then immediately reverts to a scowl. Her black bob has been sheared off and soft, ashy-blond curls grow in their place. She's wearing sweatpants and a tank top. Her face is pale and natural. She looked younger in all the goth make-up. Without the thick white powder, black lipstick and mascara, her face looks tired and undernourished, as though she's been existing on gas station cuisine for the past few months.

"What are you doing here?"

"I could ask you the same thing."

Charlotte steps in front of Tom. "What do you want?"

"You've been *here* since June? Shacked up in Tom's Barbie camper?"

"No, we've been travelling. I almost forgot what a bitch you can be."

"I'm the bitch? I'm here for our parents."

"You told on me?"

"I never told them a thing. But don't you think they're going to be curious when I arrive home alone?"

"Answer the question—what do you want?" Tom says, pushing his shoulder in front of Charlotte.

"Mind your own business. This is a private conversation."

"Charlie said it right. You are a cunt."

"She said bitch. Get your nouns right, prick."

Charlotte puts a hand on Tom's shoulder and pushes herself in front of him. "I can handle my sister."

"I want to know what I should tell our parents when they ask about you."

"Tell them I've decided to stay in Whitehorse."

"With Tom?" I say, unable to hide my antipathy. "Do you have a job here?"

"I don't know what you want from me."

"The truth would be nice."

"The truth is, you're jealous that I'm happy, that I'm with Tom."

I look at my feet, splattered in mud and shake my head. "You got it wrong, I'm actually happy that my twenty-year-old sister is living with a fifty-year-old psychotic perv, alcoholic, druggie who abandoned his wife and four kids. Who wouldn't be?"

Tom pushes his way in front of Charlotte. "Your sister doesn't want to talk to you. You need to leave."

"This is none of your business, Tom. I'm discussing private matters with my sister. It doesn't concern you. Let us finish our conversation."

"Your sister is my business."

I roll my eyes.

Charlotte whispers to Tom. He grumbles and then says, "One minute," as though it's a warning.

"Why *are* you here? Charlotte, are you pregnant?" I whisper.

She glances nervously inside the trailer and then looks me up and down, taking in my bedraggled state. "You're drenched—I'd invite you in but. . ."

"So, you are—pregnant?" Charlotte folds her arms across her chest and focuses her gaze on Shorty Bear. "Be careful, Charlotte. He already has four kids. He can't afford another—wouldn't tolerate another."

"I'm not pregnant!" she snaps and then she adds in a low voice, "Not anymore. I had an abortion—that's why I left Beringia."

"Minute's up!" Tom pushes his way through the door and places his hand firmly on Charlotte's shoulder.

"Get the fuck off me!" Charlotte suddenly snaps, shaking Tom off. I'm too shocked to smile. He stares at the top of her head, looking more confused than angry, and then retreats inside.

Charlotte's eyes are focused on Bear.

"It wasn't exactly a picnic for me at Hotel Beringia," I say.

She glances up at me, intrigued.

My wet clothes have slowly drained the warmth from my body. My legs start to shake. "I came to tell you that I'm leaving the Yukon. My flight to Vancouver leaves tomorrow." It's obvious by her intense expression that I've fucked up her plans. Missing-in-action from Beringia is the drama she's been living on.

"Okay," she says abruptly and then adds, "Thanks for letting me know."

My teeth begin to chatter. "You don't have to stay up here."

Charlotte scowls, prepared to dismiss whatever's coming next. "What do you mean?"

"I don't know what I'm doing in September either."

She shakes her head slowly. "You don't get it. You always land on your feet."

I'm shocked and a little flattered that she has that perception of me. "I do get it. I get that it's not me you're angry with—it's our parents." Charlotte narrows her eyes, trying to digest what I've said. "I haven't let you down. Our parents let you down." She shifts her focus to gaze contemplatively at the puddle next to me. "You're an adult. You can do whatever you want."

Silence and then, "But what if this is what I want?"

"Is living in a grotty RV with *him* the best you can come up with?"

Charlotte looks directly, definitely, at me. "Piss off," she says, then steps inside the RV and shuts the door.

I run, slipping in mud, with Bear beside me, to the end of the drive.

"Ireland!" Tom shouts. Bear stops at the end of the drive, trembling and whimpering.

I pat his stinky, wet head. "Sebastian really misses you, Bear."

I run toward town—stepping in muddles puddles in my haste, worried Tom might come after me. My jeans are heavy with rain; without a belt, they keep sliding from my hips. The backpack wrenches my shoulders. My spine feels as though it will snap under the pressure. I stop to breathe at the traffic light where Frank let me out.

Downtown Whitehorse streets are wide and virtually empty. The urban air is surprisingly Arctic fresh. Frank told me to be sure and find the White Pass Train Station—where the gold-fevered began their journey to Dawson. He said it's on the bank of the Yukon River. Everything in life seems to culminate at a river. Where their Klondike journey began, mine ends. It is ironic that at this moment, I possess the gold they desperately sought.

I spot a vertical, neon sign on the corner of a wide street: the Edgewater Hotel. And just as Frank said, it's across the street from the White Pass Station. Under the low sky, I haul my wet trappings into the lobby. The lights are on, but it is empty. A small

Chihuahua-cross dog darts from behind the counter, past my sodden feet, and sniffs my backpack on bird legs that could lift any minute. A woman enters through a door behind the front desk. "Can I help you?"

"I'm looking for a room for one night."

"Do you have a reservation?"

"No."

"We're full."

"Please. I've walked for over an hour in the rain. My backpack is insanely heavy. I can't keep going. I'll take anything, a broom closet."

"We're completely booked."

"Fuck—sorry, I'm really tired." I drop my pack onto the floor.

"You could try the Eldorado."

"What's it like?"

"Historical—one of the oldest standing hotels in Whitehorse."

I should have known the Arctic wasn't finished kicking me around just yet. The Eldorado would have been better off left to nature's decay—the restoration attempt is cheap and tacky. The clapboard siding has been ripped off and covered with faded yellow aluminum—Tom's Barbie palace on steroids. The hall is stinky, with a stained indoor/outdoor carpet that must have absorbed decades of cigarette smoke. The air inside the dark guest room tastes like the hall carpet smells. The only window in the room opens onto the hall. I drop my packs and then pull back the heavy curtain to allow in a little diffused natural light. A burly man stops in front of my window, dry heaves for about a full minute, then continues stomping down the hall. I shut the curtain.

I pull off the wet hoodie, jeans, and dress, and flop on top of a slippery, cigarette-burned bedspread. At least the mattress beats all the foam mattresses I've slept on this summer. My daypack is wet. I take out my damp journal and carefully slide Seb's comic book from inside its cover. Seb's creation is perfectly dry. The journal's damp leather releases an earthy, woodsy scent, creating an ephemeral, gritty, Klondike moment in the depressing room.

August 16, Hotel Eldorado, Whitehorse, Yukon: I have arrived, weary from my Arctic adventure, by way of the fabled Dawson City, robbed of one fortune, smuggling another. Eyes wide open—forward ever, martyr never.

I close the journal and turn on the cable TV with the remote.

I awake in the dark. I'm not in the trailer. My mind is confused, and I panic for a few moments, as though I've woken to find myself buried in an underground tomb. My hand fumbles for my journal on the bedside table. Its weight in my hands is instantly comforting. I follow the stream of light to the curtains and pull them open: the Eldorado. I lift my journal to my face and inhale the faint, grassy scents of the Dempster flora that I pressed between its pages: cotton grass and fireweed. I open the journal. *August 16, Whitehorse: The curtain closes on the final act of the sisters we once were. I am a sister. I am not my sister's keeper. Love and responsibility are not one and the same. Our parents will try to snap me back in line, expect me to dutifully revert to my familial role. They will try. I will let them down. Maybe I am fearless and dangerous because I am okay with that.*

I'm starving. I flip through the pamphlet on the dresser, looking for a recommended place to eat: Hey Zeus—Mexican takeaway. I haven't had Mexican food all summer. I use the Whitehorse street map from the side table to plot my walking route. I slide into my slightly damp dress and spin, encouraging gravity to pull out the wrinkles.

The rainclouds have vanished and the faraway sun shines brightly. Being alone in a city, with no pack on my back, free of all my summer burdens, feels liberating.

I order a vegetarian burrito from the Hey Zeus food truck and pay at the open window. A very pregnant woman, with long dark hair, sits sideways at the end of one of the brightly coloured picnic tables because her belly won't fit frontward. At first glance, I think that it might be Seraphina. The woman stands, turns awkwardly, and looks my way. I immediately realize that Seraphina gave birth in July, and lives in Alaska.

Leo's wife is somewhere in this Arctic city. Maybe her cowardly lion has already returned to her. Suddenly, an unbearable sadness flows through me—this is how my summer ends. My foil-wrapped burrito is ready. I grab it and trot lightly past the picnic tables. Invisible.

I wake early, at the same time I woke in Hotel Beringia for my morning shift, believing for a moment that I am in my shoebox bed. I take the sock of gold out of my day pack and shove it into my cut-offs' front pocket, and then bury the shorts deep in the middle of my big pack.

August 17, Whitehorse: A metal heavier than its weight, a treasure almost too burdensome to bear, gold's birth requires the consumption of its parent stars in a kilonova, and its ravenous energy endures in the minds of all covetous fools who believe that it can be possessed. I am not naive enough to believe that anything born from a kilonova is something to be procured. Gold flows through our blood and fires our minds. We do not possess gold, gold possesses us. The ore belongs to Beringia. I've taken temporary possession of it to set in motion the settling of a personal violation and a centuries old score—gold for a goddess. We were never Klondike geishas.

The gold is in transit, and I am its mule.

The rising sun's rays are tepid in the early hours. The sky is the palest blue, fading like the days. A faint, white, crescent moon hangs in the western sky. It's a long, quiet walk to the airport, and despite the burden of being loaded like a mule, walking is what I know.

Walking is home. Beringia remains with me as I scan the horizon for grizzle-backed mounds that might be bears, and in the forests that line the road, I watch for golden wolf eyes.

The one-room airport looks bigger than I remember. I head to the Air Canada counter to pick up my ticket. I slide my backpack on the scale and hold my breath as the Air Canada attendant weighs it. The backpack is just an ounce under the fifty-pound limit. It weighed only thirty-seven on the way up here. Reckonings are heavy. The small female attendant struggles to heave the pack onto the conveyor belt. I pray that they do not search it.

Killing two hours at the airport seemed like a good idea when I was sitting in my gloomy room at the Eldorado. I take a seat and search my pack for my journal and then take out Sebastian's comic book instead. Black combat boots stop on the green and white tiles in front of me.

"Can you give our mother a message from me?"

"What is it?"

"Tell her that I won't be coming back to Vancouver until Christmas."

"Christmas—got it." I nod.

My lack of interest seems to stir something in Charlotte. She studies my face with curious eyes. "I don't have to explain myself to you."

"Not asking you to," I say calmly.

She holds out a thin chain. "I found this a while ago. I thought of you." I open my palm and she slowly releases a delicate silver necklace into it. I hold it up to examine the tiny wolf pendant. "It's sterling silver," she adds.

"Thank you," I say, cautiously, unsure why she's given it to me.

"I know you like wolves."

"It's beautiful."

I glance behind Charlotte. Tom enters the airport, obviously looking for her but thankfully, heading in the wrong direction. "For what it's worth, I think you've made the right decision. You should stay. If it's really what you want."

Charlotte narrows her eyes. "I know what you're doing."

"What? What am I doing?"

Tom spots Charlotte at the same time she turns to march out of the airport. They meet a safe distance away. It's the first time I've seen them together in civilization. Their age difference looks awkward. His boney face looks worn out; his generic jeans hang on his skinny butt. He attempts to take her hand. Charlotte shakes him off. Tom turns and cautiously glances around the airport. I hide behind Sebastian's comic book. When I peer over the top, Charlotte's charging out the airport doors, Tom following with determined steps.

He stands just inside the doorway, heads above the airport crowd, reading the arrivals and departures sign. His left arm is tucked forward. The Arctic wind did not blow him shorter and wider like the tundra trees; it pressed him taller and thinner than the mountain man I served burnt burgers to on my first day at Hotel Beringia. For a fleeting moment, I am on Goldensides, naked under the midnight sun, with him. Excitement shoots through my chest; he loves me more. He turns around slowly and scans the airport. His jaw is ridged. His eyes are glacial. Blood leaves my head in a single wave. Leo has come for me, but love is not his guide. His fury permeates the airport lobby. I pick up my bulging daypack. Sebastian's book falls under the chair. I crouch to retrieve it and stay low trying to figure out my best option to avoid being seen.

The green and white checkered airport floor is a chessboard. I slide, moving forward and to the side, checking pawns—luggage and a stroller—placed in my way, and avoiding others—the heavy-set RCMP officer. I do not scan the chessboard floor to check his position. I *feel* him encroaching. I hear my name howled through the lobby. He is too close. The Arctic's claimed Charlotte but it's not taking me. Airport security is a few maneuvers away. My feet are heavy blocks. I move as a queen, in all directions, gliding over the squares, too fast for him to track. Invisible.

Time slows with each step. The airport lobby expands. Moments pass like seasons. I am an old woman by the time I reach the end of the short security line, fumbling through my daypack for my passport and the ticket. My aged hands feel swollen, graceless, and the pockets on the pack are too tight. The security line moves agonizingly slowly, like tundra growth. My bony fingers tremble as I hand the agent my documents. I step through security and then glance back. Leo shrugs his shoulders and raises his good hand, palm toward the sky, as though pleading for an explanation. I kiss the palm of my hand and blow a kiss in his direction. He shakes his head in disbelief and takes a step back. His eyes tell me there's more to the story. He believes we will meet again.

I made it. I am on the plane. I take a seat beside a middle-aged man. He pulls a gun magazine from his briefcase. I stuff my daypack under the seat in front and then put on my seat belt. I watch out the window as the luggage, including my muddy backpack, with Leo's gold, is loaded into the back of the plane. I will not relax until the wheels leave the tarmac. The plane fills slowly. The stewards walk past, shutting overhead compartments, as part of the cabin check, before take-off. I open the comic Sebastian made for me.

We sit on the tarmac for twenty minutes. The engines do not fire.

"We're holding the plane for a passenger. Just waiting for one last person to board. They will be arriving momentarily. We'll be on our way as soon as they board. Thank you for your continued patience," the captain says through the plane intercom.

Maybe the truth has caught up to me. Today is the day the sun and moon share the Arctic sky. Leo's told security about the gold, or he's found a way to board the plane. My heart pulses in my ears like a war drum. I glance at the man to see if he can hear it too. His nose is inside the magazine. The engines fire. Exhaust fumes circulate through the cabin. I'll die of carbon monoxide poisoning before the RCMP board and arrest me.

There is a sudden frenzy of activity at the front door. Whoever we've been waiting for is boarding. The steward blocks my view; I can't see who it is. The steward looks tense as he walks down the aisle. He reaches my seat and continues walking toward the rear of the plane. Charlotte follows behind him. I catch a fleeting, unconscious smile, as though she's pleased to see me; then she immediately stares straight ahead, pretending to be blind to me. She struts past in combat boots—wearing a denim miniskirt that was once a pair of jeans—to a seat somewhere in the rear of the plane. Our Arctic adventure ends in light.

"Flight attendants, secure doors for take-off," the speaker announces.

"You going home or away to school?" the gun magazine man asks.

"Going home to Vancouver and then away to school."

"Where's school?"

"Carleton University, in Ottawa."

"What do you study in Ottawa?"

"I'm in second-year journalism."

"Journalism, what would you do with that?"

"Investigative journalism."

A lone raven stands on the edge of the tarmac. The engines roar. The raven takes flight in synchronicity with the jet as we push through the Arctic wind and lift into the bluest sky, tail to the midnight sun.

Acknowledgements

My fascination with the Arctic began as a young child. My father returned from a visit to the Canadian High Arctic with an Ookpik—a traditional Inuit toy owl made from wolf fur—for me and each of my sisters. Not long after, my sisters and I accompanied our father, walking door to door, through our Western Canadian suburban neighbourhood, dispensing flyers in opposition to the proposed Mackenzie Valley Pipeline—a pipeline that would cut across the Canadian Arctic, from the province of Alberta, through the Northwest Territories, to the Yukon.

I had the privilege of gathering much of my Arctic research for *Hotel Beringia* in person. I am indebted to the Indigenous Peoples of the Canadian Arctic, whose cultures are the foundation for all that is great about Northern Canadian culture. I thank the Vuntut Gwitch'in Nation, Kwanlin Dün Nation, Tr'ondëk Hwëch Nation, Tagish Nation, Aishihik Nation, Na-Cho Nyak-Dun Nation, The Little Salmon Carmacks Nation, Kluane Nation, Kwanlin Dün Nation, Kaska Nation, Tr'ondëk Hwëch'in Nation, Taku River Tlingit First Nation, White River First Nation, and Selkirk Nation for the privilege to experience the grandeur of their traditional lands.

There are many people and sources that contributed their knowledge on the Canadian Arctic. Their expertise is invaluable, any mistakes are mine. I enjoyed every moment I spent on fact-finding adventures at the Yukon Transport Museum, Yukon Beringia Interpretive Centre, and Tombstone Territorial Park. I thank the park rangers for their information on Yukon geography and tundra flora and fauna, and the several cups of fresh-brewed, Labrador tea. I appreciate Parks Canada and the Yukon Government, for preserving the historical community of Dawson City, and the Yukon government for their documentation of Yukon Treaties, and the Arctic oil and gas industry. I am filled with gratitude for John Hart, who dedicated countless hours to our conversations about the political, industrial, and geographical history of the Yukon.

My most recent trip to the Arctic would not have happened without Peter Arthur, who spent many sun-filled nights sleeping in a tiny backcountry tent in grizzly bear country, and whose driving skills kept us on the slippery Dempster Highway during rainstorms. I am humbled by the wild wolf and wolf pups that I met along my Arctic journey; they profoundly changed my perception of what it means to be a person of Earth's Northern Hemisphere. I am also grateful for my earliest Yukon travelling companion, Catherine Hart, and our many Yukon adventures involving canoes, helicopters, and a hovercraft.

I am especially indebted to Theresa Hart, who insisted I put this story in print. She was available at all hours to read, offer sage literary advice, and encouragement. I thank my early draft readers: Miranda Hart and Sandra Hart for their insights and feedback. My three daughters contributed to this novel more than they know; Mistaya, Tabitha, and Penelope have taught (and continue to teach) me what it means to be a girl, a sister, and a woman in the world today, more than I could possibly learn from myself.

Hotel Beringia is a work of fiction; however, the dating of the ancient Beringian artifact mentioned in the novel, was inspired by the work of Canadian archeologist, the late Jacques Cinq-Mars. I am also thankful for the novel, *State of Wonder* by Ann Patchett, and its exploration of the fragile and ruthless egos in academia. Last, but not least, I am honoured that the writing of the novel was funded, in part, by the Canada Council for the Arts.

About the Author

Mix Hart is the author of *Queen of the Godforsaken* (Thistledown Press, 2015). *Hotel Beringia* is her second novel. She also writes poetry and creative nonfiction. Her work has been featured in *The Goose: A Journal of Arts, Environment, and Culture in Canada, Popsugar.com*, and on CBC radio *The Morning Edition* with Sheila Coles, and CBC Radio West. She holds a Master of Arts degree from the University of British Columbia, where she also pursued doctoral studies and was honoured with a Social Sciences and Humanities Research Council Doctoral Fellowship award.

Mix lives with her family in the Cascade Mountains of British Columbia.